Ashore on Stony Beach

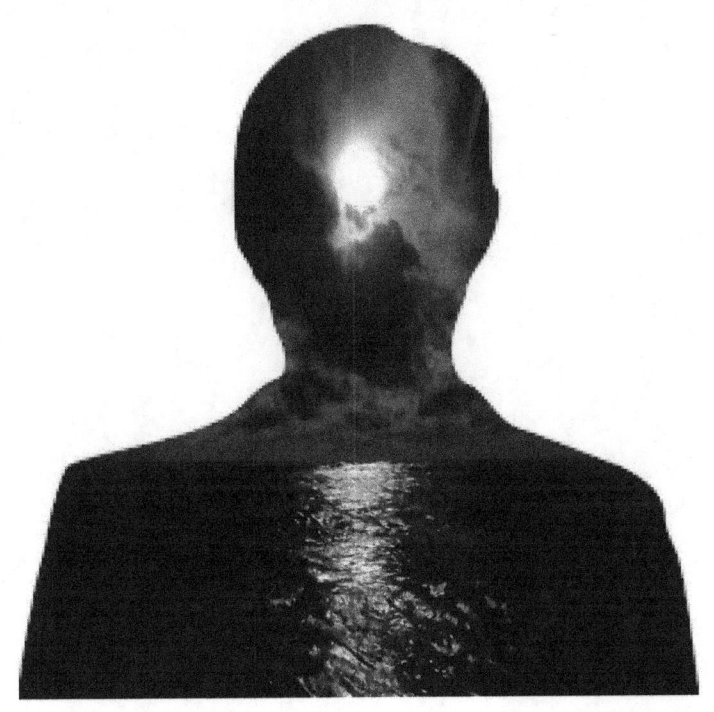

~~~ TWISTED THREADS ~~~
A Novel
SHERYLL O'BRIEN

ISBN 978-1-939351-40-1

WOODWIND PRESS

Printed in United States of America

Mom,

I know how much you love your Scots,
And now I know how much you love
Ashore on Stony Beach.

This one was so much fun writing,
and since you begged for more,
the story will continue on the pages of
Adrift on Stony Beach.

A heartfelt thank you to my team:

Andria Flores ~ Editor extraordinaire.
Nancy Pendleton ~ Goddess of the publishing world.
Jessica Champion ~ Web designer and manager.
25 Hours Consulting

Nancy Pendleton and
Jessica Champion ~ Cover design.

Acknowledgement

I would like to mention and thank
my junior year, high school teacher,
Mr. Andy Power.

I think it is fair to say Mr. Power
expected much from his students.
I know he gave much in return.

My personal Mr. Power story.

I showed up for class, having forgotten a writing assignment at home. When he finished walking the classroom collecting the students' work, he singled me out, "Miss Sneade, you didn't hand in your paper."

"No, I didn't, but there's a really good reason."

"I doubt it, but please stand and tell the class the reason."

"I was reading my paper on the way to school, and when I got to Beaver Brook, this enormous, foul-smelling, swamp monster jumped into my path, drooled and spit, then grabbed my paper and sunk back into the murky water."

"Well, that is a really good reason. Rewrite the paper and submit it tomorrow. The highest grade you can receive will be a B."

On the day Mr. Power handed back our papers, he neglected to give me mine. My hand shot up, "Excuse me Mr. Power, you didn't hand me my paper."

"No, I didn't, but there's a really good reason. I was reading your paper on the way to school, and when I got to Beaver Brook, this enormous, foul-smelling, swamp monster jumped into my path, drooled and spit, then grabbed your paper and sunk back into the murky water."

The class erupted in laughter.
Mr. Power gave me my paper the next day.

I received an A.

Thank you Mr. Power for all that you
brought to your classroom.

You demanded respect.
You easily earned it.

For a complete list of Sheryll O'Brien's books,

Please visit pullingthreadsnovella.com

Ashore on Stony Beach

~~~ TWISTED THREADS ~~~
A Novel
SHERYLL O'BRIEN

2016
Cliff Side

Welcome to Whisper Island

Esmé Baxter is behind the wheel of a Honda CRV traveling north along I-495 toward Portland. She's just crossed the Piscataqua River Bridge that connects Portsmouth to Kittery and is heading to All Points Maine. Her husband, Joe, is in the passenger seat scrolling through countless pictures of their recently purchased white clapboard, two-story bungalow with black shutters and sage green trim. Joe offers another critique of the summer home they scrimped every penny to buy, "Wind Ledge is definitely the fixer-upper we thought it was and then some, Esmé."

"Are you having second thoughts?"

"Absolutely not." He puts his cell in the glove box, rests his hand onto his wife's thigh, and takes hold of hers when it finds its way home. He gives it a gentle squeeze, "Summer on an island in Casco Bay. What could be better?"

She lifts a brow, "I think you meant to say, summer on the edge of a cliff on an island in Casco Bay. You always forget to mention the cliff, Joseph."

"Ooooo, she called you out, Joseph. That's some serious smack," sixteen-year-old Marin jokes from the backseat. "And for the record, Mom, he doesn't mention the cliff because he's afraid of heights, and so are you."

"For the record? You're starting to sound like Lawyer Jenny pointing out our questionable decision to buy a cliff hanging death-trap."

"Whatever, you're both wusses."

Joe gives his wife's hand another squeeze before she returns it to the steering wheel. An hour or so after that back and forth, she parks the Honda in the hull of the Abenaki, a car transport ferry, takes her hands from the steering wheel and smiles wide, "Okay, next stop, Whisper Island. I cannot wait to get to the bungalow!" A few minutes from shore, Esmé, the pamphlet reader of the family, has their next adventure all planned. "Joe, we should take one of the scenic cruises around the bay, or maybe go on one of these specialty cruises."

"Specialty cruises, what are those?" Marin asks as she takes her eyes away from her cell long enough to jump into the conversation.

"Mostly, they're scenic trips along the shorelines of the islands in the bay, but there are holiday cruises on the Fourth of July and Labor Day. I'm not sure we'd be interested in those, but I'm very interested in doing a Sunrise Run and a Sunset Run. And there's a Moonlight Run. Marin you'd love that one."

"Yes, yes, yes, let's do that one." Marin makes a move for the brochure.

"Go get your own, and see if there are brochures about the other islands, Peaks and the Diamond islands for starters." When her daughter is out of earshot, Esmé nudges Joe, "I was thinking."

He rolls his eyes, "I hate it when you start a sentence that way. It always ends up costing money."

"I know."

"How much and what for?"

"Not sure and for a telescope for Marin. She'd love it, and we have the perfect place for it on the widow's walk. You and I are going to be very busy getting the fixer-upper ready for the winter months, and she's going to be stuck at the cottage day and night. We might as well get her something she'll enjoy."

"She'd enjoy the hell out of a telescope. Shhhh, she's coming."

When Joe drives the Baxter Mobile off the 20-minute ferry run and onto the tiny island (three miles long, two miles wide), he parks at the first available spot at the public beach. And when they are out of the Baxter Mobile, a mad-dash to sink their feet into soft sand ensues.

"Ahhhh," is unisoned by the trio.

Esmé looks at *him* then at *her* and reads all the signs, "We are not spending the afternoon here. We have a loaded car and hours of work to do at the cottage."

Joe and Marin drop their duffs onto the sand, tilt their heads toward the sun and laugh. Esmé eventually surrenders the battle and drops her duff as well.

When father and daughter push to a standing position four hours later, Joe gathers the beach towels he'd grabbed from the Honda, Marin picks up remnants of fried dough and lemonade she got from a stand across the street, and Esmé ignores the goings on, her face pressed deep in a novel she bought at the corner store.

"Esmé. Hey, Esmé, we're leaving. What the heck are you reading?"

The captivated woman dogears a page and waves the paperback, "Penobscot Bay, a murder mystery set on an island in—"

"Penobscot Bay?" the father and daughter tease.

"Yesssss."

"Interesting choice given we just moved to an island."

Marin nudges her dad, "Yesssss, but our island is in Casco Bay."

"Oh, well, then. It's all good."

The mother gets up and huffs, "I believe it was the two of you who wanted to spend the day at the beach, I just found something really interesting to do while I was here. Now, come on. We've got hours of work ahead," Esmé's slight Spanish accent and flourish of hand movements accentuate the urgency and the finality of her words.

Joe has barely taken space behind the steering wheel when the car waiting in line inches toward the soon-to-be-vacant parking spot. Joe toots and waves to the happy beachgoer, then sets a Baxter Rule. "Next trip to the sandy side of the island, we'll be schlepped off our cliff by one of the Whisper trollies."

"Or we could bike down from the mountaintop," Marin happily suggests.

Joe and Esmé nudge one another and declare, "No way."

The Baxter Mobile inches down Main Street through the little bohemian village known as Shaky Town where shacks nestle close, and pungent smells of communal life lift and waft. They continue along Shore Drive, which is really Route 1A, past beautiful waterfront estates set on impressive lots with even more impressive views of the bay. Finally, they head outward around the easterly end of the island and upward along roads that cut through lush vegetation on one side and hug the edge of a perilous plunge on the other. Esmé inches her ass as close to the driver's side as possible and whispers, "If you get me to the cottage without our tumbling off the side, I'll do something very nice for you."

"Such as?"

"I'm not sure, but something very nice."

Marin groans from the backseat, "Quit whispering."

"But it's Whisper Island," Esmé reminds.

"I know, and I have a question."

"Imagine that, Joe, your daughter has a question."

"Yeah, yeah, I'm inquisitive. So anyway, why did you buy a cottage on the cliff side of Whisper Island when you two hate heights?"

"We couldn't afford the sandy side."
"Ah. Got it."

Owners of waterfront property on the sandy side of Whisper, as it is referred to by locals, enjoy private beach and water rights directly in front of and next to their homes. As a general rule those 'community members' are uninclined to share even a grain of sand with their fellow islanders. That means nearly all 800 residents and 2,000 annual vacationers flock to the two-mile-long public beach when they are seeking a day of fun in the sun. The Baxters, the newest family to stake claim on Whisper, do not own waterfront property on the sandy side—far from it, actually.

Wind Ledge, the aptly named Baxter cottage, pretty much says it all. Set on the *other* side of the island and on its highest cliff, Wind Ledge overlooks a mile-long shore of rocks—big rocks, little rocks, mammoth rocks that haven't moved since the Ice Age and tiny pebbles that flit about courtesy of gentle or rolling waves. There is no sand to speak of at the base of Wind Ledge, or Watch Ledge, or Walker Ledge, the three lone bungalows set high above the shoreline. There is no place for sunning or swimming on the stony beach, though there is a wide enough strip along the water's edge for a leisurely stroll, or invigorating run, or to pop-a-squat in a portable beach chair. For many decades, islanders and visitors made pilgrimages to the cliff side to bask in the serenity of walks along the bramble and to observe the majesty of panoramic views of Casco Bay. That quaint pastime was before Stonehenge—not the megalithic monument located in Wiltshire, England, but rather the kitschy version of Stonehenge known only to Whisper Islanders.

"I cannot wait to see Stonehenge tomorrow," Marin enthuses as she peers over the side of Wind Ledge—for the third time.

"Marin, please step back. We aren't familiar enough with the land, and it's too dark for us to navigate the edge safely," the very nervous mother pleads—for the third time.

"But—"

"No buts," the father chimes in.

"Fine. I'm going up to the widow's walk."

"What is it with you and elevation?"

"Just want to be as close to the moon as possible, Mom."

As soon as Marin is inside, Esmé steps near the edge, "Que la!" She jumps back, "Joe, I don't remember it being this high up, do you?"

He takes a look down and gently shoulder bumps Esmé, "Nope. I think the previous owners raised this wall after we signed the Purchase and Sale agreement."

"Funny. And please stop nudging and shoulder-bumping me. I'd hate to end my days at the bottom of the cliff because you're being cute."

Joe embraces his wife, "Don't want you tumbling over for any reason, Es." He looks again, "I doubt you and I will be heading down that ladder anytime soon."

"Or ever, but I bet Marin climbs down tomorrow."

"That's because she's not a wuss."

"Yeah."

Getting onto Stony Beach is not for the faint of heart, or the physically challenged, or for those who suffer vertigo or acrophobia. To enjoy the beach on the backside of the island you need to descend a ladder, a permanently affixed wooden structure somewhat similar to an extension ladder with foot rungs and handholds, but dissimilar in that the climbing structure is bolted to the side of a big-ass cliff. The access ladders were originally installed for emergency use—you know, in the event someone fell off the cliff there would be a way to climb down, pronounce the poor soul dead, and hoist its carcass upward. The climbing apparatus are spaced approximately one-half mile from each other, and were really not intended for access to the beach. After all, who would want to visit a beach covered in rocks?

Apparently, more people
than one might think.

During the summer of 2000, adventure-seekers started flocking to Stony Beach to spend hours erecting rock formations, taking pictures, and posting them online mere hours before their masterpieces tumbled to the surf during high tide. Ladder descending and rock building became the celebrated 'thing to do' on Whisper. Travel sites added the Stonehenge event to the list of reasons to visit Casco Bay, and flyers started popping up throughout town challenging beach bums to a day of cliff-scaling and rock erecting on the *other side.*

Competitors started hopping onto Whisper trollies and flocking to Stony Beach to build their tower, or their castle, or their expansion bridge, and if they were the Chosen One on any given day they'd walk away with the daily prize of a pound of Fiddler's saltwater taffy, or a handblown trinket crafted by local artist, Jasper Crane, or a two-gallon bucket of Gibby's ice cream, with or without toppings. Stonehenge quickly became the highlight of the Whisper community, and the Baxter family bungalow has a bird's eye view of its spectacle.

The Night It Happens
Thursday, July 21
Waning Gibbous – Illumination 96%

Since their arrival a month ago, Joe, a slightly graying, forty-two-year-old advance placement high school math teacher with sparkling blue eyes and protective nature, and whose tools of choice are a number two pencil and equations of a straight line, has done a respectable impersonation of a handyman on the Baxter fixer-upper. Esmé, his Columbian-born, thirty-six-year old middle school art teacher-wife with nutty-brown wavy hair and artistic temperament, has turned the overgrown yard into a sectioned-off garden where blooms of 'this and that' are in the contemplation-stage of taking root on the cliffy terrain. When her daily toil in the soil is done, Esmé takes to the rooftop balustraded platform known as a widow's walk to capture on canvas the panoramic splendor of the rough side of the island. So far, she's said the same thing every day before ascending to heights she'd rather not reach.

"Tell me again why we bought a place with a widow's walk?"

"For the views. You know, so you can paint them."

"Right, the views. Funny thing, Joseph, I'm having trouble viewing things with my eyes closed."

"Just stay in the center of the space and don't look down, look out."

"But if I do look down and tumble from my perch you'll catch me, right?"

"Always."

Marin is usually spared the back and forth because she spends most days on Stony Beach watching labor intensive rock construction, taking pictures of said formations and of the people who build them, and walking a half-mile from the ladder below Wind Ledge to the easterly ladder below Watch Ledge, or to the westerly ladder below Walker Ledge. She hasn't yet ventured to the public access ladder, the one used by visitors venturing to Stony Beach. That climbing structure is located at the farthest westerly point near a bend that leads to an estate known as Echo. She'd love to see what's around the bend, but it's too far a trek for the lone teen according to her parents. By late afternoon each day, when her mother is done with her painting, Marin spends time aloft, perched on a painter's stool with sketchpad in hand, reviewing the work she's done from her secret place in the bramble. Her parents think she spends her lofted time reading about the phases of the moon, but she is most often detailing one of her drawings. She smiles as she reviews her work, "Not bad, I think, but ..." She considers getting another's opinion, then squashes the idea with a heavy dose of reality, "Nope, there's no way I'm sharing my stuff with the 'talented Esmé Clemente Baxter' or anyone else for that matter." She puts her pad into her backpack and plans her evening, "Tonight I'll add an important phase to my collection: *Moonlight Over Midnight Ocean.*"

Marin heads to her bedroom shortly before 11 PM and begins a recitation of the bedroom routine of her parents, "Tidy the living room ... tidy the kitchen ... check the doors and windows ... take turns in the bathroom ... chit chat ... lights out. The snore fest should begin within ten minutes." At the twenty minute mark, she pitter-patters to the bedroom door, presses her ear tight and waits for the low, slow inhales and exhales from her parents' room. She peeks out the window at the moon then checks her watch. She cautions herself, "Wait for the snoring." It takes a few more minutes before the throaty push of her father and high-pitched whinny of her mother are heard. She moves away from the door. "God, I hope that's snoring." She shivers at the idea it could be something else then moves on.

The soon to be seventeen-year-old quickly gathers the length of her white cotton nightgown, pulls it to her waist, tucks it deep into a pair of tie dye sweatpants, pulls on a black sweatshirt with her favored thumbholes, pushes her feet into a pair of canvas sneakers, twists her shoulder-length chestnut hair through the circular opening in the back of a tie dye baseball cap, and grabs her backpack. "I am so screwed if I get caught," she says as she slides white linen curtains aside, opens a screenless window, eases her backpack onto a grassy patch below, climbs over the sill, and makes a very quiet break for it. She moves along the back of the cottage, ducks low when she inches past her parents' window, does a quick hop-skip-and-a-jump over a partially coiled garden hose, slips into a lush grouping of lilac bushes and waits. "Come on, Dad, do one of those gasping for air snores." As soon as the nighttime still is broken by the push and wheeze of Joe and Esmé, the teen hastens away from the 'fixer-upper, water view cottage' her parents scrimped every penny to purchase.

On this clandestine night of trekking the cliffside, Marin alternates between unhooking her pantleg from the bramble prickers along the walking path and stealing glances skyward. She thrills at the Waning Gibbous Moon and the long tail of light reflecting off a gentle rolling sea. "Soooo pretty." She picks up her pace, finds her space, and settles in among sweet smelling rose and lilac bushes sharing precious space with knotted Mountain Laurels. The budding artist reaches into her backpack, grabs her sketchpad and sets it on the ground, then reaches in again for her flashlight, paws around for many seconds, then cusses, "Shit. I forgot to take it from under my bed. That'll teach me, no more reading after lights out." Unable to sketch this phase, she crosses her legs in front, leans back and stares at Earth's only natural satellite. "Ninety-six percent illumination. Beautiful. If I can get back here on the twenty-sixth—" Movement just outside the tail of light pulls Marin's attention toward the water. She silences and leans forward when a boat moves into the path of light, then watches the small craft lift and rock on slapping waves. "Adrift?" Her eyes lock onto the image of a crouched person. "A man? On his knees?"

She begins to get up, an instinct stops her—she sits back down and crouches low. She thinks she caught the man's attention, she's sure when goosebumps run her flesh and her heart begins pounding erratically. She goes flat onto the ground and peers between branches of a rose vine, taking a cut or two on her face from a thorn. The man stands for many seconds looking in her direction then bends low again, seeming to wait until the boat bobs beyond the lighted swath. He takes hold of something, "A body?" He dumps it overboard. Marin's muffled shriek is masked by the splash of dead weight and roll of waves crashing along the rocky beach below the cliff—she hopes! She remains perfectly still when the boat's engine comes to life and breathes easier when the slow, rhythmic *slap, slap, slap* of the hull against water moves the small vessel toward the far end and around the bend of the island. "He knows this waterway, this rocky, rocky waterway."

The terrified teen crawls to her backpack, shoves her sketchpad inside, tosses it onto her back, and continues moving on her hands and knees until she's halfway back to her family's cottage. She's exhausted, sweaty, and filthy when she hoists one of her cut-to-shit legs over the window sill. She freezes in fear when she hears someone in the distance shout the name, "Laire!" then pushes herself up and into her bedroom, crawls into bed, and pretends she's asleep just as someone peers in her window.

"Hey, I know you're awake," he whispers.

She remains as still as death until the *slap, slap, slap* of feet move away from the white clapboard cottage with black shutters and sage green trim known as Wind Ledge.

And The 24 Hours That Follow
Friday, July 22
Waning Gibbous – Illumination 90%

Edward Kingston III, known far and wide as King, is sitting in midnight shadows near the dock of Echo, the Kingston family estate on the far westerly end of Whisper Island. He'd like to be enjoying the simple things: the near full moon and gentle slap of waves upon the shore, but two recent conversations are banging the shit out of his head…

"I don't give one holy fuck if she's carrying your child, Edward. She's a minor. I don't plan on spending the next five years trying to keep your ass out of jail, and the five after that paying big bucks to keep it safe in jail because you dicked around with a teenage girl. I've worked my whole life for what we have, and I will not let you fuck it all away. You handled an underage problem once before, so do it again!"

King found himself on the receiving end of fury during the next conversation he had—the one with a really pissed off chief of police…

"Jesus, Almighty! Did he do it?"

King didn't know for sure, so he lied. "Yes."

"And the girl is Laire MacTavish? Lachlan MacTavish's sister?"

"Yes."

There was a good bit of silence before the chief said his piece, "When this girl is reported missing, I'll have to put my most senior detective, Tom Martin, on the case. He's gonna connect the dots between Christie Anderson and Laire MacTavish. The only good news is he's retiring at the end of the year and might not make much headway before then. I'll slow him down by making sure he runs everything by me as it's happening—not like with Christie Anderson when I had to play catchup and cleanup on all of Edward's fuckups. In the meantime, tell him to take a liking to women—legal aged women. Fuck it, King, just buy him one of his own broads, or let him use one of yours. Don't call me again. I'll be in touch when I know something."

The sixty-year-old man swirls his Glenlivet on rocks, then takes a long pull.

"Those things will kill you," Edward IV says as he steps onto the dock, referring to the cigarette in King's hand, the one glowing a red tip and wafting the smell of menthol smoke his way.

"Gotta die someday, somehow, Heir. Speaking of dead broads—"

The twenty-five-year-old heir to the Kingston empire silences his sire, The King, "Don't call me that, and we weren't speaking of dead broads, and we aren't going to."

"We should talk, Edward,"

"Fine, but we won't be discussing Laire ever again. You gave me my mandate, and I followed it. Leave it there, King."

The father pulls a long drag from his cigarette, turns the butt widthwise between his thumb and forefinger and flicks it into the water. "I won't ride you about this tonight because you might need to sit with your actions, but tomorrow you should expect that I'll be loaded for bear. And while you're wallowing in misery over what you could have had with Laire MacTavish, remember this, you might have been able to keep her and your kid if you hadn't already fucked things up with Christie."

"That was a mistake. I never would have been with her if I knew—"

"Save it, Heir." King pushes from his high back, cushioned, rattan chair, lights another cigarette, grabs his highball glass, and walks away.

Young Edward plops his ass onto the vacated seat, bends forward, leans his forearms on his thighs, drops his head, and thinks—not about Christie, not about Laire, but about the other girl. "Was there another girl? It was pretty late for anyone to be on the cliff walk, let alone a young woman or teenaged girl." He replays the fraction of a second when movement caught his eye and he thought he saw a figure start to stand then crouch back down. "Was it even a female? And if it was, is it likely she would have been alone? Was she with someone else, maybe part of a couple enjoying a midnight stroll?" He gets up and paces along a retaining wall then walks down a handful of steps and paces along the water's edge. He stops and looks at the line of moonlight shining onto the bay, "Okay, I only saw one figure, so I need to focus on that. Go back to the original instinct, it was a teenage girl or young woman who stood then crouched. And if that's the case, she saw *everything*. I'm fucked if King finds out about this. Shit. Shit. Shit. Okay, think. Whoever I saw must be from cliff side. There are only three houses on the cliff with full-view of the bay, all other houses are too far inland to see anything. So unless someone from one of the lower roads made their way up for a midnight stroll along a very dark, very dangerous walking path, then it stands to reason the person on the ledge lives on the ledge. Okay, time to whittle this shit down. Watch Ledge sits at the most easternly part of Stony Beach. The bungalow is set with views over eastern waters, not northern waters where I was. If someone from Watch wanted to moon-gaze or something, they might go to the cliff walk, but that'd be more than a half-mile trek from Watch. Besides, there are only two people who live there. Correction: there's only one person who lives there." Edward's heart pounds a few beats when he runs a terrifying possibility, "If it was Lachlan MacTavish on the cliff, and he saw me dump Laire, I'm a dead man."

Edward picks up a piece of driftwood that lands at his feet and tosses it into the lapping waves. "Okay. Get your shit together. Think. Wind Ledge is very near the spot where I thought I saw something. I heard a new family moved in not too long ago, but how likely is it that people unaccustomed with the cliff walk would be on it in the dead of night?" He picks up the driftwood that's made it back to shore, tosses it into the dark waters again, and continues his contemplation. "The only other structure on the cliff side is Walker Ledge, but the folks who live there have been gone all summer." He grabs hold of the returning wood and throws it with all his might. "Fuckin thing keeps washing ashore." A chill runs his spine as the image of a bone washing ashore bangs torturously in his head. "Fuck. Work this shit. Concentrate. Okay, the whole reason I chose those waters as the dumping ground is because it's so desolate, and because it worked once before."

He climbs the stairs, takes a seat on a rattan and bounces right back up, "I should go check the area. If someone was watching, there will be signs of crushed vegetation or something." He heads toward the side of the house and is just about to get into his Jag when reason takes hold. "I can't go there now. I can't go anywhere. I need to stay at Echo. Stay where there's an alibi." His eyes are drawn upward toward the master suite. His father's plaything is standing at an open French door balcony, her naked body playing peekaboo through a sheer peignoir gown. "Shit. How long has Ruby been there? Did she see me dock? Will she contradict King's alibi when he says I was home all night. Shit. Another fucking problem."

Wind Ledge

Marin is still awake at 3 AM when she hears her parents leave their room. She pitter-patters to the bedroom door, presses her ear tight, and waits. A minute or so later, she hears the front door open, followed immediately by the squeak of the screen door and the slap of the thin wood as it closes.

"Shhhhh. You'll wake Marin," Esmé says, then spins when she hears her daughter from behind.

"Marin is already awake. What's going on?"

"We aren't really sure, but there were noises. Did you hear anything?"

Marin avoids the question by asking a couple of her own, "What kind of noises? When?"

Joe steps off the front stoop, "I'm going to walk a bit...see if he's still out there."

"He? Who?" Marin asks. "See if who's still out there?"

Esmé opens the screen door and waves her daughter onto the porch, "Let's sit on the glider and wait for your father to get back."

"From where? What's going on?"

"We thought we heard someone creeping along the back of the house and then we heard some guy call out a name. It sounded like he said 'Laire.'"

"When?"

"The first time he yelled was around midnight, then again a half-hour ago."

Marin shivers. Esmé wraps her arm around her daughter's shoulders, "Did you hear anything?"

Marin is spared an answer when her father hops onto the porch, "Some guy named Lachlan MacTavish is looking for his seventeen-year-old sister, Laire. He said he checked on her around eight o'clock and realized she'd snuck out. He thinks she might have left to meet up with some guy. She hasn't come home, and he's really freaked out."

"Seventeen?" Esmé takes hold of Marin's hand. "Mija, escuchame, por favor, please, don't ever sneak out of the house. Even on a tiny island like this, there's danger out there." Esmé leans close and brushes hair from her daughter's face, "Marin, how did you get these scratches?"

The teen who is about to lie through her teeth, lies through her teeth, "I was reading in the dark again, and when I lifted my backpack the zipper hit my cheek."

"Make sure you wash the area."

"Already did, Mom."

Joe walks past the chatting females, "Pisses me off that no one's safe anywhere. If that young man doesn't find his sister safe and sound, he's gonna be messed up for the rest of his life." Joe drills his daughter with Dad Eyes, "Lachlan and Laire are siblings, and he's torn to shit over this mess. If it were you missing, Marin, your mother and I wouldn't survive." He enters the bungalow, the screen door slamming behind him for dramatic effect—though none is needed.

Watch Ledge

Lachlan MacTavish, a young man of just twenty-four, stormed into the cottage some past 3 AM without his sister in tow. He paced an angry path that nearly cut through a black and blue tartan rug that Laire insisted they bring from the family home in Speyside, Scotland. When Lachlan first arrived on Whisper, he came alone and carried nothing from home—except a sizeable chip on his shoulder. The trip Lachlan made across the Atlantic was by plane, but it was a ferry that delivered him to his new home, so when asked, he always says, "Lachlan MacTavish arrived straight off the boat from Scotland two years past."

Lan, his preferred name, couldn't wait to step off the 'family business' in the Highland region of Speyside. He scoffs at the irony when he pulls a sip of the harsh drink he carries about and favors above all others, "The Glenlivet whisky. You walked away from the people of home who make the drink, but you couldn't walk away from the drink itself, you pisser." He goes for broke on his self-indulgence. "You just **had** to push from the Highlands, just **had** to find your own way in life." He pulls a burning swig and pushes the bruise, "And what'd you find when you turned your back on the family lot? A life without parents who up and died a year and a little after you set out on your own, and the burden of seventeen-year-old Laire to raise up, and now you've gone and lost the bonnie one." He pauses his self-recriminations at the bang on the front door, takes a quick look at the mantle clock, "Edging 7 AM." He rushes to the door, pulls it wide, and calls her name, "Laire," then stops cold when he sees an officer on the stoop. "Have you found my sister?"

The young, fair-haired man in uniform gives his head a shake, "No, Mr. MacTavish. Dispatch should have mentioned that we can't start a formal search for your sister until 24 hours of notification, but ...." the officer pauses way too long for Lan's liking.

"But, what?"

"We had a teen go missing two years ago, so we want to get ahead of this."

"This?"

"May I come in, Mr. MacTavish?"

"Lan. My name is Lan."

"Dale Jacobs, I'm an officer and rookie detective with Whisper PD. I'm stepping out of order by coming here, but I'm concerned about a possible connection between the missing teens."

"Missing teens." The words hit Lan like a sucker punch. He doubles over and tries really hard to squelch his emotions. He fails. Miserably.

LAIRE

The teen girl knows she's dead. She knew it long before her body hit the cold ocean water. Still, she wonders…

Am I to be having clear thoughts and memories?

The last of her earthly moments push hard, and the plea that fell upon deaf ears clangs pitifully…

Edward, I won't speak out that you banged me unjustly. I'll suffer the pregnancy and birth the wee one with aide of Lan. And when time rolls and I'm of age, you can claim us.

Laire had mere seconds to process her mistakes … and the things she never did … and the things she would be denied. Her final thought as Edward choked away her life was how sorry she felt for the pain she'd be settling on Lan. Her brother's name was the final word Laire MacTavish whispered to the world. And when her soul split away and her spirit stayed behind she decided…

My want for vengeance is more earthly than heavenly. It's right that I find myself fractured. I suspect if I don't find my way to forgiveness, I best prepare for a lengthy stay in the cold depths.

Laire watches her arms and one leg float freely about. She can almost feel the water splash against flesh that's grown slick and bloated. She imagines the pull of chain at her ankle…

Your anchor will keep me deep a spell, but prepare Edward, for my bones will wash ashore one day.

~~ASHORE ON STONY BEACH~~

Laire MacTavish smiles when she realizes her words can lift above the ocean floor.

Wind Ledge

Morning sun rose way too early for the Baxters. They are up and about, but move clumsily through the space they share. For more than an hour, the only words spoken were on the trite side of things, "Penny for your thoughts." … "Not worth that much." … "Pretty day out there." … "Then leave it out there." The knock on the front door and the person on the other side brings an end to the uneasiness and bangs the family headfirst into turmoil.

Joe steps outside and offers a seat on the porch, "Any news, Lachlan?"

"Lan, you should call me Lan, and sad to say there's been no word from Laire, though I got a visit at Watch Ledge in the early light from Dale Jacobs, he's a detective-in-trainin with the police department."

"So the police are involved; they're searching?"

"Not officially. The reason I'm here, Joe, is because of your daughter."

"Marin?"

"Don't know her name, but she's about Laire's age, I'd say."

"Yes. How do you know that?"

"I think I saw your daughter sneakin about your property some time past midnight. I called my sister's name thinkin, hopin it was her movin about, but I came away believin it was your girl."

"Came away thinking?"

"Sorry to say I made my way onto your property for a look, but whoever I saw from the street disappeared into your home."

Joe gets up and paces the small porch, takes an over-the-shoulder look or two into the cottage, runs a memory from when his daughter asked what the 3 AM commotion was about...

Esmé took hold of Marin's hand. "Mija, escuchame, por favor, please, don't ever sneak out of the house. Even on a tiny island like this, there's danger out there." Esmé leaned close and brushed hair from her daughter's face, "Marin, how did you get these scratches?"

"I was reading in the dark again, and when I lifted my backpack the zipper hit my cheek."

"Come on, Lan, let's walk and talk." They step off the porch and head toward Watch Ledge.

"I'm a half-mile down, we can talk there. I should be stickin close to home, I'm thinkin now."

The men walk in silence.

Joe suspects Lan's thoughts are about his sister.

Lan suspects Joe's thoughts are about his daughter.

Neither shares their thoughts until they're on the back patio of the MacTavish cliffside cottage.

"I put a burnin in your gut about your daughter."

Joe nods.

"You don't believe what I say."

"I don't want to."

"Sure. I guess I'm the one who needs to believe it, Joe. I'm hopin your daughter—"

"Marin."

"I'm hopin Marin might know Laire, or saw her about, or knows who might take an interest in teen girls."

"Girls?"

"Not sure if the conversation I had with Dale Jacobs is open for talk, but he said another teen girl went missin two years ago."

Joe drops to a seat, "Shit, Lan."

"I've been fearin all night that Laire might be in some real trouble." He moves to the edge of his place, gets lost in thought and caught by the water's move. He startles when hears his name.

~~*LAN*~~

A shiver runs and pushes him away from the ledge.

Joe notices, "What just happened?"

"I'm a bit tired, Joe. Didn't sleep, and if I did, I sure don't remember it."

"You might want to stay away from the cliff, Lan."

"Right. So, Marin, is she the type to run about?"

Joe smirks, "No." Joe scoffs, "After what you just said, I guess I might not know."

"She's not run by thoughts of boys?"

Joe smirks, "No." Joe scoffs, "Shit, Lan, I guess I don't know."

"Any reason she might've been out roamin last night?"

The father searches for a reason, "She's a studier of the moon. Maybe she snuck out to gaze a bit."

"Laire's a moon-gazer herself. Part of the teen ones, I guess."

"Marin's fascination runs pretty deep, Lan."

"Joe, I'm thinkin she could'a seen moonlight over ocean water from her window and saved herself the trouble of climbin in and out."

Joe snaps, "How do you know my daughter's bedroom window overlooks the bay?"

"I told you I saw Marin sneakin about your property, and when she disappeared, I peeked in a window to see."

Joe pushes to his feet, "What the fuck? You lurked around my place in the middle of the night, and peeped into my sixteen-year-old daughter's window? What the fuck?"

Lan followed Joe around the side of the cottage and tried to take hold of his arm, "Joe, it isn't like that."

"Better the fuck not be like that Lan. I hope your sister comes home real soon, but don't come anywhere near my place again."

Echo

Edward sneaks downstairs well before King's normal waking time. He's hoping to make a break for it—his efforts are for naught.

"Going somewhere?"

The son finds his father sitting in a dark corner, a highball glass in one hand, a lit cigarette in the other, "A bit early for the hooch, don't you think?"

"Never too early for a belt. Speaking of dead broads—"

"We weren't," the son looks around, "and we shouldn't. Not here. The walls have ears. And the windows have eyes."

"What the fuck does that mean?"

"Ruby was standing on the master balcony last night. She might have seen me pull the boat in."

"So?"

"If the cops come around—"

"The cops **will** come around."

"What makes you think so?"

"Lacklan MacTavish works for us. His kid sister is missing. The cops are going to check matters out. They are going to check him out. We're going to help the cops with their investigation."

"You're setting Lacklan up?"

"Not doing anything. Yet."

"All the more reason why Ruby might be a problem."

"She won't be."

"But—"

"She won't be a problem." King pulls some whisky, "So, where are you heading before the sun takes hold?"

"Down to the marina. I have work to do."

"Heads up. You won't be seeing Lacklan this morning. He's already called in, said he has a family situation to handle. I thought about telling him you already handled it," King laughs, "but no need to speak ill of the dead broad."

Whisper Police Department

The whole of WPD consists of 1500 square feet of office space on the first floor of Town Hall and double that size storage area in the basement. The upstairs space is for a full-time chief, two full-time officers, two part-time officers, one on-call detective who is retiring in December, one rookie detective, and a dispatcher who works some at the station, but mostly fields calls from home, day and night.

The chief is already giving orders when he passes Donna Abbott's desk, "Let's talk about the emergency call you got last night. My office."

Donna brings her log and starts talking before she even takes a seat, "A call came in at 12:45 AM from Lachlan MacTavish, he's the guy who bought old man Tanner's place on cliff side. Mr. MacTavish reported his seventeen-year-old sister, Laire, missing. He said he thinks she skipped out of Watch Ledge early that evening, but he didn't realize she was gone until 8 PM. He said he took to the area looking for her, and made several neighborhood searches in both directions, but mostly westerly toward Wind and Walker. He said around midnight he thought he saw someone move in the shadows near the cliff walk and called out thinking it was his sister, but nothing came of it. He called emergency on his way back to his place."

"Did he say where he was when he called out?"

"Somewhere near Wind Ledge."

The chief nods, his signal that the conversation is over.

Donna starts for the door then turns, "There's one more thing, Chief Banks."

"What?"

"Dale Jacobs called me a few minutes after Mr. MacTavish. He said he heard the call come in over his police scanner and wanted a rundown."

"Did you give it to him?"

"Yes, Chief. Was that the wrong thing to do?"

"No," he said the word, but he didn't mean it. "That's all, Donna." As soon as she was back at her desk, he was up from behind his, "You can reach me by phone." He walks through the squad room, sees evidence that Dale Jacobs is in, though he's not at his desk, "Where's Jacobs?" he blanketly asks.

He receives shoulder shrugs from two officers, and a muffled, "Down in storage," from an officer stuffing the last bite of a glazed donut into his mouth.

The athletic, almost-sixty-year-old, with cropped salt and pepper hair and similarly aged facial scruff, wearing his idea of uniform, faded jeans, white button-down shirt and shield, takes stairs two at a time, landing with a thud at the entrance door. He finds the facility brightly lit and calls out, "Jacobs, you down here?"

"Aisle seven, Chief."

The rookie detective is doing exactly what the chief thought he'd be doing, "You're looking at Christie Anderson's file?"

"Yes, sir. This case popped into my head when the call about Laire MacTavish came in last night."

"Uh huh."

"I was new to Whisper at the time of her disappearance, and not on WPD, but I thought there might be similarities or maybe a connection between the cases."

"Uh huh."

"I went to see Lachlan MacTavish and told him—"

"You talked to the brother of the missing girl?"

Dale gets up from his seat, "Yes, sir."

"On whose authority?"

"Detective Martin suggested I make contact. I stressed to Mr. MacTavish that WPD couldn't launch a formal search until the 24 hour mark of notification, but that we wanted to get ahead of things."

"Things. Did you mention Christie Anderson?"

"Not by name, sir."

"Pack up that file. Put it back on the shelf."

"Yes, sir."

The chief storms to the door, "You're getting way ahead of yourself, Officer Jacobs. I might need to rethink your new assignment."

Dale's ass finds his seat before any of the files find their way back to the storage shelves.

Wind Ledge

Joe Baxter has been in a foul mood since he returned from Lan's place. He hasn't gone into the cottage, or spoken with Esmé, or questioned his daughter. Two of those things are of little concern to him, the third, well that's a different matter. He's dragged his sawhorse, power saw, drill, and a whole bunch of other carpentry crap from the shed and set it outside in front of Marin's bedroom window. He answers his wife's unasked question when she comes out to putz in the garden. "I'm fixing all of the screens. Today." He has Marin's window wide open when she enters her room from the inside hallway. "Grab whatever you need and dress elsewhere." He watches her open this drawer, and that drawer, and finally the closet door. His eyes immediately go to the mound of clothes on the floor of the otherwise neat as a pin space. Her eyes go there, too.

"I should do some laundry," she bends to retrieve the pile.

"Leave it."

She halts at the abrupt directive and harsh tone. "But I borrowed some of Mom's things. She's gonna want them back."

"Leave it, and you should find somewhere else to be for the day, somewhere close."

She grabs her camera from a hook by the door, a pair of jeans and tank from the back of a chair, then addresses her father over her shoulder, "I'll be at Stony Beach."

"Stay nearby."

She nods and leaves.

When Marin starts her descent down the access ladder, Joe starts his search of her bedroom.

Cliff Walk

Edward finds the cliff walk spying spot as soon as he pushes through the bramble—then he finds something way more important. He sits his ass in her spot and stares at the sketch, the really beautiful sketch of the moon. He reads the title, "*Moonlight Over Midnight Ocean*." She was here, whoever she is. He notices the faintest scribble at the bottom of the page, pulls the paper near to read it, "Baxter? Does that spell Baxter?" He stands and peers over the ledge watching early arrivals for the rock building cult fest. "I wonder if she's down there?"

Marin notices the man standing at her spot on the cliff walk as she makes her way down the access ladder. She forces herself to keep her eyes at beach level, and counsels herself, "Don't take any pictures in his direction. If that's him, I don't want him wondering about the girl with the camera." She perches herself on a big, flat rock she favors, turns her back to the cliff and gets lost in the hypnotic roll of waves. She startles when she hears something.

~~THAT'S HIM~~

Sure she'll find someone behind her, Marin spins, nearly toppling herself from the rock. She finds no one near, but sees the man still on the cliff. She quickly snaps a few pictures while he's surveying the bramble, lowers the camera and waits until he turns to leave. She snaps a series of images of him walking away, lowers the camera when he takes one final look in her direction. She turns her attention back to the ocean, pulls her legs up, wraps her arms around her knees, and wonders about the whispered words. A chill runs her sleeveless arms. "Did that just happen? Was that a whisper? Is my mind playing tricks? Is that the man who dumped a body? Was it a body? If it was a body, then is he the killer?" A spine-gripping shiver runs quickly up and back down then settles deep as an overwhelming sense of dread takes hold, "If that man is a killer, then he definitely saw me from the boat, and he's looking for me now."

Edward notices the girl sitting on the rock at the water's edge as he starts back through the thick cover of trees. He can't tell how old she is from that elevation, but one thing he knows for sure—she looked up at The Spot. He puts to memory the things he sort of sees about the girl on the rock, "Colorful ballcap with a full brown ponytail sticking out the back. Sleeveless tank and jeans. Shoulder strap camera. Not much to go on ……. wait, jeans on a beach? During the day? A hot, hot day? Why did she have on long pants?" He gets his answer when a thorn jabs through his pantleg. "I'm wearing jeans because I'm in the pricker bushes, I sure as hell wouldn't be wearing them if I were on the beach. Maybe she's wearing jeans because she got a few scrapes from her midnight stroll through the bramble."

The killer hops into a Tacoma he borrowed from the estate grounds, pulls the sketch from his pocket, ignores the picture on the paper, and hones in on the name written at the bottom. "Baxter." He puts the truck in drive and heads back to Echo. "I need to do a little research on this." He parks on the circular drive, and when he bounds into the massive house, he slams into Ruby, who's making her way across spit-polished marble floors in clickety-clackety high-heeled sandals. He grabs hold of the wobbling woman seconds before her bikini-clad butt hits the ground. "Ruby. I'm sorry. I guess I wasn't paying attention."

The former Shaky Town beauty, who snagged a suite of rooms by shagging the ruler of Whisper, smiles wide, "I guess I'm the only one paying attention to the comings and goings at Echo." She winks an eye, sending aflutter long, mink lashes in the process. "By the way, King's been looking for you."

Wind Ledge

The Baxter Mobile is missing when Marin comes back for lunch. Hoping both of her parents are gone, she races into the house and straight to her bedroom. Her father is waiting for her, his back pressed tight against a wall, his feet crossed at the ankles. He's holding her backpack, "Guess what I found."

She looks first at the backpack, then at the mound of dirty clothes at the foot of her bed. "I can explain."

"I doubt that very much, Marin, but you're going to. Start with the drawings."

"They're just for fun."

"They're remarkable."

"Yeah?" she smiles wide.

"A conversation for another time, Marin. From the looks of things, you've been sneaking out with some regularity since we arrived on the island."

"Yes."

"And not only have you not told your parents that you have a passion and great ability for drawing, but you have also not told us anything about your secret trips out your bedroom window."

"No."

"And you made one last night?"

"Yes."

"And maybe you saw something you shouldn't have seen, or maybe heard something?"

She is soooo not admitting anything that might pull her father into this mess. "What do you mean?"

He scoffs, "Come on, Marin, you know a seventeen-year-old girl is missing."

"Yes."

"Did you see her last night?"

She is soooo not telling him Laire is at the bottom of Casco Bay. "I didn't see a girl of any age walking about, and I only heard a man's voice call out her name. I only went out to sketch the moon."

He hands her the sketchpad, "You're drawing lunar phases."

"Yes."

"Last night's moon was in the Waning Gibbous."

"Yes."

"You didn't draw the moon last night."

"No. I forgot my flashlight, so I came home."

He points to the pile of clothes on the bed. "It looks like you decided to play in the dirt first. Your sweatpants are caked with mud and debris, and there's some blood streaks inside."

"Those are Mom's sweatpants."

"Are you suggesting your mother got them dirty and bloody?"

Silence.

"Perhaps the blood is from pricker scrapes."

Silence.

"Like the ones on your cheek."

Silence.

"No explanation for the condition of those clothes, Marin?"

She starts spinning a tale. "When I realized I couldn't draw – because I couldn't see – because I didn't bring my flashlight – I stayed a while and watched the moon, but now that you mention it – I think the dirt was from the other day – from Stony Beach – from right after high tide – I remember scraping my leg on the big rock – you know the one that's really rough on the sides, but really smooth on top – the one I like to sit on – I think last night I just threw on whatever I found when I knew you and Mom were asleep, it must have been the same sweatpants."

Joe raises his hand when he hears the Baxter Mobile door shut. He addresses his daughter. "Your mother is not to know about this. When I am ready, when I have enough facts, I will tell her. Until then, you will act as if nothing is wrong. We both know you're very good at fooling your parents, so continue on that tract. Tidy this place and do your laundry. And most of all, Marin, keep your butt in your room—tonight and every night. Is that clear?"

She nods. She waits until he leaves. She cries.

Day Two
Saturday, July 23
Waning Gibbous – Illumination 83%

   Chief Vernon Banks knocks on the front door of Watch Ledge at precisely 12:45 AM, 24 hours after Lachlan MacTavish reported his sister missing. The chief paid a similar call to Christie Anderson's family two years before, so he recognizes the terror in the young man's eyes. "Maybe I should have called first. There's no news, Mr. MacTavish. May I come in?"

   Lan steps aside and points to the comfort room.

   "I wanted to tell you that an official search and investigation has begun and ask if you've heard anything or have any information that might help us find ...." The chief's eyes fall on a bottle of whisky and half-drained glass. "Have you been drinking, Mr. MacTavish?"

   "No."

   "When was the last time you partook of the hooch?"

   "Does that concern ya?"

   "It might."

   Silence.

"Were you drinking the night Laire went missing? Maybe that's why you didn't know she snuck out?"

"Chief Banks, I think you should set your questions about Laire and unworry yourself about my occasional pull."

"I've read the information Officer Jacobs wrote up on his visit here last night, so I'm good on those particulars. If you don't mind, I'd like to take a look at Laire's room." The chief pulls on a pair of latex gloves and retrieves a large, rolled plastic baggie from inside his jacket. "If you'll point the way."

"Top of the stairs, room on the right, overlookin Cliff Road."

Lan takes a seat on the fireplace hearth and listens to footfalls moving through his sister's room, his missing sister's room. He freezes when he hears the creak of a floorboard in *his* bedroom. "The man's steppin afoul." Lan is near to the bottom step when the chief appears at the top.

"I've collected a few things, Mr. MacTavish." He holds out the plastic bag, "As you can see I've taken Miss MacTavish's hairbrush, toothbrush, a notepad, and an earring."

"An earring? Let me see."

"Does it look familiar? Maybe a family heirloom? It looks expensive."

"Haven't laid eyes on it before. Where's the match?"

"A very good question. Most likely it's in her bedroom, but I don't have time for a formal search. Depending on how things move on this case, I might be asking for a CSI tech from Portland PD to come over. I'd appreciate your staying out of your sister's room. If you don't comply with that request, you could be charged with interfering with a police investigation."

Lan takes a quick look up the stairs, then a long look at the back of the retreating chief of police.

WPD

King is sitting behind the chief's desk when the lawman returns from Watch Ledge. "Get up, and don't come in here and give the cops out there the idea we're friends, or worse, that you're running things. Right now they think you're an asshole big shot who doesn't know his place. If you don't get your ass out of my chair, I'll be putting it into a cell for the night to set the record straight."

"Yeah? What record is that, Vernon?"

"That I think you're an asshole, and I'm definitely the one running things."

King pushes up and moves opposite the chief. "Don't forget you're up to your ass in this, Vernon."

"I'm not even ankle-deep in this shit, King. If you want to go toe to toe you'd best know this, I could put you and Heir away for life. So tell me,

Edward Kingston III, are you done trying to put me in my place?"

"What's got you so riled up?"

"The fuck fest you dumped at my doorstep, you degenerate bastard."

King pushes to his feet, "I should fuck you good, Vernon."

"Sit your ass down and listen up you son of a bitch, if you so much as look at me sideways, those dipshits out there will receive every bit of information I have on you, and you'll spend the rest of your days behind bars. Mark my words, King, you and Heir will spend the rest of your days in adjoining cells if you fuck with one more girl on my island."

King laughs, "MY fucking island! And the cell right next to mine is reserved for you, Vernon."

"Don't count on it. Now get your goddamn ass out of my office and get Heir under control."

Echo

Edward bolts upright in bed when something very soft brushes his cheek. Light from the moon illuminates a naked Ruby. "Jesus, put that shimmer robe back on. If King finds you here, he'll kill the both of us."

"King isn't coming home tonight."

"Why not?"

"He has business in town. We both know what that means."

"You think he's with someone else? A woman?"

"Of course, a woman. There isn't a woman alive, or dead, who's managed to keep King faithful."

Edward knows that's true, although he only recently learned that his father cheated on his mother.

Ruby crawls onto the bed, slides her hand beneath the sheet and takes hold of Edward's very hard dick. "So much bigger than King's and I don't have to wait a half-hour for the little blue pill to do its job. Now, speaking of job."

Edward enjoys the hell out of Ruby's mouth work, smiles wide when beams travel the ceiling and wall silently announcing the return of The King to his castle. Edward pulls Ruby from his dick, "Straddle me." He goes balls deep and waits for King. Edward has more than a mouthful of Ruby's tit when his father eases the door open, gets an eyeful of his son and his whore, gives a thumbs up, and leaves.

Ruby spent the night in Edward's bed, he spent the night in Ruby, and King spent the night in the guesthouse. Father and son meet on the rattans just after dawn, one is sipping a coffee, the other is already one finger into his morning libation. King raises his glass to his son, "Getting Ruby into your bed took less time than I thought."

"Yeah, she struck while the iron was hot. You haven't been staying away much lately, so she—"

"Struck while the iron was hot," the father laughs.

Edward gives his head a good shake, "Are you sure you want to let this one go? I mean damnit to hell, she's good."

"I'm not letting her go, Edward, I'm just sharing her. You sex her good from time to time, make her think you two are clandestine lovers, she loves that shit. Toss a few trinkets and promises her way, and she'll give you a good alibi, a good blowjob, and anything else you want. And if there comes a day when Ruby disappoints either of us, I know a guy who handles these kinds of things."

Edward has a push of regret, "I don't handle shit, King. And I definitely didn't want to handle Laire."

"Because of the kid?"

"Because she was Laire. I would have been right with her."

"You would have been in jail." King gets up and calls over his shoulder, "Forget her. And by the way, Vernon sent a message."

"Yeah?"

"He said to stop with the jailbait, or he'll put your ass in prison. Take the warning, Edward, quit fucking juvies."

Edward kicks back in a chaise and immediately falls into the sleep of the dead, the one he missed out on the night before. He is woken by a soft brush across his cheek. He opens his eyes expecting to find Ruby. He finds no one. A shiver runs when he hears her voice.

~~TURN AROUND~~

He looks behind and all around. He finds no one.

Wind Ledge

Joe spent a very sleepless night walking the floors. He's starting another day in a pissed off mood and Esmé is having no part of it. She follows him to the porch, takes hold of his hand, and leads him to the driveway. She leans her butt against the Baxter Mobile, "Okay, spill. What did MacTavish say that put you into this mood?"

He shakes his head, "Let's walk a bit. I don't want Marin overhearing."

"She's still asleep."

"Good, it's been a rough couple days, but let's walk a bit anyway."

Esmé pushes from the bumper, and takes hold of her husband's outstretched hand. She thinks she feels a slight tremble, "Joe, what's going on?"

"Lan thinks—"

"Who's Lan?"

"MacTavish. Lachlan goes by Lan."

"Okay."

"Lan got a visit from an officer at Whisper PD who told him another teenage girl went missing two years ago."

Esmé's hand tightens, "Joe," the word catches, "is the girl still missing?" her voice elevates.

"Lan didn't mention, so I checked online. Christie Anderson was seventeen when she went missing during the summer of 2014. Her parents said she left to meet up with some friends at the beach and was expected back at midnight. When the mother woke on the couch just before dawn, she realized Christie never came home. She called the police, but by then, she'd been gone almost fourteen hours."

"Do the Andersons live on the island?"

"No, they were vacationing in Shaky Town, and witnesses say Christie was last seen waiting for a cliff side Whisper trolly at 9 PM."

"Weeknight or weekend?"

"Not sure, why?"

"I don't know what the trolly schedule was back then, but the last trolly off cliff side is 10 PM on weeknights, and midnight on weekends. Makes you wonder where she was going for such a short period of time." Esmé is quiet for a few. "I just assumed the situation with Laire was a one-off, a terribly sad event. Now that I know there was another girl who went missing, I'm worried about Marin."

Without realizing it, Joe and Esmé walked from the access ladder by their cottage to the one near Walker Ledge. "Shit, Esmé, we're a half-mile from home. Marin's alone." They take off running.

Marin goes outside sure she'll find her parents having coffee on the patio, "Huh." She heads around the corner to check on the Baxter Mobile, "Huh." Then she walks back to the patio to look up at the widow's walk, "Huh." She stomps back inside wondering how she could have missed them, "Mom. Dad." Silence. "The cliff walk? Did Dad tell Mom about my sneaking out at night? Are they trying to find my sketching spot?" She heads outside again, makes her way to the ledge, and looks westerly through the bramble. Something on Stony Beach catches her eye. She jumps back from the ledge when she sees a man sitting on her rock looking up at Wind Ledge.

~~NOT HIM ~ LOOK AT~~

Marin turns and runs into the cottage. She bumps hard into her parents when she rounds a corner. She screams, then dials it back a bit when she realizes it's them.

Esmé takes hold of her daughter's shoulders. "What's wrong? You look like you've seen a ghost."

"I ……. I ……. I couldn't find you. Where. Were. You?"

"We went for a little walk and—"

"And you left me alone!?" she shrieks. "Do you know what could have happened with him right out there?"

"Him? Who? Right out where?" Joe presses.

Marin pulls herself together, "Not him-him. I don't know him-him. But *him*-anyone." She stomps her feet in frustration. "I can't believe you two left me alone in this cottage with a kidnapping, murdering *him* out there." She storms to her room.

"Kidnapping? Que la?" Esmé repeats.

"Murdering? Que la?" Joe repeats.

Esmé makes a move to follow their daughter. Joe stops her, "Let her live with the fear for a minute. She needs to know—really know—how high the stakes are."

"I think she knows, Joseph. In her mind, she's already decided what happened to Laire."

Joe grunts, "Yeah."

Esmé tears, "Marin's right, you know. We never should have left her alone."

Joe nods, "And now that we know two girls went missing, we won't be leaving her alone ever again."

Echo

Edward returns from his walk on Stony Beach, heads to his home office right off his bedroom, and goes online. He stares at the flashing cursor in the search engine for several minutes, then talks himself through his plan, "Okay, make a list: 1. I need to find out who bought Wind Ledge and whether the family staying there are the owners or renters. 2. If I find out the people there have the last name, Baxter, I need to know if one of them is an artist. 3. I need to know if the girl on the cliff walk, the girl on Stony yesterday, and the girl from earlier today are the same girl. Okay, quit talking about this shit and find some answers." His fingers fly over the keyboard, and in a matter of minutes he learns all he needs to know—for now.

"Joseph and Esmé Baxter recently purchased Wind Ledge as a summer vacation place. Their primary residence is in Oxford, MA. They are both teachers in the Oxford Public School system. He teaches high school math. She teaches middle-school art. Huh. An artist with the last name Baxter. Looks like I'm onto something." He sits with that information for a while, "I've been thinking the figure that night was a teenage girl or a young woman, but Esmé Baxter is only thirty-six, and she could be a youthful thirty six." He runs the scene through his mind's eye again, "It could have been a woman, I suppose .... but the girl on the beach yesterday and the one standing on the cliff edge today is definitely a teenage girl." He continues his internet search and hits paydirt, "Marin Baxter, sixteen, almost seventeen. She's the one I saw yesterday on Stony Beach and today on the cliff at Wind Ledge. But is she the one who was on the cliff walk, and did she do the moon sketching? More likely it was Esmé

Baxter. I need to do some checking on the Baxter Babes."

Primrose Priscilla

Dale Jacobs is just getting his feet back under him and firmly planted after the ass-reaming he took from the chief. He knows he's taking a risk, a really big risk when he drives the length of a tree-lined cul-de-sac, and pulls to a stop at the home of retiring detective, Tom Martin. He's about to ring the doorbell when Tom comes from around the corner of the house.

"Heard your Harley, Dale. You here about Christie Anderson and the new girl?"

"You heard about the dustup at the station?"

"What dustup?"

"Got my ass removed from the rookie detective position. The chief didn't tell you, Detective?"

"Nope. The chief and I aren't exactly on speaking terms. Do me a favor, Dale, when we're out of the station, call me Tom. I've only got until the end of the year at WPD and maybe if enough people call me by my given name, I might start thinking like a civilian."

"I sure hope you'll let me pick your 'detective brain' a bit before you go all flip flop beach bum."

"Come on around back."

When they get there, Tom's lovely doppelganger of Mary Tyler Moore, gushes a bit over the young man who's paid a visit. She settles the men with tumblers of iced tea, then heads back inside, but not before she gives a warning, "Stay under that umbrella and out of direct sunlight, Thomas."

"Will do, Priscilla." Tom takes a sip, "So you're thinking there's a connection between the two cases?"

"I got a nudge when I heard the call come in about Laire MacTavish. I made the mistake of talking to her brother before the clock ran out on the 24 hour timeline. But my instinct tells me the two cases are connected. I was in the storage unit reading Christie Anderson's file when the chief appeared, already hot under the collar. I didn't have enough time to make any real determination about the cases. And by the way, I might have told the chief you told me to talk to the brother."

Tom laughs. "One, you might have just gotten my ass fired. Two, your instincts are right. Three, I've got Christie Anderson's files inside. Come on." Tom opens a screen door that leads to a screened-in room that leads to a basement office. He points to several carboard boxes. "That's them. Took me a damn long time to copy that shit and get it out of storage. Have a look through, take notes, and we'll talk when you're done."

Dale made it through a single box and jotted several pages of notes when he heads outside for a talk. He finds the detective in the screened-in porch waiting on his lunch. "Take a seat, Dale. The Missus prepared some grub. We'll eat and talk."

Dale smiles wide at the plate that's handed him, "This is hardly grub, Tom."

Priscilla chortles, "Don't pay attention to my husband, Dale, unless he's talking about an investigation. Then you should take every word he says as fact. Now eat up. Dessert will be out of the oven in an hour."

The men take turns eating and talking.

"Laire MacTavish was noticed missing by her brother Lan around 8 PM. He doesn't know exactly what time she left."

"Why?"

"MacTavish might have had a few drinks. There was a near empty Glenlivet bottle in the den, and he had the smell of booze on him when I showed up."

"MacTavish is about your age, right?"

"Yeah."

"Do you know him?"

"Nope."

"Continue."

"There's not much else from our meeting. I told him I was training to be a detective, and that the formal investigation couldn't begin for 24 hours, and that we wanted to get out ahead a bit because of the other missing girl. That's when MacTavish lost it a bit."

"Yeah. You might not have wanted to lead with that. As soon as you mentioned the other missing girl, you put him on notice that he might be looking down a long life of not knowing about his kid sister."

"What should I have said?"

"As little as possible. Let the other person talk. Take it all in. Prompt them toward questions that need answering. Let's try something. Answer my questions, keep it brief."

"Okay."

"What time did you arrive at the MacTavish place?"

"A couple minutes before 7 AM."

"Did you have to wait for him to answer the door?"

"No, he pulled it wide, practically before I stopped knocking."

"Did he ask why you were there?"

"No, he immediately asked if we'd found his sister."

"Did MacTavish invite you in?"

"No, I asked if I could go in."

"Where'd he take you?"

"To his den. It's the space where most people would set a more formal living room."

"How so?"

"The room is at the front of the cottage, to the left when you first walk in. It has really nice hardwoods and mantled fireplace. Islanders have the whole beach living thing going on, still most places have that room set somewhat fancy."

"Interesting. Okay, based on what I asked you, tell me what you know."

"It's unlikely MacTavish slept upstairs if he slept at all. He was awake at 7 AM and eager to find his sister on the other side of the door when he opened it. He didn't invite me in ……. I don't think he kept me outside because he was hiding something—"

"Why?"

"Because he took me to the room where there were obvious signs he'd been drinking."

The detective nods, "Keep going."

"When I mentioned the other missing girl, he totally lost it. He became very emotional. It was as though ……."

"Grab hold of that thought, Dale, and walk it through."

"It was as though he never considered his sister might not be coming home until that very minute."

"You need to remember that Lacklan MacTavish was hit with something when you mentioned the other missing girl."

"Guilt?"

"Could be, but what's the source of his guilt?"

Dale shrugs. "Maybe he thinks he didn't take good enough care of his sister, and now Laire might be in over her head."

"What's your gut telling you, Dale?"

"Lachlan isn't involved in the disappearance of Laire MacTavish, but beyond that I've got nothing."

"That's plenty. Make sure you remember what your gut just told you, especially if Lachlan

MacTavish becomes the focus of the investigation."

LAIRE

Lan heard my whisper. He'd been drinking his fair share and probably thinks it was the drink talkin, but he heard me. And the girl heard my whisper. She knows deep down that the man on the cliff walk is the one who tossed me asunder, but she needs me to help settle that thought a bit. And Edward heard my whisper and felt my touch upon his cheek. Should'a smacked him a right one.

She wonders then decides a few things...

Marin heard only part of what I said when she was looking at the man on the rock. I tried to tell her that he wasn't the one who took my life, that it was the man standing and staring up at her. The one with the blue ballcap on. But she only heard part of what I said? Is it because she's young, and the whole lot of us hear what we want to hear and let the rest fall upon deaf ears? Lord knows, I ignored Lan's warnin words about the dangers of a lass flauntin her belongins. Even pitched a hissy when he made me cover my parts before goin to the Kingston party at

Echo. A lot of good coverin my parts did when Heir's wooin words stripped away my clothes and showed me what for, takin my virginity along with my heart—and knockin me up right and tight.

Day Three
Sunday, July 24
Waning Gibbous – Illumination 74%

Esmé plans to spend her Sunday perched upon her artist stool with brush in hand and eyes set on the wonder of Casco Bay. Joe jumps at the opportunity to spend the day with Marin away from Wind Ledge. They pack a beach bag with towels, sunscreen, and a Frisbee, then hop the first Whisper trolly that passes by. Their trip to the sandy side of the island begins with a pass by Watch Ledge. Joe notices Lan sitting on the front stoop. He ignores the man's half-hearted wave.

"Who's that?"

"Who?"

"The man who waved?"

"I didn't see anyone."

"Back there. At Watch Ledge."

"Huh. Didn't see anyone. I must have been daydreaming."

"Really? Because it looked like you leaned forward so the guy couldn't see me. Who is that guy? Do you think he has something to do with that girl's disappearance?"

"You saw Lachlan MacTavish."

"The missing girl's brother?"

"Yes."

"That's him?"

"Why?"

She shrugs. "He's young. You should let him know you didn't see him wave, or he'll think you're rude."

"Not sure you should be counseling me on what I should and shouldn't be doing, Marin."

Widow's Walk

Esmé takes a long look at the work she's done since arriving at the cottage in June. A handful of canvases line the walls of her art studio which is really the second-floor master bedroom. Nearly all of the paintings are of the shoreline and ocean at different times of day.

The artist offers some criticism, "Mira, Esmé, you're easing into a comfort zone with your work. You need to step away from the land and seascapes and toward something else for a while, at least for a few pieces." She makes her way to a painting across the room, the only piece that's completely finished. It's of her daughter sitting on what has become her favorite rock looking out at the ocean. "This is really beautiful if I do say so myself. Joe is going to love this. It'll be the perfect Christmas gift, especially if we spend the holiday here where I painted it." She pulls her shoulder-length, nutty-brown, wavy hair into a high ponytail, puts on a pair of glasses, and reads the title of her work, "*Girl on a Rock*." She continues her assessment. "The essence of Marin shines through, yet the girl could be anyone."

She opens a door very near the bedroom fireplace, turns on an overhead light, climbs five stairs, opens another door and steps onto the widow's walk. She inches her way toward the railing and looks at the people moving about on the beach below. She jumps back to the center of the platform when a swirl of nerves takes hold. "God, I hate it up here, but I love it up here. I wish I had Marin's constitution. Nothing about heights bothers that kid." Esmé thinks about the painting of her daughter again, smiles at her accomplishment, and makes a mental note that she wants to compare the finished work with the photograph she used as inspiration. "I took that picture of Marin when we came to Whisper to sign purchase papers." Inspiration strikes again, "I should take a few shots of people on the beach and paint from those."

She runs to the first floor, finds Marin's camera hanging on a hook in the bedroom, and heads outside to the platform area just above the access ladder. She steps back and changes plans when she scrolls through pictures her daughter already took. "Wow, these are really good. Marin has quite the eye for photography," she stops talking when she finds the perfect images for her work.

She moves through seven frames and decides three things: "The zoom capability on this camera is awesome. Marin really knows how to best optimize the camera's features. She chose the perfect subject matter." The artist analyzes the form, "Intense body language. There's an almost palpable energy pulsating off him … an edginess that pushes against the wistful tranquility of the rose and lilac bushes surrounding him. These shots tell a story, a contradiction, a mystery." She laughs when the novel *Wuthering Heights* pops into her head. "Instead of Heathcliff in the moors of England, I've got him on a cliff in New England." She abandons her photography session and heads to the widow's walk.

Sandy Beach

Joe lets his soon-to-be seventeen-year-old daughter enjoy the first part of her day at the beach doing a bit of seventeen-year-old stuff: sunning, swimming, and strolling along the surf. She builds a sandcastle, tosses a Frisbee, and does her fair share of people watching—most particularly male people watching—though it doesn't seem like the normal kind of watching done by teenage girls, of which the high school teacher has some point of reference. In fact, the father notices his daughter tense and practically shrink into herself when a guy walks by and looks her way. The father nudges his daughter's shoulder, "You should come clean, Marin."

"About?"

"Whatever it is you know, or think you know, or saw, or heard, or all of the above. I already know you snuck out of the cottage, and

I'm pretty sure you only did it so you could sketch the moon, but I also know you were out of the house at the same time a teenage girl went missing. If you found yourself in the wrong place at the wrong time, and if you saw something that could put you in danger, you really need to tell me."

He is met with silence. Lots and lots of silence.

Joe nudges again, "When you're ready to talk, I'm ready to listen. For now, I need you to listen, really listen. Okay?"

"Okay."

"Your mother and I have been married almost eighteen years, and in all that time I haven't lied to her or kept secrets from her. Not once, Marin. And now, every word that comes out of my mouth is a lie. I hate what I'm doing, and I will pay dearly when all of this comes to light. So, while you're stewing about whether to tell me or not to tell me what you know, make sure you consider the collateral damage being caused on this end."

Marin pushes from the sand, grabs and rolls her towel, stuffs her things into the beach bag and starts marching away, "I want to go home."

Joe follows her to the trolly stand, arriving in plenty of time to see Lachlan MacTavish being escorted into Town Hall.

Marin doesn't miss a beat, "Hey, isn't that him?"

"Yes."

"And isn't the police station inside Town Hall?"

"The police station and the county court."

"Do you think they found his sister?"

"Don't know what to think, Marin."

It isn't until the trolly is nearing Shaky Town that father and daughter Baxter realize they'd hopped onto a sightseeing trolly, so instead of a thirty minute trip to cliff side, they expect it will be more than an hour before they make it home. Under normal circumstances neither would mind, but living in a world of normal circumstances seems to have ended when Laire MacTavish went missing.

Joe does the whole shoulder nudge thing, "There's something else."

"Okay."

"I took your sketchpad and hid it."

"Why?"

"Until I know what's going on and can tell your mother everything, I can't risk her finding your work and learning that you were sneaking out at night. I'll take very good care of the pad and will return it to you in time."

"Okay." She thinks for many minutes then pushes in, "The cottage isn't very big."

"No."

"But you found a hiding place that Mom won't find."

"Yes."

"Cottage or shed."

"Nice try."

"Did it work?"

"Nope."

Whisper Police Department

Officer Dale Jacobs pretends to be busy when Lan is walked into the police station by Chief Banks. He keeps his eyes averted until the office door closes behind the two men, then shuts down his computer and heads out of WPD. He makes a quick call to Tom Martin from outside his patrol car, "Lan MacTavish was just escorted into the chief's office."

"Uh huh. Are you on patrol?"

"Until seven."

"Make your way to Watch Ledge and leave a note for MacTavish with my address and the suggestion he visit tonight. Tell him to take a trolly and to come after dark. You come, too."

"How late is too late?"

"For you, it's never too late. For MacTavish, it'll be too late if Banks makes a move on him tonight."

Chief Banks drops Lan off at Watch Ledge a little before 7 PM, "You should get yourself a lawyer, Mr. MacTavish."

Lan slams the door.

The chief heads directly to Wind Ledge, "Time to check out a few things." He steps onto the front porch and knocks then walks around back when no one answers. He finds the Baxter family roasting marshmallows over a firepit, "Sorry to interrupt."

The family of three shoot to their feet. Joe approaches the chief, "No worries, Chief. Joe Baxter, and that's my wife, Esmé, and our daughter, Marin."

"Vernon Banks. Wish I could welcome you to Whisper in a friendlier way, but I need a few words with you, Joe."

Esmé and Marin head inside, and the men take seats.

"I spent some time with Lacklan MacTavish, and I'd like to check a few things, after I hear your recollection of things."

Joe nods. "Esmé and I were awakened when someone outside yelled something. We didn't know at the time that the shout came from Lachlan MacTavish and that he was calling his sister's name."

"What time was this?"

"Around midnight. Then, a little after 2:30 AM we heard the same thing. Esmé and I got up and waited a bit, then I headed out around three to see if I could find the guy who yelled and to see if he needed help."

"And?"

"A guy introduced himself as Lachlan MacTavish and said he was looking for his seventeen-year-old sister, Laire. He said he checked on her around eight o'clock and realized she'd snuck out sometime before that. He said she might have left to meet up with some guy and hadn't come home yet. He was starting to freak out."

"Some guy? Any idea why he thought that?"

"No."

"Okay. Continue, Joe."

"I returned to Wind Ledge and stayed here until Lan showed up the next morning."

"What time was that?"

"Around eight."

"Just go ahead and talk. If I need to push in, I will."

Joe nods and quickly decides he's not going to tell everything he knows. "Lan said he stopped by to tell me there wasn't any news on Laire, but an officer stopped by to say the police would begin a formal search later that night. I got the sense he just needed someone to talk to, so I went with him to his place. When we got there he said he feared his sister was in real trouble."

"Did he say why?"

Joe *could* say that Lan told him about the other missing girl, Christie Anderson, or that Lan saw Marin sneaking around the house at midnight, or that Lan peered into her bedroom window, or that Marin might have seen something or maybe knows something— instead, Joe simply says, "No. MacTavish didn't say why, but I got the sense that Laire being gone so long was starting to settle badly."

"Your daughter, Marin, she's about the same age as the MacTavish girl."

Joe nods.

"Do you suppose the two girls know each other or maybe met, seeing as they're contemporaries and they're both from the cliff side?"

The father wants to say, "No chance," but he really can't be sure, so he simply says, "Unlikely. We've been here little over a month and it's been all Baxter hands on deck settling in and fixing up the place."

The chief takes a surveying look, "You're doing some good work, Mr. Baxter."

"Time will tell, Chief. I'm pretty inexperienced with the power tools, so you might want to hold your praise until we see if my work makes it through the winter intact."

The chief smiles, "Sure can get rough on this side of the bay during winter months, but you'll be heading home at the end of the summer for your teaching jobs, right?"

Joe feels the sting from knowing he's been researched by a lawman, but he doesn't let it show. "We're heading back by September, but we hope to spend holiday weekends and maybe Christmas here."

"Better book your holiday ferry passes now or you might be out of luck."

"Good to know. Thanks."

The chief gets up to leave and tosses a final question, "Any chance Marin was out that night around midnight?"

Joe laughs, "Absolutely no chance." As he watches Chief Vernon Banks head to a WPD Range Rover an unsettling thought finds his lips.

"For fucks sake, I'm lying to the cops now."

Primrose Priscilla

Lan MacTavish waited a good ten minutes after the chief drove away before hoofing it a half-mile down the road to hop a trolly. He grabs a seat, pulls the note Dale left, and silently rereads the instructions and address. Then not so silently he laments, "This shit day can't be done soon enough." He hangs his head when he remembers his sister is gone and silently prays the day never ends. An uneasiness roughs his gut as he follows flagstones around the side of the pretty yellow house surrounded by lush yellow primrose bushes. He starts right in when he sees Dale, "I thought you were workin the case."

"Chief got pissed that I told you about Christie Anderson. He pulled my training spot and benched my ass."

"Sorry for that, but I had my ass carted to the police station, and when the not-so-friendly encounter ended, the chief told me to get a lawyer." Lan notices the other man for the first time, "Shit, who's that now?"

"I'm Detective Tom Martin, and for the record, you weren't here and we never talked. Got it?"

Lan checks with Dale who nods. He addresses the detective. "Are you of the Scottish clan MacMartins?"

"I am."

"And your motto be?"

"Sure and steadfast."

"We'll see, right? Straight up MacMartin, I'm keeping more shit silent than I'm airin, so let's have a go of it, Detective."

Tom points to a seat, "You're gonna tell us about the shit you're keeping silent later. Right now, tell me about the meeting you had with the chief."

"He grabbed me from home and rode me to town and locked me inside his office and asked me a second go of queries. He asked when the last time was I saw Laire. I said, mealtime around 5 PM. He asked what time I realized she was gone. I said, around 8 PM. He asked what I was doing between 5 and 8, and whether I'd been drinking. I suggested it was none of his business if I'd been bending the elbow with Glenlivet."

The detective leans forward and puts his forearms onto his thighs, "Continue."

"He asked where I work, and I said, the marina. He asked if I worked that day, and I said, yes. He asked what Laire did during that day. I said, I didn't know as I was workin. He asked if I saw her before I went to work, and I said, I hadn't. He asked when I arrived on the island. I said, two years past. He asked if I spend time on the sandy side or in Shaky Town. I said, most of my travels are from Walker Ledge to the marina and back, but that I've spent time at the beach and at Diggers."

Lan gets a nudge.

"Somethin else. The chief took a plastic bag with an earring out of his desk drawer."

"What earring?"

"The one he found in Laire's room—"

"When was he in your sister's room?"

"He came to the house 24 hours after I reported Laire missing."

"You called 9-1-1 at 12:45 AM."

Lan nods.

"Chief Banks went to Watch Ledge at 12:45 AM?"

Lan nods.

"Continue."

"He said an official search and investigation was on and that he'd read the report Officer Jacobs wrote up and—"

"I didn't write a report."

The young men look at the older man who grunts, "Continue."

Before Lan has a chance, Dale's phone rings, "It's the chief. I need to..." he steps away.

Tom nods to Lan to continue.

"The chief asked if I'd heard anything or had any information that might help. He looked about the room we were in and asked if I'd been drinking, and when the last time was I partook of hooch. I told him to unworry himself about me and set his questions about Laire. That's when he went up to her room. That's also when he stepped about in my room."

The detective pushes in, "What makes you think he was in your room?"

"I heard the squeak of a floorboard I shoulda fixed a right time ago. He moved about for a bit, and as I was nearin the stairs to find out why he was nosing about, he came down with a plastic bag that held Laire's toothbrush, hairbrush, a notepad, and an earring. He said he only found one, and it looked expensive. He asked if it's a family heirloom."

"Is it?"

"Tellin you the same I told him, I never seen it before. My ma might have handed off jewelry to Laire, but Mother MacTavish never pierced her ears and took a right fit when Laire did. The earring the chief showed me had a piercin post." Lan suffers through an emotional pull then pushes through. "Right before Chief Banks left, he said he might have a CSI tech come from Portland, and that I should stay out of Laire's room."

The penny drops.

"Detective Martin, I'd say the chief was more interested in me during his visit than he was in Laire."

"Uh huh. Talk about that."

"I mentioned my fear that she went off to meet a guy. He made a note, but didn't ask more. And he never mentioned the 9-1-1 call I made. I think that shoulda been discussed."

The detective notices Officer Jacobs' head nodding as he returns, "You want in, Dale?"

"I heard the 9-1-1 call come in and gave dispatch a call right after, asking for a rundown. Donna said she received a call from Lachlan MacTavish saying his seventeen-year-old sister skipped out of Watch Ledge sometime early evening, that he made several neighborhood searches in both directions, and that around midnight he thought he saw someone move in the shadows on the cliff walk. So, he called out thinking it was his sister, but nothing came of it. He called emergency on his way back to his place."

Detective Martin takes over, "Did Dale accurately describe your conversation with Donna Abbott?"

Lan nods. "Except I said someone moved in the shadows **near** the cliff walk at Wind Ledge."

"And the chief didn't ask you about this?"

"No."

The detective mulls a bit. "Tell me about the shit you're keeping secret."

Before he has a chance to begin, Dale gets a second call. He waves his phone, "I need to take this."

Tom nods, "Take it out of earshot of Mr. MacTavish." He nods to Lan to continue.

"After my call to emergency I moved about Cliff Road and through some of the lower neighborhoods. Around 3 AM, I was approached by a man who identified himself as Joe Baxter from Wind Ledge. I told him my sister was missing, I was searching for her, and that I thought I saw someone near the backside of his place around midnight. The talk was brief, but it gave me reason enough to go back to his place the next morning. I suggested the person near his place was his daughter. He didn't take too kindly to the suggestion, but wanted to discuss it. We went to Watch Ledge, and I set it all out. I told him I saw his daughter sneakin about his property some past midnight and that she disappeared through a bedroom window before I could talk to her. He didn't take kindly to my sayin I peeped in."

"I imagine he didn't."

"True statement, I wasn't thinkin straight at the time, but I could tell the girl wasn't sleepin. She was out and about that night, for sure."

"How'd you leave it with Joe Baxter?"

"He told me never to darken his doorstep again."

"What other secrets are you keeping, Mr. MacTavish?"

Dale enters the space again and feels the tension, "What'd I miss?"

"Nothing. Mr. MacTavish was just about to tell me **all** his secrets."

There's something in Tom Martin's tone that sets Lan thinking. The detective cuts to the chase. "I already know about the dustup in

Speyside, and I know you knew Christie Anderson."

Lan pushes to his feet and walks away.

Tom calls out after him, "I know this shit because WPD marked you as a suspect in Christie's disappearance."

Lan spins and spews, "I barely knew her, and I stopped seeing her when I found out she was a minor. I hadn't a single thing to do with her goin missing."

"I knew that then. I know that now. I also know you're going to be the fall guy for two missing teens, so sit back down."

Day Four
Monday, July 25
Waning Gibbous – Illumination 63%

It's after midnight when Dale and Lan leave the detective's home. Lan doesn't wait for the questions he knows the officer wants to ask about the dustup in Speyside. "Do you know anything about the law of heraldic arms?"

Dale laughs his, "No."

"A bit of history then. Scots are all about displaying their coat of arms, a heraldic designed shield with crest, motto, and tabard of family colors."

"What the eff? Are you speaking the English language right now because I don't think I got one bit of that."

Lan laughs for the first time in Lord knows how long. "Listen up and grab what you can. In Scotland and other places for sure, the coat of arms is serious business, passed down through ancestral rights and protected by the Lyon Court, a standing court of law which regulates heraldry. A man who fucks with a Scotsman's coat of arms ends up a dead man, or one wishin he were dead, or one who could spend enough time in jail to become dead."

"I'm guessing you fucked with someone's coat of arms."

"The someone was he who put a roof over me head since birth."

"Your father?"

"Sir Ian MacTavish himself. In right defense I was drunk on the Glenlivet when I took the family tartan of red, blue, and black, tossed it on the ground, and pissed a fine lot upon it while chantin the MacTavish clan motto, 'non oblitus.'"

"Feel free to translate."

"Not forgotten."

Dale gives a hearty laugh, "Bet your father hasn't forgotten that bit of disrespect."

"I suspect not even while he's tossin in his grave."

"Sorry, Lan."

"Your sorrow is appreciated."

Dale pulls to the trolly stand on the street below Cliff Road and pushes in, "You ought to stop drinking, at least for the time being. You need to keep your wits about you. If the detective is right about Chief Banks setting you in his sights, you'd better be clear-headed from now on. And you'd better never mention tonight's meeting."

Lan nods and starts to get out.

"Another thing, Lan, you and I are going to talk about Christie Anderson and why you didn't tell me the other night you knew about her."

Wind Ledge

Marin fell into a deep REM sleep the minute her head hit the pillow around 9 PM. She's wide awake at 1 AM frantically searching for her camera. She's looked in her drawers three times each, rifled through her closet more times than she can count, emptied her backpack compartment by compartment, and even snuck into the living room as soon as the groaning and wheezing of Joe and Esmé began, and nothing. "Did I lose it?" She replays her steps after the last time she used it. "I took pictures of the guy on the cliff walk and brought it home. I know I hung it on the hook where I always keep it." Dread settles deep and hard, "Did my father see the pictures and take the camera? Did he hide it with the sketchpad? Shit! What the hell am I supposed to do without my drawings and my camera?"

She tidies up a bit then crawls back into bed, bounces right back out and stands at the window, "Waning Gibbous at 63% illumination." She begins to cry, "I didn't get to sketch this. My collection, *Moonlight Over Midnight Ocean*, isn't complete, probably won't ever be complete, at least not this summer." It takes a minute for her disappointment to ebb, then she grasps onto what's really important, "Laire has been gone for four nights." The confused and tormented teen leans her elbows on the sill and replays the events of that night. A shiver, or two, or three runs when she gets to the part where the body splashed into the ocean. She covers her ears and shakes her head, "Maybe I should say something. Maybe tell someone that I saw *something* being dumped into the water. And if it turns out it's Laire, as awful as it would be for her brother to know she's dead, he would probably be better off in the long run." She pushes aside curtains that are being lifted by a breeze and tries to get lost in lunar beauty. When…

~~NOT YET~~

An icy cold runs her length sending Marin quickly to bed. She pulls the covers overhead and shakes herself into a fit of exhaustion.

Echo

Ruby takes advantage of an empty house and heads to Edward's suite. She heard him at his computer the other day muttering stuff about the Baxter family so that's where she goes to find information. She sneaks through his bedroom to his office, shuts the door behind her, runs her fingertips over the mousepad, only to find the computer screen stays dark. "That was a bust." She pulls open a few desk drawers and flips through a few file folders, "Kingston Marina – Big Diamond, Kingston Marina – Little Diamond, Kingston Marina – Peaks Island. Holy shit. King is ready to buy three more marinas. That will put him at seven locations in Casco Bay. He'll own a huge amount of water rights and chunks of shoreline. And what's this? He's buying into the Casco Bay Ferry Lines, too. I wonder if people know about this? I wonder how he's doing this."

She scoffs at her wonder, "He's doing it because he's Edward Kingston III. The man among men, ruthless men." She puts the folders back and quickly looks through the final two. "Nothing about anyone named Baxter." She's ready to abandon her search when she sees a lone piece of paper on the printer tray. She raises a brow when she reads it, "Baxter Family." The section on Marin Baxter is bolded in red print. "Date of birth September 1, 1999, so she's almost seventeen. She's from Oxford, Massachusetts, but lives at Wind Ledge with her parents, Joe and Esmé." Ruby puts the paper back, sneaks out of Edward's suite, and hustles to King's room when headlights rise from the circular drive.

She's stepping into the shower when King moves in behind her, "Make room for me." He presses her against a wall and starts banging her pussy while her head is banging something else, *Why is Edward researching a teenage girl?*

Watch Ledge

Lan thinks about bringing his stash of whisky back out of the cupboards when news about his sister hits the airwaves.

Breaking News: Another teenage girl goes missing on Whisper Island. Laire MacTavish, a cliff side resident, went missing early Thursday evening from Watch Ledge where she lives with her brother, Lachlan MacTavish. Police are releasing very little information and caution people from making a connection between this missing girl and Christie Anderson who went missing two years ago. When asked if there's been any progress in the Anderson case, Chief Banks barked his usual, "No comment," and headed inside WPD. This is Roxanne Carmichael for WCWI, Channel Four news.

The very pissed-off brother of the missing teen picks up the phone and calls a young woman he works with and sexes up from time to time, "I suppose you heard?"

"Yeah, Lan, I'm so sorry. Can I do anything?"

"Tell the Kingston's I'm takin the week off. If it don't settle with them, tell them to send me my last check."

"I'm sure King will be fine with this, Lan."

"Don't care, Danielle. I've got to go."

"Take care … and Lan, stop by if you need a shoulder."

"Think you should be expectin me, Danni."

Kingston Marina

King tells Chief Banks about Danielle's call. "MacTavish is taking the week off. He said I could fire his ass and send him his last check if I objected to his calling in."

"Don't fire him. Give him the time he needs. It'll be a lot easier for us to keep an eye on him if he's here eight hours a day."

King nods.

"Did you give Edward my message?"

King nods, pulls a sip, and takes a drag.

The chief tosses the bagged earring onto King's desk, "Look familiar?"

The man who purchased the earrings doesn't have to pick up the baggie to recognize it, "Where did you find that?"

"In Laire MacTavish's bedroom."

"Where's the other one."

"Don't know," he lies. "I'm guessing from your reaction Edward gave them to the girl."

"They were his mother's." He pauses to reflect. "Heir said he was really into this girl. He must have been serious about her if he gave her something of Kathleen's."

Vernon shakes his head, "That woman was too good for the likes of you."

"Still pining?"

"Stopped pining twenty-five damned years ago, you miserable son of a bitch. All I can say now is, I'm glad she isn't here to see what a colossal mess you did raising her son."

"Fuck you."

"More like your son is gonna get fucked if Laire showed those earrings to anyone, or bragged about bedding a Kingston."

"Edward said the girl only hung out with him or her brother, and the latter of those two was pissed as a fart half the time—the dead bitch's words by the way. So it's unlikely she told anyone anything. Have you started framing MacTavish?"

"I'm not doing shit until I know for sure Laire didn't tell anyone about Edward. I had Lan at the station last night and when I dropped him back at his place, I told him to get a lawyer."

"Why the fuck would you tell him that?"

"If he hires legal representation and the press finds out, they'll hound him and me to find out why. Then we'll muck the waters by letting Roxanne Carmichael at WCWI know we were looking at MacTavish when Christie Anderson went missing."

"You said you couldn't build a case against him for Christie."

"I said Detective Thomas Martin knew there wasn't a strong enough case against MacTavish to bring charges."

"Yeah, well, Tom's still around, and he's not gonna let a guy go down for a murder he didn't commit."

"First of all, King, the **only** thing anyone knows is that Christie went missing. No one knows she's at the bottom of Casco Bay, so no one at this point will be going down for murder. As long as her bones stay where they are, there's no need for the WPD to reopen the investigation into her disappearance. It doesn't mean we can't have the press churn the waters a bit. My plan, right now, is to sit on the Anderson investigation until Tom retires. Between now and then, we see if we can build a case against Lachlan MacTavish for the disappearance of his sister, Laire." The chief takes the bagged earring off King's desk and delivers a directive, "Tell Edward to keep his dick in his pants. I'm warning both of you, this is the last time you're pulling my ass into one of these shit fests."

Watch Ledge

Lan spent much of the morning on the widow's walk thinking about the call he made to the marina, wondering whether the Kingstons would let him go, wondering whether his finances could hold out if he needed an attorney, and wondering if he should take the chief's advice and hire one. He takes out his cell and gives Dale a call. It goes straight to voicemail. His ire kicks up good until he reminds himself, "Dale said not to leave a message if he didn't answer, said he'd see the number and get in touch when he could." Lan pulls a slip of paper from his pocket and dials that number.

"Detective Martin."

"You said I could call."

"Yes, Priscilla, dear, I know it's you, I have caller ID, you know. And you also know I'm at the station." He laughs, "No, I suppose it doesn't matter. So, what can I do for you, dear?"

"Should I hire a lawyer?"

"Absolutely not. I mean it Miss Prissy, no retirement party. We've discussed this matter, and I'm sure we'll be doing so several more times, but now is not one of them. I'll talk to you when I get home. And by the way, I'll be doing some snooping to see if you're trying to pull the wool."

For the first time in days—four days—Lan feels like he might have someone on his side of things.

Wind Ledge

Esmé nudges Joe and motions with her head in Marin's direction. It's the third time she's called his attention to their daughter, the one who's butt hasn't moved off a chaise lounge all morning. "Que es esta?" the mother asks on her way into the cottage.

"No idea," the father answers when she comes back outside.

"Did something happen at sandy beach, yesterday?"

"No," he lies.

"Maybe the visit last night from Chief Banks upset her."

"Maybe the wall-to-wall news about Laire and Christie is upsetting her."

"Maybe being stuck on this island with nothing to do is upsetting me," Marin pushes from her chair and storms into the cottage.

"Well, that's new," Esmé chuckles.

A shiver runs Joe, "Welcome to the adolescent angst of high schoolers, a little later than normal, but whatever…" the teacher scoffs.

Esmé takes hold of her husband's hand and gives it a squeeze. "I'll be right back." She doesn't bother checking the first floor, or the second. She goes directly to the widow's walk where she finds Marin standing at the railing looking out to sea. She knocks on the doorframe. "Can I come out?"

"It's your studio."

"What's got you in such a mood?"

Silence.

"How come you're not on the beach?"

"That isn't a beach. It's just a pile of rocks."

Esmé pushes a huff, "Well, this is more serious than I thought."

"I'm just bored. Can't I just be bored—by myself?"

"Yesss, but I have a better idea. Put on your sneakers and get ready, we're going into town."

"Why?"

"I have an errand. Come on."

She groans and rolls her eyes.

Watch Ledge

As soon as his wife and daughter head to town, Joe puts his tools into the shed, locks the house, and goes for a walk that ends up being a half-mile sprint in an easterly direction. He knocks on the front door of the MacTavish place and when he gets no answer, he heads around back, where he finds the patio and yard empty. "Maybe Stony Beach," he moves toward the cliff, then stops when Lan calls down to him from the widow's walk.

"Up here, Joe. Head through the house, you'll find the walk stairs in the master."

"Came to check on you," Joe says when he steps outside.

"Appreciate the effort. You've checked, now you can leave."

"Chief Banks came by Wind Ledge."

"And?"

"I found myself lying to him."

"Welcome to the club."

"I don't want to be in this club, Lan, and I don't even know how I got into it."

"Because you know Marin snuck out that night, and you think she knows somethin and you're tryin to protect her."

"Yeah."

"Finally admittin Marin's sneak-about, are ya, Joe?"

The father nods, then shakes his head.

"Take a seat and answer me straight. Did you put me in a poor light durin your account of things with the chief?"

"If you're wondering if I told him you peeped into my teenage daughter's bedroom window in the middle of the night, the answer is no."

"Because to say that, you'd have to tell the chief Marin snuck out."

Joe nods. "Did you tell the chief about Marin?"

"No, and he didn't ask, which is an odd matter."

"Why?"

"When I made the emergency call about Laire, I told the dispatcher I thought I saw someone walkin the cliff shadows near Wind Ledge."

Silence.

Joe breaks the silence. "Okay, let's recap. You called 9-1-1 to report Laire missing, and during that call you told a police dispatcher you saw someone, not a girl, but **someone**, lurking about Wind Ledge at the same time you were looking for your missing sister."

Lan nods.

Joe gets off his seat and paces a bit. "When the chief was leaving my place, after our conversation turned toward house repairs and holiday ferry trips, he abruptly asked if there was a chance Marin was outside around midnight the night Laire went missing. You didn't say it was a young girl lurking about, so why did the chief ask specifically about Marin?"

"Could be I wasn't the only one who saw her."

Joe hangs and shakes his head, "This is getting worse by the day."

"I can attest to that. The chief has settled on a suspect."

"Who?"

"Me."

Joe spins toward Lan and nearly chokes on his words, "Chief Banks thinks **you** had something to do with your sister going missing?"

Lan nods.

"Why?"

"I'm thinking it's because I knew Christie Anderson."

"The other missing girl?"

Lan nods.

"For fuck's sake, MacTavish, that girl was seventeen when she went missing. How the hell old are you, anyway?"

"At the time, twenty-two, and I hadn't an idea she wasn't legal. We met at a pub in Shaky Town, dated twice at the public beach, and when I learned of her age, I walked away."

Joe gets lost in thought. *Lan was five years older than Christie. I'm six years older than Esmé. She was eighteen when we met, so legally we were okay, but shit. As far as Lan meeting Christie in a bar, I can see how his not knowing she was underage could happen.*

"Where are your thoughts, Joe?"

"Just trying to figure how these cases could be tied together. It doesn't make sense, to me."

Lan gives a shrug, "The problem for me, Joe, is while the law is tyin them together, the chief is loopin a noose around my neck."

Down On Main Street

It took a half hour for Esmé to travel the few miles into town. Marin laughed herself sore at her mother's inch down the Walker Ledge side of the cliff where the roads are a bit wider and the downward plunge a tad bit briefer. When they finally make it to Main Street, they have three dozen or more cars trailing behind them with drivers in all sorts of pissed off moods. Esmé parks at the municipal lot and huffs away from the Baxter Mobile. "That's it. I'm not driving into town ever again, pinche high-ass cliffs this side, that side, que la?"

Marin laughs at the little Spanish rage, "You drove in the other day by yourself to get something for Dad?"

"Something for you, and I won't be giving it to you unless you promise to keep quiet about our trip off the cliff today."

"What trip?" Marin nudges.

"Good, Lord, you're like your father with the nudging."

Marin's thoughts go to her sketches, *and a lot like my mother the artist.* She is so lost in thought that she nearly ass-plants when her mother pulls up short and drags her into a store.

"Ah, Mrs. Baxter, your order arrived." He takes a quick peek at Marin. "This young woman has to be your daughter."

"Yes."

"You two could be twins, and I'm not just saying that."

The mother laughs amusedly. The daughter smiles politely.

"Can I talk about your purchase in front of ……."

"Marin. And yes, please go ahead."

"Great. Your Smartphone-app-enabled refractor telescope arrived on the postal ferry."

"Smartphone. Refractor. Telescope." Marin whispers and almost two-steps her excitement.

Esmé smiles at her daughter, addresses the man, "Yes, I received a call from one of your clerks saying I could get it today."

"Just let me grab it from back."

"A telescope? For me?" the doppelganger daughter squeals and adds a booty-shake to her two-step before the store owner returns.

"Here you go." He slides the rather long box onto the counter, apologetically preempting the question he knows is on the horizon, "I'm sorry, but I'm the only one in the shop, so I won't be able to walk it to your car."

Esmé smiles, "No problem. The two of us can manage."

The two of them manage to
smash it to the ground.

The man into whom they awkwardly plowed bends to help them, "I'm sorry, I didn't see you." He looks at the rather long box on the sidewalk, "And I should have. I guess I was paying more attention to my cell than to where I was heading." He reads the label, "A telescope.

Oh, I'm really sorry. This must have cost a pretty penny. I'll replace it, of course." He lifts the box, gives it a shake, and listens to the clink of broken glass clank from within. The very handsome young man with wavy brown hair and to die for dark-brown eyes introduces himself. "I'm Edward. If you come back into Bert's, I'll have him put another order through, on me."

Esmé and Marin follow him inside.

"Ah, Mrs. Baxter, did you forget something?"

Edward sizes up the two Baxter Babes and answers Bert's question, "They didn't forget a thing. I forgot to look where I was heading and knocked this box to the sidewalk. The telescope inside is smashed to pieces. I want to replace it."

"Sure, no problem, Mr. Kingston." He addresses Esmé, "You don't need to wait. I'll put the order through and call you when it arrives. I'm sorry for the inconvenience."

The mother and daughter smile, offer their thanks to Edward, and head to the fried dough and lemonade stand up the street. While they're enjoying cinnamon-sugar-covered-puffed-yumminess, Edward is purchasing a telescope and planning a cliff side visit.

Primrose Priscilla

Detective Tom Martin gets right to it when the young men arrive, "Lan, about your call this morning, I'm reiterating, do not get a lawyer, do not call a lawyer for a consult, and if a lawyer materializes out of thin air and knocks on your door, don't answer it. The press is already connecting Laire to Christie. If the vultures get wind that the brother of one of the missing girls is lawyering up, they'll start digging in your sandbox, and when it's leaked that WPD checked you out at the time of Christie's disappearance, the public will demand that her case be reopened, and you'll be labeled a person of interest."

"And if the chief wants another talkin, should I have a legal mind present?"

"Ask him if you're under arrest. If not, suggest he keep you informed about your sister's case, then shut your mouth. You should be calling the station with regularity asking if there's anything new on Laire. If Banks arrests you, don't say Word One without a lawyer, and get one from the mainland. Okay, now I'm putting you on notice about two things, stop your drinking, and put your temper in check, especially when you're with the chief."

"Doin both is a tall order."

"Do them. Now, I need you to tell Dale about your involvement with Christie Anderson. You go the rounds with him, Lan. It'll prepare you for what's to come."

The young man gets up and paces some, then sits back down, "Long and short, Dale, I was new to the island and spendin some time in Shaky Town. I met a lass in a pub and took that she was legal age."

"What pub?"

"Diggers."

Dale nods. "Go on."

"Christie was a really sweet girl who trusted without reason."

"Was? Christie was?"

"Was as a former fancy, not meaning she's dead, Dale."

"Yeah, well you better clean that shit up before someone else picks up on it."

Lan nods.

"Explain the trust without reason comment."

"Christie didn't know me five minutes and she was runnin her mouth about everythin except her real age. She said her family was stayin on the island for a month, and when she got back home she'd be headin back to college where she was settin to study finance."

"Where?"

"Where what?"

"Where did she say her family was staying, and what college?"

"The backend of Shaky where the road starts curvin toward the cliffs, closer to Shaky than the dunes, and she never said what college. We hit it well, so I asked if she wanted to meet up at the beach the next day. We spent a few hours swimmin and all, and she suggested she come around my place that night. I was rentin Watch Ledge at the time from old man Tanner, and didn't think it right to shag at his place, so I declined her generous suggestion."

"Did you tell her you lived on cliff side?"

"No need to tell about my livin arrangements when I put a kibosh on a shag." He notices the look between the two lawmen, "Feel like discussin the look between you two?"

"Keep going, Lan."

"We went to the beach again the next day, that's when I found out her real age and left. Then a couple days went by before I headed to Diggers. Christie was there with some guy, sittin on his lap and shit."

"Did you get a look at him?"

"The back of his head is all and that was covered by a navy ballcap. I'd finished an ale and was readyin to leave when she made her way past to hit the loo. I left and never saw her again."

"Do you know the dates you were with her?"

"I'd just started a pay job at the marina and was on a four day on/four day off rotation. The beach dates were on weekdays, and the trip to Diggers was Sunday, the day she went missing."

Detective Martin pushes in, "Thursday, July 21, Friday, July 22, and Sunday, July 24."

Lan and Dale share a look. Lan connects a very unfortunate dot, one that could be used against him in a circumstantial case, "Christie and Laire both went missin in July."

Tom nods.

Dale comments, "Some fuckin coincidence."

"I'm supposin coincidence isn't a right defense in this kinda crime."

"Nope. That's just one of the problems facing you," Mr. MacTavish.

Lan nods, "You'd did some investigatin on me, Detective."

"I did."

"And how'd I fare out?"

"Convicting you would have been tough, but throwing suspicion your way, no problem. Christie was underage, and that's always a driving force behind these investigations. She turned seventeen the month before she came to Whisper, and though she told you she was starting college in the fall she was actually heading into her senior year at Andover High in Massachusetts. As soon as she hit the island, she became well-known at Diggers, a not-so-fine-establishment that never turns away a patron, even an underage one. The few witnesses who remembered seeing you two together described it as being brief, and a few of those same people remembered seeing the two of you on a very public beach."

"And these witnesses, they saw her with others?"

The lawman nods.

"And they musta gave descriptions of the lot."

The lawman nods.

"Lookin forward to hearin the stuff that could tie me up, Detective."

"The last time anyone saw Christie alive was when she was waiting for a cliff side Whisper trolly, or sitting on that trolly, or getting off the trolly one street below Cliff Road."

"If she was headin to cliff side to meet someone, it wasn't me."

"Yeah, but we never found a single thread to pull, not on any other mystery man. Christie's trail turned to ice at the trolly stand."

"And now?"

"Two years have passed. That's plenty of time for witnesses to remember this or that, and for evidence to materialize. More to the point, Lan, a second girl's gone missing, and you know this one too."

LAIRE

She's been dead four days and has refused that many offers to reunite with her soul. Her thoughts on the subject flow as freely as the water in her grave...

I'd have to abandon my spiteful ways in order to be whole again. Lord should know I'm not one to let go of a wrong. I'm sure as hell not about to start whilst my bag of bones is tethered to the ocean's floor. I need to taste a bit of vengeance against Edward before I let bygones be such.

Laire looks upon her anchored leg and wonders…

The metal bind is doin a right job of keepin my body in place, but it doesn't stop my spirit from travelin a bit.

She ponders the things she can do and wonders about the things she can't…

I can be heard, so long as the person is near the ocean.
I can be felt, so long as the person is near the ocean.

But I can't read thoughts or know the deeds of the livin ones unless I hear words of sin and sorrow—like when the chief told King to get Edward under control, and the brutes' words of plottin to frame Lan for Edward's crimes, and Joe's comin around to seein things my brother's way, even when he learned Lan knew the spirit one…Christie.

She locks her glare on bones scattered in the ocean's silt…

Christie Anderson. I know your soul and spirit are as one. What I don't know is if you went heavenly the day you died or if you fractured for a bit.

I don't know why you didn't help your bones find their way ashore.

But be sure the problems for my brother are many if your bones start headin that way now. The Kingstons are plannin a frame for him as soon as your parts start driftin. The plotters and framers against a MacTavish are right bastards, they are.

Wind Ledge

Joe is surprised by the 9 PM knock on the front door, surprised again when he finds a young man standing on the porch, surprised even further by the long box that is sort of pushed his way.

"I'd shake your hand, Mr. Baxter, but I've already smashed one of these today, so you might want to take it before formal introductions take place."

Joe heard all about the telescope drama in town, so he readily complies, takes the box, sets it on the porch, and offers his hand. "Joe Baxter, and you're, Edward?"

"Yes. Edward Kingston. Have we met before?"

"Nope. That's the name I was given of the man who murdered Marin's telescope."

Edward's dark eyes flash.

"Sorry, just a little telescope-smashing humor."

Edward smiles, a really great smile. "I hope you don't mind my getting your address, and I hope this delivery isn't too late."

"Not at all, come on in. Say hello to Esmé and Marin."

Mother and daughter have been on their feet since the knock, the younger of the two has been two-stepping and booty-shaking in place ever since.

"Not sure how you managed the quick turnaround, Edward, but we sure appreciate your efforts," Esmé smiles wide.

"I had business this afternoon in Portland, so I made a stop at Bert's mainland store and picked it up."

"Business in Portland," Joe repeats, "the ferry service must come in handy."

"It would, but I work for the marina, Kingston Marina, so I tend to use one of our boats." Edward laughs, a really great laugh when he realizes the Baxters don't recognize his last name, "You sure are new to the island if you haven't heard the name Kingston."

"We don't get into town much," Esmé smiles.

"And when you do, you're accosted by a telescope-murdering man."

They enjoy the laugh.

"You know, I don't get to the cliff side often, but I'm sure there's plenty here to keep you busy, and the telescoping will be amazing."

"Telescoping for Marin, I'll be doing repairs. We bought quite the fixer-upper," Joe offers.

Edward takes a quick look, "Well, the place looks great, especially the fireplace. I'd bet the water stones used in the hearth come from Stony, and that's a beautiful mantle." The impromptu deliveryman steps toward the door, "I'll let you get back to your evening, and I hope you enjoy your viewing, Miss Baxter."

"Oh, I will!" Marin two-steps again. "Thank you so much, Mr. Kingston."

Edward smiles and breathes a bit easier with the surety that neither of the Baxter Babes recognized him as the man dumping a dead body into the ocean. He reminds himself on the way to his car, "I was pretty far away from the cliff, and when the body hit the ocean the boat was out of illumination, so maybe there's nothing to worry about." He takes another look at Wind Ledge, "For Esmé and Marin Baxter's sake, there better not be." On his way off Cliff Road, he passes a familiar car; the drivers recognize one another.

"Shit, that's Edward Kingston. What the fuck is he doing on cliff side?"

"Haven't a clue, but he saw the two of us together, Dale."

"Shit!"

Lan quiets and leaves Dale to his thinking.

His thinking makes way to carping, "I've already had my ass reamed by the chief for talking to you. If word gets back I'm driving you around, I'm screwed."

"Bloody hell."

"Yeah."

Echo

Edward parks on the circular drive and heads to the rattan for a load off. He pulls the moon sketch from his pocket and notices something written on the back, "July 19, Full Moon, 100% illumination." He compares the sketched moon to the one currently overhead and though it's in a different phase, he can see the talent of the artist. "This is really beautiful, expertly done."

"I agree," Ruby says from behind.

He folds the picture and returns it to his pocket, "Where's King?"

"In town. What were you looking at?"

He points skyward, "The moon."

"On the paper, in your pocket?"

"Starting to see why King is spending time away, Ruby."

She runs her fingertips down his arm, straddles him, gives a gentle ride, and removes her top.

He takes hold of her breasts, molds a bit, takes one of her nipples into his mouth, and does a little sucking and a little motorboating. She reaches down, unzips his pants, and guides his fully erect dick in. He watches her ride him, runs his hands along her womanly shape, reacts to the lift and sway of her breasts. He's ready to unload. When…

~~*KING'S WATCHING*~~

Edward quickly pushes Ruby off, packs himself away, and waits for his old man to make an appearance. What he gets instead is the sound of Laire's laugh. His head spins toward Ruby who has parked her perfectly round derriere onto a nearby chaise, "Did you just laugh?" he stammers.

"No, and I didn't climax, either. Why'd we stop?"

Edward looks over his shoulder, "I thought I heard King. You should go inside, Ruby. Now." As soon as the door slams behind her, he takes the sketch out of his pocket and gets an unsettling nudge. "Okay, one of the Baxter Babes was on the cliff walk July 19th, the day of this drawing, so it stands to reason that one of them was there on July 21st to do another drawing. Could be either babe. The mother is the same height and weight as the daughter, and she's an art teacher, so she probably drew this picture. But the daughter is really excited about the telescope, so she might have an interest in skygazing stars and planets, so there's nothing to say she didn't sketch the moon. Shit! I'm back at square one. I haven't a clue who was on the cliff that night."

"What night?" King asks from behind.

Edward folds the paper, puts it into his pocket, pushes from the rattan, and barks, "I warmed your plaything, go finish her off, and stop with the creeping around."

Day Five
Tuesday, July 26
Last Quarter – Illumination 52%

Dale Jacobs answers the incoming call from Lan who asks if there's news about his missing sister. The officer makes sure his answer is overheard by Detective Martin, "Sorry to say there's nothing new to report on Laire MacTavish. We'll be in touch."

"In touch with who?" the chief asks from behind.

"Lachlan MacTavish. He called to check on his sister's case."

"Is this the first inquiry from him?"

"Not sure, but it's the first one I fielded."

The chief tosses a blanket question to the squad, "Anyone else get a call from MacTavish?" He's met with shaking heads all around. "I want to know if and when he calls again."

Watch Ledge

Joe doesn't bother with door knocking or bell ringing; he immediately heads to the patio and takes a look upward. "I'm coming up, Lan." On his way through the kitchen, he pours himself a mug of coffee. When he gets to the widow's walk, he takes a load off.

"Feelin at home, I see."

"Yeah. What do you know about Edward Kingston?"

"Which one? Though I think the same for the father as the son."

"Which isn't much, I'm guessing."

Lan shrugs, "The son is a bit of a doucher, but the father's business side borders on the ruthless. He's liked in town, though."

"The son bumped into Esmé and Marin in town yesterday and accidently knocked a telescope they were carrying to the ground, smashed the thing to shit. He offered to replace it, and came over last night to deliver the new one. He said he picked it up on the mainland."

Lan nods, "Sounds about right. He goes to Portland a lot."

"On business."

"Some, but there's talk his woman lives there."

"And yet he took time to get the telescope. Kinda nice for a doucher."

"A broken clock hits the mark twice a day, Joe. Tell me, have you hit the mark about Marin bein out that night."

Joe pulls a long gulp of coffee, sets down the mug, and comes clean. "I found a sketchpad full of drawings in a backpack that belongs to Marin. The sketches are of lunar phases and are dated on the back. She's been sneaking onto the cliff walk since we arrived in June. I'm sure that's where she was coming from when you saw her."

"Her thing with the moon, that's why you got her the telescope?"

"That, and I took her sketchpad."

"So you took her reason for sneakin out?"

"Yeah, but I took it mostly so Esmé doesn't find it. She doesn't know Marin was out the night Laire went missing, and I don't plan on telling her until Marin comes clean."

"You thinkin your lass saw somethin?"

"I don't know what to think."

"I sure would like to know, Joe."

"What if it's bad news?"

Lan pulls a long, slow inhale and looks out toward the bay. "It'd be the worst thing to know, but if fate's been unkind to Laire, I need to know and then find the bastard who hurt the bonnie one."

"And?"

"And I'd allot some fate in return."

Wind Ledge

Esmé and Marin set up the telescope on the widow's walk after clearing a space at the top of the stairs for nightly storage. Then the mother gets ready for some art time and the daughter heads to Stony Beach for a ladder-to-ladder stroll. Her trip sets her in an easterly direction toward Watch Ledge, the really beautiful bungalow set on an easterly angle and buffered on three sides by bushes of pale yellow primroses, various shades of lilacs, fuchsia rhododendrons, and groupings of gnarl-branched Mountain Laurel readying for their annual burst of snowball flowers. She takes her eyes off the foliage long enough to see her father sitting with a man on the widow's walk. "Dad's with Lachlan MacTavish," she groans.

~~FIND OUT WHY~~

Marin spins about looking for the whisperer, spins a second time for good measure, then heads toward the access ladder. She's stepping onto the tiny platform at the top when Joe sees her. "Marin?"

She moves onto surer footing and gives a wave.

Lan pushes in, "Have her come up. Let me see if I can work her emotions about Laire. See if she budges."

Joe steps to the railing, "Come on up. The widow's walk access is through the master, the same as at Wind Ledge."

As she moves through the house, she is overcome by sadness, and guilt, and fear. She turns around, rushes from the bungalow, gives a wave to the perched men, and heads back to Stony Beach.

"Well that was weird," the father opines.

"Somethin put a scare into that girl, Joe, and we need to know what for."

109

Esmé has been perched upon her painter's stool, staring at the pictures of Cliff Man for nearly an hour. She's sketched multiple outlines of his body from each frame and is satisfied with the detail from the neck down, but the finer details of the face are obscured by shadowing from a ballcap. The artist gets a bit discouraged when she zooms in, "There's just no good shot of his face. The clearest is a side view, but the features are blurred, probably by movement, maybe his, maybe Marin's. Still, the essence is there. It's tense, determined. Or at least that's what I'm getting." She jumps off her stool at Marin's interruption.

"You're talking to yourself, again." It's then that Marin notices her camera. "You have it!? I thought—"

"What? You thought what?"

"I thought I lost it. I pulled my room apart looking for it."

"Oh, I'm sorry, Marin," she hands the camera off. "I thought I'd take some shots of people on the beach, maybe step away from painting land and seascapes for a while. I should have asked if I could use this before taking it."

Marin hands the camera back, "No, go ahead and use it. If I'd known you had it, I wouldn't have wasted time looking—"

The conversation is interrupted by Joe, "Thought I might find you two perched up here." He hugs his wife and eyes his daughter—a myriad of questions banging through his head. "Hey, Marin, why don't we leave your mother to her work. You can help me with the fireplace downstairs."

Esmé pushes in, "Joseph, you should hire a professional to inspect the fireplaces before you do anything to them."

"I will, but we can do some cleaning before then, and there's a loose piece of mantle I should shore up. Marin can help."

The teen rolls her eyes, not because she's being recruited for work, but because she's in for a fireside grilling. "I'd rather be burned at the stake," she mutters.

"What's that?"

"Nothing," she rolls her eyes again and lets out a long sigh.

They're barely to the living room when Joe pushes in. "So what happened at Watch Ledge? I wanted you to meet Lan MacTavish."

"I didn't know what to say to him."

"Hello is a good place to start, Marin."

"And then what? Sorry your sister is missing? Bet that sucks? Did they find her body?" She pulls up short and turns a thousand shades of red.

Joe points a finger at his daughter, "That. That right there. That's the second time you've suggested Laire MacTavish is dead. Why do you go there?" The father closes the space between them, lowers his voice, and raises his intensity. "What. Do. You. Know? Tell me." A knock at the door interrupts the heated exchange. "Go to your room and stay there."

She goes, but she does not close her bedroom door.

Joe pushes the screen door open, "Can I help you?"

"Mr. Baxter, my name is Detective Tom Martin, do you have a couple minutes?"

"Sure, come on in, Detective. I suppose this is about Laire MacTavish."

"It is."

"I've already spoken with Chief Banks."

"I know. I just have a couple follow-up questions. It'll only take a minute."

Joe nods and points to a living room chair. The detective parks his duff and removes a small notebook from his breast pocket. He takes a quick look around in the meantime, "During the emergency call Mr. MacTavish made at 12:45 AM to report his sister missing, he said he made several neighborhood searches, stopping at his place on each pass by. He said around midnight he thought he saw someone move in the shadows near the cliff walk and called out thinking it was his sister. According to your report to the chief, you put Mr. MacTavish outside Wind Ledge at approximately midnight."

"Yes, but I didn't know it was Lan MacTavish at the time, I only knew it was someone shouting a name."

Detective Martin nods, "You have a teenage daughter, is that right?"

"Yes."

"Any chance she was outside your bungalow and Mr. MacTavish saw her?"

"No chance," he lies.

"Did you check on your daughter?"

"What?"

"When you heard a man calling out a name, did you check to see if your daughter was tucked in safe and sound?"

"No, but given what's happened, I guess I should have. I just never thought Marin would—"

"Sneak out."

Joe can tell the detective, or the chief, or both of them suspect Marin was out that night and that she might have seen something.

The detective hands him his card, "If your daughter gives you information, please give me a call." He leaves.

"Shit, the walls are closing in on Marin." The father heads toward his daughter's room and before she has time to shut the door he accuses, "You were listening to that conversation."

Silence.

"The police want to know who was near the cliff walk that night. They are not going to stop pushing for an answer. I can't make you talk, Marin, but I can send you and your mother back to Oxford. I need to do everything I can to keep you safe, and if that means sending you off Whisper, you can bet your ass I will do it." He slams the door on his way out.

Watch Ledge

Lan is finishing lunch when Detective Martin bangs. The lawman is already talking when he steps inside, "I just came from Joe Baxter's house. He didn't say so, but he knows his kid was the one you saw on the cliff walk."

"I know. He told me when we talked earlier."

"He needs to push in on that girl and find out if she saw anything."

"He knows, and he agreed to let me have a go of it, but Marin got spooked."

"She definitely knows something. I need to work the father a bit. You need to bring him to my house."

"When?"

"As soon as you can. Dale's on nights the next four days, but I don't want to wait. We'll have to fill him in later."

"I'd say it's right good that Dale isn't seen with me."

"Why?"

"Edward Kingston saw Dale givin me a hitch home last night."

"Kingston the third or fourth?"

"Heir."

"In town or on the upward roads?"

"Near to my place."

"What was he doing on cliff side?"

"Don't know, but Dale was right up concerned about it, sayin right off that the chief did some ass chewin on him for talkin to me the night Laire went missin. He was put in a twist that the chief might hear we were drivin about."

The detective nods and agrees, "Might be better if we meet without Dale for a while, put a little distance between you two. In the meantime, talk to Joe Baxter and set something."

Lan readies to walk the detective out—the man has no intention of leaving, "I've been digging in your sandbox, Lan, and you have a real problem if things go sideways on Laire."

"**A** problem? I was thinkin I had a mountain's worth."

"In a nutshell, you made it quite known that you did not want the responsibility of your kid sister when your parents died. Folks back in Speyside are quick to suggest you would have placed her with just about any relative, but there were no takers."

"Sad to say, the talkers are tellin it the way it was. Not proud of my ways back then, but I was just settin on my own at twenty-three, had just gotten a foothold in the States, had saved a pretty penny for a down payment on Watch Ledge, and settled into a thing with Danielle—"

"Rayburn?"

"Yeah, and the thought of bein stuck down with a teen, especially a headstrong teen like Laire, wasn't my cup, you know."

"Yeah, well, the running of your mouth about the burden isn't going to sit well with either side in a court of law."

"The milk's been spilt, Detective, so what're you plannin?"

"Nightly prayers your sister shows up alive."

"Already prayin that's the way of things, Detective."

Echo

Ruby is just stepping into the shower after her Bodaciously Beautiful Booty workout when she hears a news report about two missing teens, Christie Anderson and Laire MacTavish. She walks butt-naked to the bedroom and bumps into King. "Did you hear that report—about the missing girls?"

"Yeah. Days ago. Where've you been, Ruby?"

"You know I don't watch T.V. When did they go missing?"

"The Anderson girl disappeared in 2014, and the MacTavish girl went missing sometime last week."

"MacTavish? Why does that name sound familiar?"

"The girl's brother works at the marina. You probably heard me or Heir mention him."

Ruby spins on her heels and heads for a shower. She's so deep in thought, she doesn't hear King's parting compliment, "Your ass is looking great, Ruby. Remind me to mess with it when I get back."

Booty Babe shuts the shower door, leans against the wall, and wonders, "Did Heir take those underaged girls? Did he get them on a boat and maybe stash them somewhere … like Portland? He makes the run from Whisper to the mainland all the time, and he supposedly has a woman there—who **no one** has ever seen. What if he's keeping a couple of underage girls for shits and giggles—wait, the first girl went missing in 2014 when she was seventeen. She's no longer jail bait. So maybe she left Heir and he needed to replace her and took the second girl. That fits with the timing. Is that why he's looking at Marin Baxter? A replacement for next year?" She shakes her head and sets herself right, "For Christ sake, Ruby, Edward Kingston IV can have any woman he wants. There's no way he wants juvies." She gives her hair a good lathering and herself an equally good tongue lashing, "You're stringing a whole lot of shit together based on nothing but a piece of paper with information about Marin Baxter. That paper also mentioned her parents, Joe and Esmé Baxter. The research could be on the parents, or the whole family. That makes more sense than the juvie crap. Although, King only bangs young women, really young women. Could be a father/son fetish."

Shaky Town

Lan knocks on Danielle's door a little before 11 PM. He doesn't say a word, he just wraps his arm around her waist, pulls her close, and holds on for several minutes. "I'm hopin you can see your way to a bit of company." She steps aside. He steps in. In a matter of minutes, he slips in.

Edward Kingston IV was stepping out of Diggers when Lan's BMW tooled past. He remembers Laire saying she insisted her brother buy the gorgeous ride with a piece of their parents' 'willin money'. Heir hops into his Jag, waits a few, then drives past a cute little waterfront shack he knows belongs to Danielle Rayburn. He hits paydirt when he sees her car and Lan's Beemer parked side by side. He checks his watch and places a call, "MacTavish is with Danielle."

"Then I've got some work to do. Let me know if he leaves her place."

"Let me know when you're done, or else I could be here all night."

Officer Dale Jacobs starts his patrol a little after 11 PM just as a moonlight cruise on the Abenaki sets sail from the docks. He looks skyward, "A half-moon, a two-hour cruise on a beautiful night, not a bad way to spend an evening. Of course that's not how I'll be spending my evening." He does a slow drive down Main Street, loops around and heads to Shaky Town as per his normal routine. He pulls to a stop near Diggers, watches the comings and goings, decides a couple girls heading in might be underage, makes a note on his police log as per WPD protocol, then moves along. He's just about through the bohemian village when he recognizes several vehicles, "Lan MacTavish's black Beemer parked at the Rayburn shack," and a little further up the road, "Edward Kingston's navy Jag parked at the Beach Bum a little eatery at the tail end of Shaky Town." His recitation of who's where on Whisper is silenced by dispatch. Dale listens to the call then makes his way out of Shaky.

Wind Ledge

Joe finds Marin on the widow's walk peering through her telescope at the moon.

"She's beautiful," the male mathematician suggests.

Marin chuckles, "Well, yeah, if you're assigning antiquated male/female roles to the planetary system, I suppose 'she' is beautiful. Breathtaking, actually. The Buck Moon, though not in full phase, is in Aries at Last Quarter and at 52% illumination."

"Show off," he gazes a bit at the satellite object. "She really is breathtaking. You know, Marin, that little dissertation you just did on the moon proves you are a very intelligent young woman." He pauses to correct himself before she starts in, "You are a very intelligent *person*, which means you know full-well that keeping secrets is never the smart thing to do. So heed this warning. I'm giving you one week to come clean. If you do not, I'm sending you and your mother home. I'll follow when I finish up some things that need repair before winter."

Marin steps away from the scope and into his arms, "Okay."

"Okay, you'll tell me?"

"Okay, I'll leave."

Joe steps from his daughter's embrace and heads downstairs, "Well, that backfired spectacularly."

Marin gets back to her viewing. "It's almost midnight." She flashes back to the night she saw the man dump a body overboard and lets her mind wander and her thoughts find flight, "I wonder if it was Laire MacTavish."

~~IT WAS~~

Marin startles and gives a quick rub along her gooseflesh arms. "Am I hearing things, or am I so upset I'm imagining things?" She shakes it off and gets back to her viewing.

~~WATCH LEDGE~~

Marin turns her telescope easterly and finds an opening through the array of flowering bushes. She zooms in tighter and tighter on a figure moving quickly in and out of view. She pulls away from the eyepiece and cautions herself. "You've already seen too much on this island. Don't snoop. Don't." She spins the scope back toward the bay, "Ahhhh, the moon, a bringer of light." She steps away from the scope and looks with her naked eye at its splendor. "I wish I had my sketchpad." She thinks of her sketches, her incomplete collection: *Moonlight Over Midnight Ocean*. She wonders where they are and wishes she could finish her work. "Maybe I should tell what I know."

~~LOOK FOR ME~~

Marin obeys. She steps back to the telescope, looks through the eyepiece and sees a cloud, or the rise of mist, or the spray of a wave—something that resembles .... "Is that?" The terrified teen straightens at the ghostly image of a teenage girl. "Laire MacTavish?" She makes a hasty retreat from the widow's walk, lands with a thud at the bottom of the access stairs, and bangs clumsily as she moves through her mother's studio. She's more than a bit winded and struggling mightily with her emotions when she takes the corner into her room. She pushes the door closed behind her, presses her back tight against it and breathes, rapidly and raggedly. She turns on both lights, then from the safety of her bed, she manipulates an app on her cell phone to operate the telescope located two stories above. She positions it away from the ocean that may or may not be lifting spirits and toward the easterly set bungalow that may or may not have a burglar. She presses record zooms in as tight as she can, and watches someone in jeans and a

white long-sleeve T-shirt and a black ski mask
ruin Watch Ledge.

Day Six
Wednesday, July 27
Waning Crescent – Illumination 40%

Lan slides his arm under the slumbering Danielle and rolls her into the crook of his shoulder. He brushes her light blonde bangs away and kisses along her brow, "I needed you, your ear and—"

"My fun parts," she moans and nestles.

"Was thinkin your tenderness, but your fun parts, too." He kisses her temple and fingers her long hair. "I don't deserve your kindness, but I sure do welcome it, Danni."

"Mmm. You're welcome here anytime, Lan." She rolls a bit. He waits a bit, then gets out of bed when her slumber recaptures, shoves his ass into his jeans, leaves a penny on her nightstand, eyes the jar she keeps them in, settles with the smile it brings him, and slips out the slider off the living room. He's back at Watch Ledge in minutes and back to the reality of his world—and it sucks.

"Fuck. Fuck. Fuck." He steps over and around broken glass and toppled furniture and things belonging in cupboards and on shelves. He lifts a jacket of Laire's from the floor, shakes it, hugs it, and hangs it onto the back of a chair. He takes hold of the last MacTavish family photo ever taken, traces his finger along a corner-to-corner crack, then drops his ass onto the couch and breaks a bit. "Good thing I have an alibi for last night, otherwise I'd be pullin the blame for this mess."

Wind Ledge

The Baxter family is woken minutes before 7 AM by the steady knock of Lan MacTavish. Joe might have invited him in if not for the anger pulsating off the young man. Lan pushes his way in anyway.

"What's going on, Lan?"

"Someone trashed my place last night."

"Were you there?"

Lan scoffs, "I'd be more than pissed right now, Joe, if I were home during the raidin. I found the place tossed after spendin the night with," he stops himself when he sees Esmé and Marin out of the corner of his eye. "My apologies for wakin you." He turns his attention back to Joe, "Any chance you heard a fuss from Watch Ledge sometime between midnight and five?"

Joe shakes his head, then silently checks with Esmé and Marin. The older of the two shakes her head, the younger of the two turns beet red. She slips from the room when Lan receives a call.

He looks at caller ID, "I need to take this. MacTavish."

"Lan, it's Dale. There's breaking news about—"

Lan moans.

"It's not about Laire, but a young woman's been found murdered ... You know her, Lan, from work."

"Danni," he whispers.

"What?"

"Nothing. How? When?"

"Strangulation. Not sure exactly when, but recent. News should be breaking any minute."

The wind pushes from him. Hard. He drops his duff onto a chair and his head into this hands.

Joe and Esmé wait silently for an explanation.

Marin races to the widow's walk, turns the telescope away from Watch Ledge and toward the ocean, runs back downstairs to her mother's art studio, grabs a tarp, runs back up and covers the scope, then makes a mad dash to her bedroom. She is about to look at the captured images from the night before on her cell phone when her mother knocks on the door.

"Can I come in?"

"Sure."

Esmé takes a seat on the foot of Marin's bed, "Mira, there's some news."

"About Laire?"

"No, about a different woman, a young woman." She pulls a cleansing breath and touches Marin's shin. "I don't know much, but a young woman named Danielle Rayburn was found dead in her home in Shaky Town this morning."

"How?"

Esmé shakes her head in disbelief that the two are having this kind of conversation so early in the morning on the vacation island that held so much promise a month ago. "She was strangled."

Marin tears, then remembers the call Lan got. "Does Mr. MacTavish know her?"

Esmé nods.

"Was he with her last night?"

Esmé's face does a whole lot of pinching up, "Why would you ask a question like that?"

Marin stammers a bit, "Because … because he said he was out last night while his place was being tossed."

Esmé nods, "Right, he did say that."

"Is Dad still with Mr. MacTavish?"

"No. Your father is up on the widow's walk."

Joe's been leaning against the house for the last several minutes trying to work through a nudge of suspicion. His eyes haven't left the tarp-covered telescope, even though the bay moves with shimmering waves in the early morning light in the distance. He talks himself through the mounting concerns he has about Marin. "Pretty sure you saw something the night Laire went missing, and now I'm wondering if you saw something last night." He pushes from his lean-to, untarps the telescope, turns it toward Watch Ledge, and follows Lan MacTavish step-for-step in and out of view as he cleans up his home. "Shit! Marin saw—"

"Marin saw what?" Esmé asks from the doorway.

Joe covers the scope, takes his wife's hand, and leads her to their daughter's room. "Marin, start packing. You and your mother are leaving Whisper." He leads Esmé to their room, "Please start packing."

"Joseph Baxter, I will do no such thing, not until you tell me why Marin and I have to leave," her upset words heavily accented and her hands in a flurry of gestures.

"Are you serious? We've been on this island for five weeks and a seventeen-year-old girl went missing, a twenty-four-year-old woman was murdered, and another missing girl's file is in the damned Lost and Not Found bin at the police department. I need to stay here and get Wind Ledge set for the winter, but I do not need you two here to do it. And as soon as I finish what needs to be done, I'm coming home."

Esmé replays the events of the morning, then lets her mind bang against everything that's happened since Laire went missing. "Joe, do you know something that you're not telling me?"

"No."

Her eyes hood in doubt. "Is Marin in some sort of trouble?"

"No."

"Joe," the word gets caught on emotion. "Can't we stay a few more days?"

"No. Please pack, Es."

Echo

Ruby wakes with a start to find sun streaming in the window and a disheveled Edward walking from her en suite. She pushes up, grabs a coverlet, and whisper-shrieks, "What are you doing? King might find us. Wait, what time is it, and when did you get here?"

He laughs, "Nice try, Ruby." He reads the confusion, or the faux confusion on her face, "Seriously? You don't remember last night? I must be losing my—"

"Quit fooling around, Heir. We didn't do anything last night." She pulls the coverlet away from her body and finds plenty of evidence to suggest they did. "A hickey? Seriously? How the hell am I supposed to hide this from King?"

"Same way I'm gonna hide this," he points to the love bite on his shoulder.

Ruby isn't looking at his shoulder. She's trying to find a memory of their being together. She runs her hand through her hair while she scans the room. "Wine glasses? And an empty bottle of..." she pulls the weighted bottle near enough to read without her contacts, "2005 Chateau Mouton Rothschild? Jesus, Heir, this is from King's private collection." A flash of memory, "King brought this up last night." A silent search for more, "He opened it. We had a glass." She tries to find more in her fuzzy-brain.

"Come on, Ruby, I brought up the bottle. We had a glass."

She reads the label again, "King is more likely to kill one of us for the booze than the bang, and I'm thinking I'll be the one heading six feet under." She pushes from bed, runs to the en suite, locks the door, and steps into the shower. She lets the water beat against her face for several minutes, desperate to grab hold of a single memory of her night with the son of the man who owns the estate she's living in, not to mention every other damned thing on the island of Whisper.

When she returns to the guest suite, Edward and every bit of evidence of their night together is gone. She pulls a deep breath and is exhaling it when a knock comes on her door.

"Ruby, it's King."

She pulls a tee over her head and is stepping into thong panties when she beckons him in, "Morning, King."

"Sorry I didn't come for you last night, but I didn't get in until very late."

She smiles, "You said you'd be late, so I crashed early."

"Listen, I have a meeting in Portland and thought you might want to come, do a little shopping, or primping, or whatever, then we can get dinner and spend the night at the condo if Heir isn't using it or at The Coastline."

She thinks about the hickey.

He never expected her pause, "Do you have something else to do, tonight?"

She laughs, "No. Of course not. I'm just doing a mental check of my monthly cycle. I know how you are about menstruating women."

He storms out, "Forget it. I'll see you tomorrow, or whenever you're off the rag."

Ruby is shaking when she takes back to her bed. She's there hours and still working her way through her confusion when she takes a remote from her end table, presses a button, watches doors on an enormous armoire slide open, and a T.V. automatically turn on—just in time for the noontime news—breaking news.

...Danielle Rayburn, employee of Kingston Marina was found murdered in her Shaky Town shack this morning...

Ruby slumps against the backboard, "Danni. Oh, Danni." Her eyes fill, she bats away a tear that slides, and she wonders, "What the hell is going on?" Ruby's shaking returns full-force.

Week One Comes To An End
Thursday, July 28
Waning Crescent – Illumination 29%

The Baxter family are asked to turn their Honda around and proceed off cliff side via the opposite end of Cliff Road, the side that leads past the marina. No one speaks while Joe does a five-point-turn on the narrow road, not until they are well past Wind Ledge.

"Que la? Why do you suppose there are so many police cars at Watch Ledge?" Esmé asks with a look over her shoulder at the flashing lights.

"I don't know."

"Do you think there's a break in Laire's case? Do you think they found her?"

"God, I hope so."

"I don't," Marin whispers.

Joe looks in the rearview mirror, "What did you say?"

She looks out the side window, "Nothing."

By the time Joe returns to the Baxter Mobile after escorting his wife and daughter onto the Abenaki, news of an arrest in the Danielle Rayburn murder has broken.

Police made an arrest in the murder of twenty-four-year-old Danielle Rayburn earlier today. A Shaky Town resident for the past three years, Ms. Rayburn was found dead in bed yesterday morning. Lachlan MacTavish, also twenty-four, was arrested at Watch Ledge, his home on the cliff side of Whisper. Police are providing little information, but have confirmed that Lachlan is the brother of Laire MacTavish, the teenage girl reported missing one week ago. Those close to the deceased Ms. Rayburn say she and the suspect worked together at Kingston Marina and have been in an on-and-off romantic relationship for nearly two years...

By the time Joe settles back at Wind, he is overcome with a glut of doubts and emotions. "Lan? Is he responsible for Christie Anderson being missing, and for his sister's disappearance, and for the murder of Danielle Rayburn?" The sorrowful man makes his way to the back patio where he stands for some time watching the churn of the ocean before he settles on another question, "Or is he being setup?"

Portland, Maine

Jenny Stuart, who describes herself as a 'Lipstick Power Suit' lesbian, and June Fletcher, who describes herself as a 'Chapstick Activist' lesbian help schlep the baggage of their best friend, Esmé, and her daughter, Marin, to Jenny's Mercedes SUV. The women readily agreed to fetch the Baxter women as soon as they received Joe's call. They settle momma and daughter in back, park their asses in front, and when Jenny puts the car in drive, June declares, "This vehicle is safety bound!"

Once at highway speed, Jenny sets the cruise control and a few rules. "Okay, no one needs to talk about the island on this trip home, there will be plenty of time later for my questions—"

"Be prepared, she has a legal pad's worth," June butts in.

Jenny continues, "But you should know there's been an arrest in the Danielle Rayburn murder. We just heard the breaking news report."

Esmé leans forward. Marin looks out the side window.

Jenny continues, "An on-and-off-again boyfriend of hers, some guy named—"

"Lachlan MacTavish," Esmé exhales his name. She thinks she notices a gentle shake of Marin's head. She gives a gentle rub along her daughter's thigh, "We don't have to discuss this if it bothers you."

"It doesn't," she lies. She zones in and out of the back-and-forth, then bangs into a memory…

Marin leaned forward when a boat moved into the moon's tail of illumination and watched the small craft lift and rock on slapping waves. "Adrift?" Her eyes locked onto the image of a crouched person. "A man? On his knees?"

Could that have been Lan MacTavish, the man who came to Wind Ledge yesterday morning? She lets the rest of the memory bang while holding that question…

The man stood for many seconds looking in her direction, then bent low, waited until the boat moved beyond the lighted swath, took hold of a body and dumped it overboard. Then he moved the small vessel toward the far end and around the bend of the island.

"Toward the marina."

Esmé nudges her daughter's leg, "What?"

"What?"

"You said something about the marina."

"That's where the dead woman worked."

"Yes." The mother changes the subject. "We're going to have to rent a car since your father kept the Baxter Mobile. Any preferences?"

"Nope."

Jenny looks in the rearview mirror and catches concern cross Esmé's face. She pushes in with an idea, "Hey Marin, my niece, Jade, is in for the weekend. We're going to StrangeCreek in Greenfield tomorrow for the festival. Are you up for three days of camping out and listening to some really good music?"

Esmé answers for her daughter, "Pues, si! She'd love to. Right, Marin?"

"What?"

"StrangeCreek. You were bummed you couldn't go, and now you can."

Marin makes a very quick decision. "Actually, Jenny, I'd love to go."

June jumps into the fray, "You can come too, Es, we'd just have to take two cars."

"Nope. I've got some painting I'd like to get done before school starts." Her mind drifts to the images of Cliff Man and her forefinger reflexively draws him onto her thigh. She wipes the invisible image away with the palm of her hand when Marin looks over.

"What are you doing?"

"Practicing the outline of my painting."

"It looked like you were drawing a man."

"I was. I told you I wanted to do things other than land and seascapes. I'd say that's a good thing given I'm not bayside anymore."

"Yeah. Good thing."

Week Two – Day One
Friday, July 29
Waning Crescent – Illumination 20%

Joe is trying to tamp nagging doubts and banging thoughts with the deafening sounds of a whole shitload of power tools set ledge side. He silences the saw when he catches movement out of the corner of his eye—the ones he rolls when he sees the badge and gun on his visitor. "Shit."

Detective Martin laughs, "Can't tell you how often I get that response when people see me."

"I bet." Joe tosses the freshly cut short end of a 2x4 onto a pile near his shed, unplugs the saw, brushes off a good amount of dust from his pantleg, and points to a seat, "Take a load off."

"Any chance I could have something to drink, Joe? This is gonna take a few."

"Lemonade or iced tea?"

"Lemonade. Thanks." The detective is reviewing several pages in a pocketsize notebook when Joe returns. "Lan's in some real trouble, Joe. Off the record, I don't think he's good for any of the shit he's going down for, but make no mistake he's going down."

"If he's innocent, then—"

Tom laughs. "There are plenty of innocent people in jail." He pauses for a sip and a look at the ocean. "Lan could have easily become one of the imprisoned innocent men two years ago when Christie Anderson went missing. There was a push for answers by the people who work really hard prompting people to vacation on Whisper. They were clamoring for an arrest, especially since the missing girl was a vacationer and a teenager." Another sip. Another look at the water. "The waves are kicking up a bit."

Joe takes a look. "Forecast is for rain later."

"Mmm. You know, two things weighed heavily in Lan's favor back in 2014: the fact that Christie became a regular at Diggers, a pub in Shaky that's big with tourists and is known to let underage patrons in, and that witnesses put the teen with lots of different guys. More than a few guys might have become persons of interest, but they ferried off island before we knew much about the girl or the circumstances of that night. Anderson was my case, Joe. I worked it 24/7 for more than a year. I was pulling threads that made sense and snipping ones that popped up out of nowhere. I was so leaned in to the case that it was impossible for the chief, the mayor, and the town bigwigs to get the arrest they wanted."

"Lan."

"Yup. This go around, I'm being pushed aside because I'm retiring in a handful of months, but it's obvious there's a concerted effort to get Lan MacTavish for everything."

"They want to sweep everything under one rug."

"Yup. They've got him behind bars for Danielle. That arrest was easy, and the conviction will probably be quick and easy too. Depending on what happens with Christie and Laire, things might go a bit slower, but they'll get him for those girls, too."

"Why do they want Lan?"

"Scapegoat is my guess."

"Because they know who the killer is?"

"Maybe, but like I said, the Whisper economy depends on vacationers, and people like you who ferry in and buy real estate. Neither of those two things are going to happen if people think there's a killer on the loose. Lan is an easy fix. To varying degrees, he knew all three victims. Others probably fit that profile, but no one is going to take the time to look."

Joe takes a sip or two and processes a thought or two. "It would take some well-connected, influential people to frame someone for murder."

"Uh huh."

"You know who they are." It wasn't a question, though it should have been.

"Point a finger at any of the houses from the east to west bends, and along Shore Road and you'll find well-connected, influential people living inside. More than a few are rumored to partake in a dirty dealing from time to time and nearly all of them work overtime to shutter salacious secrets inside beautiful sandy side waterfronts." He drains the rest of his lemonade, then runs the back of his hand across a bit of water condensation that finds his chin. "I could shake a stick and find plenty of people who harbor suspicions about this guy or that guy— and rightly so, but they keep their mouths shut— and rightly so. As for my suspicions of who has enough clout to push these cases forward, I'll be keeping my mouth shut on that. In the meantime, I'll work the evidence, and if I'm lucky I'll get to stay on this case until I retire. If so, I'll have access to information and get a chance to document things behind the scenes. Maybe when I'm off the force, I'll push all-in with an investigation of my own." The detective puts his little notebook away. "Like I said, Lan's in some serious trouble. He thinks your daughter can help him. I'm pretty sure you think so too."

Silence.

"I heard you drove your wife and daughter to the ferry. I also heard your wife doesn't know anything about what's going on, unless you said something before she left."

Silence.

"Well, they're off island now."

Joe nods.

"Makes me wonder why they up and left this beautiful summer place. It's gonna make a few other people wonder the same thing, Joe." He pauses for effect, though he need not. "When you're asked about their departure, and you will be asked, you might want to say your daughter got bored and missed her friends back home, and that their trip mainland is temporary. Understood, Joe?"

He nods.

"There's something else." Tom Martin looks upward. "The telescope on the raised walk. Is that new?"

"We got it for Marin on Monday."

"From Bert's Electronics in town?"

He nods. "It was delivered that night."

"Huh. Didn't know Bert delivered to the cliff side."

"He doesn't. Edward Kingston brought it out."

Tom Martin laughs big at that one, "Really? There's got to be an interesting story coming."

"Esmé and Marin were carrying the telescope out of Bert's, and they had a run in with a guy on the sidewalk. The telescope paid the price. The guy escorted them back into the electronics store and put in a replacement order. We expected Bert would call when it arrived from the mainland, but Mr. Kingston delivered it that night."

"King, the father, or Heir, the son?"

"The son. Anyway, he said he made a trip to Portland, got a replacement from Bert's store there, and delivered it that night."

The detective remembers something Lan said during a recent conversation…

"Edward Kingston saw Dale giving me a hitch home."

"Kingston the third or fourth?"

"Heir."

"What was he doing on the cliff side?"

"Don't know."

"Well that explains that."

"What?"

"Lan said he saw Heir on cliff side the other night. I found it odd." The detective takes a look upward, "Any chance there's a visual into Lan MacTavish's house from up there?"

Joe is quick to answer—too quick to answer, "No."

"You sure about that, Joe?"

Silence.

"Because if someone other than Lan was in his house the night he was visiting Danielle Rayburn, and someone can testify to that fact, it'd certainly help keep him out of a courtroom. Right now, Lan's been fingered for tossing his own place, and he can't prove otherwise."

"What reason would Lan have for doing that?"

"Two theories: he freaked out and tossed his place after strangling Danielle because the walls were closing in, or he tossed it early in the night so he could suggest a mystery someone was in his house while he was in bed with Danielle. Look Joe, the bottom line is this: if your daughter knows anything about anything, she needs to come forward. Otherwise, she's going to help convict an innocent man."

Silence.

For many uncomfortable minutes.

"You know, I think it's a good thing you sent Marin away. She'll be safer on the mainland. Come to think of it, you might want to head that way as soon as you can."

Silence.

The detective takes a long look out at the bay and pulls a deep breath of ocean air, "Sure is pretty on this side of the island. You know, you've got the whole cliff side to yourself now."

"How so?"

"With Lan in jail, Watch Ledge is empty. And the Parkers, the folks who own Walker Ledge, they aren't expected back from Fresno until September. So that means it's just you out here. Hope you don't mind the solitude, Joe." He taps the shoulder of the silent man on his way past, "Give me a call when this conversation settles a bit." Tom is nearing his truck when he hollers back, "Sooner is safer, Joe."

Week Two – Day Two
Saturday, July 30
Waning Crescent – Illumination 11%

Marin is climbing into Jenny's SUV long before the sun has a chance to claim the day. She and Jade squeal their delight at seeing one another again, and the four of them do an out-the-window final wave to Esmé.

"Okay, we're off," June gives a squeal of her own. "I love, love, love StrangeCreek!"

"We know," the others sing in unison.

"I've been going to The Fest every year since 2002—"

"We know," another chorus.

"But this is my—"

"Twenty-fifth year camping at Kee-wanee," they unison.

"Make fun if you will, but I've seen some great New England bands at The Fest, and I kissed my first and last boy at camp Kee-wanee."

"We know."

Things settle after their back-and-forth and remain pretty quiet during the hour-plus drive. Marin is by far the quietest of the group. When the SUV exits the Mass Turnpike for the back roads of Greenfield, Jade nudges Marin's knee.

"I heard about the murder on Whisper. I'm glad you're okay."

Marin tears and turns away.

Esmé ran to her studio at the back of the house overlooking a small yard and thickly wooded area the second the SUV turned the corner out of sight. She took the pictures of Cliff Man she printed from Marin's camera, set them onto a table next to the already prepared easel, and got to work. Many hours in, she heads inside for a cup of coffee and a suppertime chit-chat with Joe.

"Hi, babe. I miss you."

"Yeah," he grunts.

"Que la? Not the response I was expecting, Joseph."

"Sorry, Es. I guess the shit fest up here is getting to me."

"Any more news on Lan since we talked last night?"

"Nothing since Detective Martin's visit yesterday."

"You never said why he stopped by?"

"To see if we heard anything at Lan's the night his place got tossed."

"I didn't. Did you?"

"Nope. That's what I told him."

"And Marin never mentioned anything, so I guess the Baxter family isn't going to be much help."

Joe grunts.

"Do you think Lan MacTavish killed Danielle Rayburn?"

"Not sure what to think."

"Lan was in our house."

"I know."

"Around our daughter."

"I know."

"Joe, I'm glad Marin and I are home, but I'm worried about you being there all alone."

"You don't know how alone I am. Detective Martin said I'm the only one on the cliff side. Lan's in jail, and the people who own Walker Ledge are away until September."

"Oh, Joe. I'm not sure I like this. Maybe Marin and I should come back to the island."

"I'll be fine, Es. I shouldn't have told you because now you'll worry."

"You should have told me. We don't keep secrets, remember?"

He remembers. He changes the subject, "Hey, did Marin get off alright?"

"They left this morning. They've pitched their tents, set their campsite, and are heading to the nighttime concert as we speak. There are seven bands tonight. By the time they hit their sleeping bags, their ears will be ringing."

He laughs. "This is good for Marin. She deserves to put some time and space between everything that's happened at Whisper. By the way, Es, I looked at some of your work in the master upstairs. Your land and seascapes are breathtaking."

The artist smiles at the compliment and is relieved she had the good sense to hide *Girl on a Rock* under Marin's bed before she left.

"Thank you, Joe, but I'd say you're a bit biased."

"I should have prefaced, *objectively speaking*, your land and seascapes are breathtaking. If things settle, we should think about moving here permanently. I could teach at the high school, and you could paint, paint, paint."

She laughs her wonderful laugh, "Marin has one more year before college. Let's table this discussion until January and then really consider it. We could sell the place in Oxford, use that money to pay for UMass Amherst. I believe it's still the only college on your daughter's list—"

"I'm not sure about that, Es."

"Why? Is she thinking of applying somewhere else?"

"She hasn't said anything outright, but I saw a handwritten list of other schools in her room. And the other day when we were at the beach she said she loves the ocean and that she's been reading a lot about marine biology."

"Huh, I wonder why she never said anything."

"Maybe because of the stuff going on up here."

"Maybe."

Silence.

"Joseph."

"Yes, Esmé."

"I **really** want to move to Whisper. We could set ourselves on the island, and Marin could spend summers and holidays there. If she's into marine biology, then what better place for her to study and to have fun? She'd have a body of water to explore and play in."

Joe gets a good kick, "Seems you've already entertained this idea and are ready to put a plan in motion."

"I have and I am."

"Okay, let's make a promise. Come hell or highwater, we move to Whisper next summer and make this our permanent home."

"Deal." She ends their call with, "I love you, Joseph."

As soon as he ends the call, he steps outside to make sure everything is put away for the night and decides to fold and store a few sand chairs when he hears distant thunder. "Rain clouds are moving in." He looks skyward, notices Marin's telescope on the widow's walk, runs into the house and up to the platform to haul it inside. He's folding the tarp and looking out at the bay when a mist rises from the ocean. "Aw, shit. I wish Esmé and Marin were here. That rising cloud looks like .... a woman, a beautiful young woman."

~~*LAIRE*~~

The whisper hits him with the force of a sledgehammer. He bangs back against the house just as the sky opens with torrents of rain and rolls of deep thunder, the kind that shake all the way to your bones.

~~I'M HERE~~

Unable to move inside, Joe Baxter stands in the pouring rain as reality bangs his head and breaks his heart, "Laire MacTavish is dead. Her body was dumped in the bay. And Marin saw it all."

~~YES~~

Week Two – Day Three
Sunday, July 31
Waning Crescent – Illumination 5%

Dale Jacobs bounces from his seat the minute Detective Martin arrives at the station, "The chief called looking for you."

"I was on Cliff Road."

"Again? Did you have another talk with Joe Baxter?"

Tom shakes his head. "Nope. I was having a look around the perimeter of Watch Ledge."

"Did you find anything?"

"Nothing to indicate a break in."

"You don't think Lan killed Danielle, do you?"

"Nope. I don't think he was involved in Christie's disappearance either."

"That shit show was before me, so I'm not really sure why you think that."

"The people in Diggers the night she went missing were vacationers, so they couldn't ID the guy she was with, other than to say it wasn't Lachlan MacTavish. Fred Fuller, the owner of Diggers at that time, said Christie became a regular faster than most patrons could drain a shot, that she spent time with more than a few guys, and the night she went missing she was sitting on the lap of some guy. Fred said he never saw the guy's face, so he couldn't help much. I think he saw plenty, but he didn't want to help because he was being squeezed pretty tight about the teens in his place."

"Not much to go on."

"Nope."

"And what about Danielle?"

"What about her?"

"Why do you think Lan isn't good for her murder?"

"How about you tell me why you think he killed her, Dale."

Silence. A prolonged bit of silence.

"Okay. I don't have all the facts of the case, but this is what I heard. Lan spoke with Danielle on Monday when he called the marina and said he was taking the week off. He said the conversation was cordial and that Danielle expressed her concern about Laire and offered her help."

"Right."

"Lan described his thing with Danielle as being friendly and comfortable, and it involved some 'sexing up' from time to time."

"Right."

"And not only did he say he was there the night of her murder, but he also admitted they had sex, and he left a penny on the nightstand, something they did as a sort of joke."

"Right."

"And he said he stopped by her place without calling."

"Right." Tom watches Dale try to arrange the facts in a way in which Lan comes out looking bad. After a bit, Dale pushes in. "All of that tells me Lan and Danielle were on friendly terms and comfortable with one another. It tells me that it's very plausible he woke her long enough to say goodbye, then slipped out her slider, pulled it closed behind him, and headed home."

"Like he said."

"Yeah."

"Now work the other angle, the one that leads you to Lan as the killer."

"He had opportunity, and he's under a lot of stress."

Tom nods. "Not much to convict. Now work the possibility that someone else was there? Who else had opportunity?"

Silence.

Tom nods, again, "We don't know if someone else was there. We don't know if someone went in after Lan left, but we do know he presented opportunity to someone else by leaving the slider unlocked." The detective waits for the officer to process a bit then adds, "He said he arrived at Danielle's around 11 PM." He stops talking when Dale starts nodding.

"Detective, I can't say for certain when he got there, but I saw his BMW at her place when I started patrol."

Tom gives a nod and continues, "Lan said he stayed until 5 AM, headed directly home, and found Watch Ledge trashed. He waited a couple hours before knocking on the Baxter's door. Joe Baxter confirmed a 7 AM visit from Lan telling them about the house trashing incident and asking if anyone heard anything."

"Yeah?"

"They said they hadn't. Not long after he got to the Baxter's place, Lan said you called to tell him a woman he worked with was found murdered."

"Yeah, that's right."

"And?"

"I think he whispered her name. Then he asked how and when she was killed. I told him strangulation and that news should be breaking any minute. He hung up."

The detective grabs a pen from his desk and starts tapping it on the corner of a leather blotter. It's something he's wont to do when he's processing or looking for a thread to pull. The younger officer waits a few, then pushes in.

"I know I'm not a rookie detective anymore, and you might not be able to tell me, but I was wondering something."

"What?"

"When you met with Mr. Baxter, did he tell you why he sent his wife and daughter mainland?"

"He said the kid was bored and missed her friends back home. He said they'd be returning at some point."

Dale is silent for a few then, "You don't think Lan is good for Christie, or for Laire, or for Danielle, and I'm guessing you don't think he's good for the house trashing."

"Nope."

"But he's been personally involved with all of the women, and he lives in the damned house that was tossed. You know what the chief would say to that."

Tom laughs. "I do, but why don't you give a whack at it."

Dale puffs his chest a bit, "No need looking beyond the obvious suspect, Tom. If there are hoofprints in Central Park go look for a damn horse not a zebra. Then I think he'd say something like, we were looking at Lachlan MacTavish two years ago for Christie Anderson. Maybe if we pushed harder back then, we wouldn't have two dead women."

Tom pushes from his seat, **"Two dead women? Who the fuck's the other dead woman?"**

"I thought you heard, Detective. There's nothing conclusive, but a bone was found on Stony Beach. The chief, and every other WPD officer, is on scene. A CSI team and medical examiner from Portland are heading this way. It's gonna be a damned shit show."

"The bone. Where? When? Exactly."

"Not sure when it washed up, but it was found on the shore of Echo."

"The Kingston estate."

"Yes, sir, right by the family dock."

Echo

Detective Tom Martin takes a lean-to against a big-ass weeping willow that's throwing a wide circle of cover from the on again, off again rain. He watches the goings on at the shoreline that sits just below a wide expanse of perfectly manicured lawn, "Haven't had a damned blade of grass in my yard in thirty-five effing years. Pretty proud of my crabgrass though. It's green and lush enough, and the important thing is Miss Prissy gets to keep her shade trees, so it's all good." He stops his grousing at the throat-clearing that comes from behind.

"Talking to yourself, Tom?"

He looks over his shoulder, "Always good to see you, King," he lies, "though the circumstances—"

"Suck."

"I'd say so. Who found the bone?"

"Yours truly. I was heading to the dock to check on the tarp on Heir's boat." King slides a pack of cigarettes from his pocket, taps the bottom several times, flips the top, pulls a filtered menthol, and lights it.

Tom lives vicariously through the process, "Damn, that still smells good."

King laughs, "Nowadays, the only men who smoke are widowers. Be thankful you've still got Priscilla chasing your ass on this habit cause these are gonna kill me."

"Thankful for Miss Prissy every day, King."

The owner of the estate pulls a long drag and gives his head another tilt, "Have you been to the shore yet?"

"Nope."

"Has news hit the airwaves?"

"It hadn't when I got here."

"Did the chief call you?"

"Nope. I heard about it from Dale Jacobs."

There's a pause and a tilt of the head. "That's Matt Jacobs' kid?"

"Yeah."

"Last I heard the kid lived in Portland with his mother .... what's her name?"

"Connie."

"Right, Connie."

A Priscilla memory pushes in on Tom...

"You can't be Matt and Connie's boy?"

Dale smiled wide, "Yes, ma'am."

"Well, I know your mother, or I should say, I knew your mother quite well when you all lived on Whisper. Sorry to say we haven't been in touch for quite some time, but I may just give her a call and say I've met her fine looking son."

Tom makes a mental note to ask Priscilla about Mr. and Mrs. Jacobs and whether she made that call to Connie. He gets back on track. "Officer Jacobs came to Whisper direct from the police academy a year or more ago."

"Good for him. Is he a good cop?"

Detective Martin reads a whole lot of shit into that question and answers it without bias,

"He gets the job done. I suppose time will tell if he's a good cop or a bad cop."

King gets the message, "You're a good cop, Tom. Bet that'll sit well when your ass is parked on a chaise come retirement. When's that happening?"

"The day I turn sixty-five and not one minute past December 31st."

"The end of the year. The end of a career. Can't come soon enough."

"For either of us."

King laughs big and walks away.

Wind Ledge

Joe wanted to call Esmé the minute he heard the news about a human bone being found on the shore of the Kingston estate, but she called earlier from the Mass Pike saying she was on her way to StrangeCreek for a surprise visit with the girls. It's well past 10 PM when he finally hears from her.

"I'm home, safe and sound."

"Did you have fun?"

"Yesss. We had a blast. You'll be happy to know that Marin is back to her old self. I'm really glad she had time away with Jade. They are two peas in a pod, and very whisper, whisper, conspiratorial. Like sisters. It was wonderful to see. Speaking of whisper, anything new on the island."

Silence. Deafening silence.

"Joseph ……. what's happened?"

"A bone washed up on shore."

"Oh, no. Laire?"

"I don't think so. The news anchors say authorities think it most likely belongs to Christie Anderson because it's completely without—"

"Que la! Good Lord, Joe. Stop! Just stop. I get it, and I'm sickened by it all."

"I know. Let's change subjects." A roll of thunder and crack of lightning dim the lights for a second or two. "You should see how menacing the ocean looks tonight. It's rained on and off for most of the day, so there's quite the churn going on. And the waves lift and curl in really odd shapes, you know like clouds do, but these materialize and disappear in an instant."

"Ooooo, I bet it's great. I wish I was there to see it."

"Too bad you didn't leave Marin's camera behind, I could have taken some great shots for you to work off of. Speaking of that, you never told me what you were working on yesterday?"

"When I was at Whisper, I found some really great pictures on Marin's digital camera. Most were of people on Stony Beach building Stonehenge monuments, but the picture I chose to paint is of a man on the cliff walk where the rose and lilac bushes sort of duel for prominence, the place you and I stopped on the walk we took right before signing papers to buy Wind Ledge. Anyway, Marin took a series of pictures of a man standing at that particular area; the subject matter and framing are nearly perfect. They really tell a story of intense contemplation and mystery."

A thought bangs hard in Joe's head. "Hey, Es, I'm gonna cut this short. I want to watch the light show for a while. The rain has stopped, so I think I'll head outside and commune with nature."

"Okay. Have fun, and be safe. Love you, Joe."

"Ditto, Esmé." He sprints to the kitchen, grabs a flashlight from under the cupboard, heads to the living room, grabs Marin's sketchpad from his secret hiding place, and flips through the pictorial collection: *Moonlight Over Midnight Ocean*. He analyzes every shot, "They're all from the same location, the one Esmé just described as being in Marin's camera." He processes for a few seconds then returns the sketchpad to its hiding place. "If Marin took pictures of the cliff walk, she took them from Stony Beach—there must have been a reason why she pointed her camera upward. Shit, I wish I could see those shots. Mental note: have Esmé text them to me tomorrow. For now, I can go to the spot and get a firsthand look."

Joe has a momentary nudge of fear at the lilac bush entrance, stops for a second, then heads through. He counsels himself along the way, "Just stay far away from the ledge." He moves slowly, mostly because it's dark and slippery, but also because his pantlegs keep getting hooked by prickers. On occasion he takes a look at the sliver of moon playing peekaboo behind moving clouds. He can't help but get caught in the beauty and majesty, "No wonder Marin snuck out at night. It's really beautiful here. From this height, it feels like you could reach out and touch her—that's why Marin's sketches are so amazing." He laughs at his antiquated female identification of the moon, then quickly grabs his wits about him when he slips on a rain-soaked rock. "Jesus, Marin, you were nuts to come out here to draw." He bends for the fifth or sixth time and unhooks his pantleg from a bramble—and stops for the third or fourth time thinking he hears something in the trees and bushes. When he turns toward the ocean, he hears her warning.

~~GO HOME~~

A shiver runs and fear grips him deep. "Shit, that girl of mine is either fearless or clueless coming here in the dark—for that matter, so am I."

Those are the last words
Joe Baxter utters.

The lawman moves swiftly away from the newest Whisper Island murder scene. He pushes through the bramble toward Walker Ledge, gets into a WPD vehicle parked on the gravel driveway, edges it onto Cliff Road, then creeps down the westerly side of the island past the Kingston estate and marina. He places a call, "Baxter's been taken care of."

Heir moves to the window and stares out at lightning that etches across the black-as-ink sky. "Good to know, Dale. Now what?"

"We wait for his wife to report him missing, or for someone to find him on Stony. Though I doubt anyone will be venturing to Stonehenge tomorrow. It's supposed to piss-pour rain all day."

Edward releases a devilish laugh. "The breaks keep coming our way, friend."

"We're not friends, remember?"

"Right, we're brothers."

2017
Sandy Side

Welcome Back to Whisper Island

Esmé joins her daughter at the ferry's railing. She puts her arm across her shoulder and pulls her near, "I know you didn't want to come, Marin, but I need you with me, and I think your being part of the decision-making process about Wind Ledge is really important."

Marin nods, the slight movement unleashing tears that run her cheeks and silently plop onto hands that are death-gripping a blue rail at the bow of the Abenaki. The daughter leans her head on her mother's shoulder, and the two get lost in thought. Within minutes, the contour of Whisper's shoreline begins taking shape, and a voice startles from behind.

"Mrs. Baxter, Miss Baxter, I don't mean to intrude…"

Esmé turns toward the man, Marin quickly eyes him and walks toward Jenny and June, who remain seated on a bench but have tuned into the conversation. Esmé croaks her recognition, "Detective Martin."

"Retired, ma'am."

She smiles, "Yesss. I heard you left WPD. Well, good for you. I hope your days are full and pleasurable."

"Yes, both." An uncomfortable pause hangs a bit. The detective bats it away, "It's been some time since you've been to Whisper."

"Yes," her eyes sting.

"The Missus and I sent a card, but I want to express my condolences personally."

"Thank you. I did receive the card and a lovely note from your wife ... I'm sorry I've forgotten her name."

"Priscilla."

"Yesss, that's right, Priscilla. I think I should have reached out."

"Ma'am?"

"To you. About things." Esmé raises a trembling hand and clutches the collar of her jacket, "Joe said you and he spoke ... shortly before he—"

Tom nods.

"And I wanted to ... hear your side ... to get your thoughts about Joe ... you know, to see if he was okay ... or ..." She gives her head a little shake and looks toward the island for a minute. "But, Chief Banks insisted that he and I be the ones to talk about Joe. I suppose he was right since you were set to retire, and it was easier to only have to talk to one person, but ..."

The detective waits for her to get where she wants to go. It's a short wait.

"I know you aren't with the WPD any longer, Detective, but—"

"I'd like to talk with you, too, Mrs. Baxter. It might help us push through the weeds on things."

"Yesssss. I have so many questions. There are things that don't settle well, things I haven't been able to understand or explain." She looks at the dark ocean then to the lights along the sandy side of the island, "My friends say I may never have answers or understand what happened and why it did, but if talking with you gives me one answer or sheds some light on some point of confusion, it would lift some of the heaviness and channel the regrets I have. At least, I hope it does."

Tom puts his hand onto Esmé's, "How about we both do a little talking and a little listening?"

She wipes away tears that hold promise, the very first of their kind since the passing of Joseph Peter Baxter.

The Night They Return
Thursday, June 29
Waxing Crescent – Illumination 37%

Marin walks quietly to her bedroom, leaves both lights off, climbs onto the bed, presses her back against the wall, and starts doing what she's done nearly every day since her father plunged to his death—at her spot, the one where she used to sketch the moon, the place where she saw the dumping of human remains, the place where Cliff Man stood. She clings to her cell phone and fingers through countless pictures of Whisper Island—a place that took so much from her. She unleashes her nightly verbal attack at the cause of her pain. Her recriminations are quick and orderly and are marked by a heavy dose of self-loathing.

"The death of Joe Baxter is your fault, Marin Baxter. The husband of Esmé was alone on Whisper Island because you, his only child, didn't confess about the man in the boat, or the man on the cliff walk, or the man tossing Lan MacTavish's bungalow. No matter how many times Joe Baxter asked you to come clean and let him help you sort things out—You. Kept. Quiet. He told you he was going to send you home if you didn't tell him what you knew. He told you he had to keep you safe.

Well, he sent you home. He kept you safe. And he stayed behind and paid the price. You left your father alone. To shoulder your secrets. They made him a target. Joseph Peter Baxter did not accidently fall from the cliff side of Whisper. He was pushed. And if by some huge twist of fate his fall was an accident, you still put him on that cliff. You sketched the moon from that spot. The Spot where he was standing before he crashed to the rocks below. The Spot he **never** would have been anywhere near had you not snuck out and gone there in the first place. You sent your father in search of answers—you sent your father to his death. You might not know why he chose that night to venture out, but you are the reason he did. And now, Marin Baxter, you and your mother are back on Whisper Island, and you're still keeping secrets—deadly secrets."

She silences when there's a knock on her door and a whispered, "Goodnight, Marin. I love you."

Primrose Priscilla

Tom Martin is in his favorite chaise on his crabgrass lawn looking at the moon and rehashing his trip to prison...

"How are you Lan?"

"Strugglin with a life I didn't set for myself." **He scoffed,** "I heard some shit that if you can't do the time, then don't do the crime. Damned right sentiment, but I don't believe there's a sayin about my current fate."

Tom wanted to commiserate with the broken young man, but decided that wasn't what Lan needed, "Have your pity-party after I leave, I've got some questions."

"You still pushing in on Danielle's murder?"

"On that murder, on Christie's murder, and on your missing sister."

"I'm already payin for Danielle's murder and suspect the WPD will set me here for another life of time for Christie's killin. In the meantime, I'll keep prayin Laire's alive somewhere."

"I know you aren't guilty of killing Danielle or Christie, and I'm completely sure you had nothing to do with Laire's disappearance, so all I need to do is find the right fucking threads and start pulling."

"Appreciate your efforts, Tom."

"Then help me out."

Lan shook his head a good spell then finally nodded.

"I think the best way to get you out of here is to prove you had nothing to do with Christie Anderson's murder. Part of the reason you're sitting here is timing. You were arrested for the murder of Danielle Rayburn on July 28th. Three days later, Christie Anderson's tibia washed ashore. When she went missing in 2014, you were a recent arrival on the island, an easy target. Transients are looked at with suspicion by small communities. Can't get much smaller than 800 islanders."

"Can't tell if that's the good news or the shit news, Tom."

"It's news that levels the playing field some. The press has gotten wind that you were being looked at in

2014." **Tom leaned in and lowered his voice,** "Roxanne Carmichael from WCWI has left a couple messages for me saying she wants to discuss the case with the detective of record back then. She'll get a return call from me if I get wind the WPD investigation is starting to stink or I happen upon a good thread to pull."

"Explain."

"The press and the public know that you met Christie Anderson at Diggers. They know she was underage. They know you and every other guy she met there didn't know she was underage. They know the two of you spent a couple days at the beach together. And they know Christie was last seen on a trolly heading toward the cliff side. They don't know you turned down her offer to have sex. They don't know you left her when you found out how young she was. They don't know you never told her you lived on cliff side. And they don't know you saw her at Diggers sitting on the lap of another guy. That last bit of information could swing both ways with a jury, but right now, that information isn't for public consumption."

"I doubt my words on all that will cut sway with the public or a jury."

"The reason I'm pushing in on Christie is because I don't want WPD bringing charges against you—I certainly don't want you in a court of law answering those charges. I'm aiming to keep WPD from mucking with evidence and pushing the case forward. I want them to have to hold the line on what they've got against you, which isn't enough to do shit.

And while I keep them tethered to the case I built, I'll be conducting my own investigation, starting now."

"Okay."

"We never interviewed you in 2014, so I never knew you saw Christie with a guy who wore a blue ballcap. The former owner of Diggers said Christie became a regular pretty quick, was friendly with a few guys, and the night she went missing she'd been riding the lap of one of them. He said he never saw the guy's face. I think he saw plenty but didn't want to help with the investigation because he was being squeezed pretty tight about the teeny-boppers in his place."

"Okay."

"Is there anything else about that night?"

Lan went quiet for some time, "I was finishin an ale and was readyin to leave when Christie made her way past to hit the loo." **He stopped and turned his head as though trying to catch a thought,** "She stopped for a second and suggested we meet at the beach the next day." **He straightened in his seat,** "A waitress bumped into her with a tray of drinks. Didn't cause a mess, but a bit of a splash. I think the waitress apologized and said she was new. She offered to get Christie's next drink."

The detective nodded and jotted the information in his pocket notebook.

Tom takes a long look skyward and gets lost a bit, then concedes, "The waitress might be a thread." He takes out his little notebook and flips back a few pages, reads something he wrote on his last prison visit, "Legal papers placing Watch Ledge and Lan's finances in my

hands. Papers need to be signed on July 3rd."
He mulls that a bit and settles on a thought,
"First thing I do when I get into Lan's place is
search for the missing earring." He takes his
pocket pen and jots and talks his way through
two reminders from today's meeting. "Locate
Fred Fuller and push in about the guy in the navy
blue hat with Christie the night she disappeared;
get the name of the waitress who was new to the
establishment." A thought pushes its way
through his fatigued brain, "Damned weird
seeing Esmé Baxter on the Abenaki tonight, of
all nights." He startles a bit at the touch on his
shoulder.

"You're talking to yourself, dear."

He places his hand on top of his wife's, the
hand he's held through thick and thin for nearly
four decades, the one that's grown soft and a bit
wrinkly, and whose fingers have started feeling
the ache of age. "Hello, Miss Prissy."

Mrs. Martin looks skyward, "Waxing
crescent."

"Mmm."

"She's beautiful."

Tom lifts his wife's hand and gives it a
tender kiss, "She pales in comparison, Priscilla."

The wife of the detective does something
she's not wont to do; she pushes in. "You know,
Thomas Alan Martin, you talk during your sleep."

"Do I, now?"

"Yes, and I suppose I shouldn't listen, but
I do. And certain things you say about the
terrible fates of Lan MacTavish and Joseph

Baxter get a good tossing in my head from time to time."

"Do they, now?"

"Yes. And of all the things that concern me … and there are so many … the one that lifts my interest most is ……."

"Go on, Miss Prissy."

"Why is it Joe Baxter was on that dark, dangerous cliff, at night, after a soaking rain? To my thinking there isn't a single good reason."

"Keep going, dear."

"It couldn't have been for moon gazing."

"Why is that?"

"If memory serves, the moon was a sliver of a thing that night, and besides, it's never good to go gazing or cliff walking after a driving rain."

He nods, "Anything else been bothering you, dear?"

"Do you think Mr. Baxter chose to be on that cliff because he planned to end his life?"

"Nope."

"Do you think Mr. Baxter accidently fell from that cliff?"

"Nope."

"Do you think he knew something … maybe something that could have helped Lan MacTavish?"

"Nope. But I think his daughter, Marin, knows something and Joe knew that."

"Well, I'd say Marin had better stay off Whisper."

"I'd say that's very good advice. Unfortunately, Esmé and Marin Baxter returned to the island today and are back at Wind Ledge."

The fear of that announcement traveled through Pricilla Martin and was expressed by an involuntary squeeze of her husband's shoulder by her aging hand.

Wind Ledge

Marin has yet to settle. It's 3 AM and she's pulled her ass out of bed and is beginning her search for her sketchpad, "The thing that started this whole fucking mess." She's talking herself through her search plan as she opens this and moves that, "My bedroom. My parents' bedroom. The living room. The kitchen. The first-floor bath. The pantry. The front porch. My mother's second-floor art studio. The second-floor guest room. The second-floor bath. The linen closet. The stairway and hallway leading to the widow's walk. I think that's it for inside the bungalow, then there's ...." Marin is on her hands and knees peeking under the foot of her bed when she sees a tie tape art portfolio her mother uses to protect and carry her artwork. She slides it across the floor causing several dust bunnies to hop about, bats them away and places the hidden treasure onto her bed. She pulls the end of the tie, lifts the top flap, and slides out one of her mother's works. She gasps when she reads the title, *Girl on a Rock*, and tears when she sees herself perched upon 'her rock' looking out at Casco Bay. Marin is overcome with emotion, talks haltingly through sobs, "We … were so … happy then." She puts the painting onto the bed and slides it away from her falling tears and then moves the portfolio aside. An amber-colored envelope slides from within. The name Joseph and the words I Love You are written in her mother's calligraphy. "Mom did this piece for Dad."

Marin falls apart.

LAIRE

The bitch who's fine with my brother languishing in prison has ventured back to Whisper. A fair warnin, Marin Baxter, an unkind fate will befall those who've played a hand in Lan's unfair punishment. And fate will be my calling.

It's been nearly a year since Joe Baxter's death. His daughter refused to make the trip when her mother received word of the accident or when the wife accompanied her husband on his final trip mainland. Marin remembers the thought that banged when she saw the bronze urn set on the mantle in the family home in Oxford, "All snug as a bug in an ash container." A single tear rolls as she offers an explanation, "I tried really hard to come get you, Daddy, I just couldn't. And I've tried really hard to store my

173

memories of what happened here in an urn of their own. But they're back with a vengeance, and I'm scared, Daddy." On her next full breath, Marin remembers the echoes that rose from the sea—the ones she's sure belong to Laire MacTavish. She drags her ass to the window, pushes aside white linen curtains, and gazes at a crescent of lunar light.

~~WELCOME BACK MARIN~~

A death-shiver runs and settles deep. She pushes it away and answers back, "I know that's you, Laire, and I know what you want. I will help your brother. I just need some time. Please believe me. Please trust me." A moment or two hangs, then in the fractured light of a waxing crescent moon over gently rolling ocean waters, a rise of mist, or the spray of a wave—something that resembles the ghostly image of a teenage girl moves across the night sky. "Laire, is that you?" Marin whispers.

~~IT IS~~

And The 24 Hours That Follow
Friday, June 30
Waxing Crescent – Illumination 47%

Officer Dale Jacobs, aka newly reinstated rookie detective Dale Jacobs, overhears a very early morning call. He immediately makes a very early morning call, "We have a problem."

Edward pushes up against the headboard, rubs his hand through his hair, and checks the time on his cell, "Shit, Dale, it's not even seven."

"And yet the chief of police is already at his desk talking to someone, most likely our sire about the Baxter women."

Heir is fully awake now, "What about them?"

"They're back on Whisper. They arrived last night with two other women and all of them are staying at Wind Ledge."

"Well, so much for your plan. You know the one where we kill Joe Baxter so his women get too scared to come back to the island. Guess that didn't work for shit, Dale." He silently runs a couple possibilities then offers them up, "Maybe they're here to do some memorial ritual, or to pack up the house, or to put it on the market, or maybe—"

"They're back to nose around."

"About what?"

"Joe's fall from a cliff he visited on a rain-soaked night in pitch darkness. Look, I lucked out when he left the cottage and went to the cliff walk. It made for an easy kill. One heave-ho and it was over. But I didn't consider the aftermath. I didn't play the scene out."

"And if you had?"

"I would have anticipated The Big Question: why was he outside his bungalow in the middle of the night standing on a cliff? That was the question WPD asked over and over. We couldn't come to a consensus, and it was eventually determined that it was an unanswered question, one that didn't alter the finding that Joe had an accidental fall. But that question still lingers. I can only imagine how many questions his wife and daughter have. Maybe they're back on the island to demand an investigation. "

"His fall happened almost a year ago, Dale, and you said Esmé has talked to Chief Banks about it several times already."

"Yeah, but maybe she wants more answers, or better answers. Or worse for us, maybe the daughter is ready to tell people she saw a man in a boat dumping a body into the ocean." A flash of anger takes hold of the younger brother. "Jesus, Edward, you need to stop killing your bitches. You just aren't cut out for a life of crime—which I find very surprising since you're King's son, but let's leave that conversation for another time and recap."

"Let's not."

"First, you're seen leaving Diggers after spending time inside with Christie, you're seen picking her up from the cliff side trolly stand, you're seen having sex with her in the dunes at Cliff Cove, then you're seen killing her—granted I was the one who saw all this, but there could have been others. Then you ask me—"

"My brand new brother—"

"To help you dump the dead bitch. Tell me Edward, what was your plan before I showed up?"

"Plan?"

"What were you going to do with the dead body of a teenage girl?"

"Probably something stupid—"

Dale laughs, "No question it would have been stupid, but really, go on."

"I probably would have buried her in the dunes."

"Good thing I happened by then."

Edward gets a good laugh in, "Not sure what fucked me up more, Dale, finding out I was capable of murder or finding out King's other son was perfectly fine with dumping a body at sea."

"Genetics. A damned good thing, I guess. Not sure I would have helped you, Edward, but you sort of had me over a barrel. I was *thisclose* to getting what I wanted—"

Edward scoffs, "A lowly public servant job at WPD?"

"Not just that, asshat. I wanted a chance to fuck with King, the bastard who knocked up my mother and fucked up my father."

"King is your father."

"No. He. Is. Not."

Edward Kingston IV waits a bit before pushing in. "Let me tell you about your bio-dad, Dale. If Edward Kingston III finds out you told me you're my brother after you two entered a deal to keep that bombshell quiet, he's gonna cut off your balls, dip them in bronze, and put them on a mantle somewhere."

"Yeah, well, he hasn't figured it out so far, and he won't find out if we keep our distance and you stop fucking up. Right now, Edward, there are two things hanging over our heads: finding the second earring you stupidly gave to your teenage baby mama, and getting rid of Marin Baxter. If we take care of those two things cleanly, we should be walking away scot-free."

"Fuck, Dale. Do we have to kill Marin?"

He lets some silence hang, "Miss Baxter's demise is necessary and imminent, but I have a few questions first."

"What?"

"When did you learn about Laire's kid?"

"The week before she died. She told me she missed her period then showed me a positive pregnancy test."

"She bought the kit and took the test by herself?"

"That's my guess."

"Do you think she went off-island to buy the test kit?"

Edward's response is immediate, "No way. Laire hated open ocean waters and stayed as close to shore as possible."

"The irony of that is staggering."

"Fuck you, Dale."

"Later. Let's get back to business. There are two pharmacies in town, which means Laire went to one of them to purchase an OTC test kit. If a store clerk rang it up, the possibility that Laire was pregnant would be common knowledge by now. So I think Laire had a pharmacist handle the purchase, meaning he or she would be legally bound to keep quiet about it. Bottom line for us: there's a person in Whisper who knows the missing teenage girl might have been pregnant and someone got her that way. And more important to us is the only way to bury a secret is to bury the secret-keeper."

Edward scoffs, "Two things about that. Laire was smart enough to keep that purchase private, and you're Exhibit A when it comes to not being able to keep secrets."

"Two things about that. Fuck you, and your teen crush wasn't smart enough to keep from getting knocked up." Dale knows his verbal punch hit its mark. "Sorry if that cut too close to the bone, brother. Oops, my bad, I shouldn't have mentioned bones when they're washing ashore on Stony Beach."

"Fuck you, Dale."

"Trying to keep us both from getting fucked, Edward, so let's push in. Any idea what Laire did with the positive test strip?"

"She showed it to me."

"And then?"

"Let me think…"

"You knocked my knickers right and tight, Edward," Laire said whilst waving a pregnancy stick featuring a bright blue plus sign.

An involuntary smile spread across Edward's face seconds before reality churned his innards, "Fuck, Laire, I thought you were on the pill, how—"

"I'd say the baby blockers didn't block shit. What be your intentions about this?"

It didn't matter what Edward IV's intentions were; it only mattered what Edward III wanted…

"I don't give one holy fuck if she's carrying your child, Edward. She's a minor. I don't plan on spending the next five years trying to keep your ass out of jail, and the five after that paying big bucks to keep it safe in jail because you dicked around with a teenage girl. I've worked my whole life for what we have, and I will not let you fuck it all away. You handled an underage problem once before, so do it again!"

It was Edward's and Laire's final moments together that mattered most…

"Edward, I won't speak out that you banged me unjustly. I'll suffer the pregnancy and do the birthin of the wee one with aide of Lan. And when time rolls and I'm of age, you can claim us."

"Or—"

Dale knows where his brother's thoughts have gone, "Push that shit aside and concentrate. Do you know what Laire did with the pregnancy stick?"

Edward slides open a bedside table drawer. Anguish hits his heart when he sees the bright blue plus sign. He removes the stick in question with a shaky hand. "I haven't a clue where the test stick is."

"Shit. Looks like I'm gonna be busy for a while. I have to make another trip to Watch Ledge to see if I can find the earring and a pregnancy stick, and I need to make another heave-ho trip to Wind Ledge."

"Before you do anything to that girl, are you sure it was Marin on the cliff that night?"

This time it's Dale who takes a memory trip...

He edged through the bramble toward the moving beam of light coming from the direction of Wind Ledge. He stepped between two gnarled Mountain Laurels and waited for Joseph Baxter to near. His prey stopped at a clearing, turned toward the bay, and started muttering. Dale halted his step to listen.

"Jesus, Marin, you were nuts to come out here to draw. Shit, that girl of mine is either fearless or clueless coming here in the dark—for that matter, so am I.'"

Dale shakes off memories of Joe's scream and the thud of his body, then answers Edward's question, "Yeah, I'm sure it was Marin on that cliff."

~~MURDERERS BOTH~~

"What did you just say!?" Edward barks.

"I said I'm sure it was Marin on that cliff."

"No. The other thing."

"I didn't say anything else. Shit, Edward, are you hungover? Maybe you should move back to Whisper and dry up and shit."

"I'm not hungover. Maybe I—" before he finishes his sentence, a wind lifts off the ocean sending floor-length gauze balcony sheers whipping and snapping. The noisy gust fills the room and swirls paper files to the floor. Edward watches in amazement, remaining speechless until he feels a forceful whip-slap across his hand. He drops the pregnancy test onto the bed, "What the fuck?"

Dale loses his patience, "Get your shit together, dry your ass out, and get it back to the island, or you'll fuck everything up and we'll both be doing time with Lan MacTavish."

LAIRE

The evil doin brothers are plannin death for Marin. If fate turns in their favor, she'll be joinin me in the depths and Lan will spend the rest of his earthly days behind bars.

The spirit one throws a warning.

Try your mightiest, but know this—a fate such as mine will not befall Marin Baxter! I will block your treachery as sure as I am of the clan MacTavish.

~~NON OBLITUS~~
~~NOT FORGOTTEN~~

Primrose Priscilla

Tom steps next to his wife who's building a morning pot of coffee, "I wonder how many of those you've assembled over the years?"

She gives a little chortle, "Detectives wonder about everything."

"They do. Right now, I'm wondering what you remember about Connie and Matt Jacobs."

Another chortle escapes, "That would require some gossiping, and we both know your feelings on that subject."

"Humor me."

Miss Prissy spends a few minutes organizing her thoughts. "I mostly knew Connie from the quilting club, and for a short while she was part of the 'Cemetery Walkers' or the 'CWs' as we referred to ourselves back then. As you'll remember, Connie was a real looker." The Missus gives the Mister a squinty-eye when he sort of groans his remembrance. "Watch yourself, Mr. Martin."

"Will do, Miss Prissy."

"Connie and Matt struggled with infertility for years," she pulls a quick breath, then yanks at the thread that binds the Jacobs and Martin families.

Tom places his hand onto his wife's shoulder. She pats it three times, "That's all water under the bridge now, Thomas."

"I know, Priscilla."

"Anyway, a year or so before Connie's fortieth birthday, she and Matt happily announced a pregnancy. The quilters' were swift to wonder who the father of the baby was."

"Odd thing to wonder."

"Not when the pregnant woman had previously told everyone her husband was sterile—and before you ask, I never mentioned our fertility issues."

"Wasn't going to ask, dear." He ponders some before pushing in, "Did the quilters speculate who might have fathered Dale?"

"Of course we speculated. It became our favorite pastime after we contemplated how Connie explained the pregnancy to her husband."

Wind Ledge

Esmé Baxter spent an agonizing day on the appropriately named widow's walk and a heartbreaking night alone in the bed she once shared with her husband Joe. Marin Baxter spent a guilt-ridden day and night alone in her bedroom, remembering every minute of every day she and her father spent on Whisper. Their friends, Jenny and June, stood at the ready should either Baxter woman need them.

Day Two
Saturday, July 1
First Quarter – Illumination 57%

Esmé is eager to get into Marin's room to get the *Girl on a Rock* painting from under the bed. She abandons her plan when there's no answer to her quiet knock. She's heading to the living room with a cup of coffee in hand when Jenny and June come down from the second-floor guest room. She turns and heads back to the kitchen, "There's a fresh pot of coffee. I hope you two slept well—both nights. I'm sorry I left you to yourselves, but I needed some time."

"No worries. We explored the island a little, went to the public beach, and just relaxed. The best part of our stay so far was spending time in your upstairs studio with your paintings," Jenny smiles. "Your work is really beautiful, Es. June arranged them along the walls as though they're in a gallery, which they should be, by the way. After oohing and aahing we spent some time last night sitting on the widow's walk." The women clasp hands, "It's so beautiful up there."

June agrees then confesses, "I hope you don't mind, but we pulled the telescope out and used it."

Jenny laughs and corrects, "I used it. June snooped with it."

"Snooped with it?"

"Yeah. Did you know you can see right into the bungalow next door?"

Esmé plunks her mug onto the table sending hot brew in several directions, "Que la? You can see into which bungalow?" she snaps.

"Ummm," June looks for the sun over the ocean to get her bearings, "The one east of here."

"Watch Ledge, that's the MacTavish place." She raises her hand to halt the discussion and lets her mind grab hold of a memory…

The Baxter family was woken minutes before 7 AM by the steady knock of Lan MacTavish.

"What's going on, Lan?"

"Someone trashed my place last night."

"Were you there?"

Lan scoffed, "I'd be more than pissed right now, Joe, if I were home during the raidin. I found the place tossed after spendin the night with," he stopped himself when he saw Esmé and Marin out of the corner of his eye. "My apologies for wakin you." He turned his attention back to Joe, "Any chance you heard a fuss from Watch Ledge last night?"

Joe shook his head, silently checked with Esmé and Marin. The older of the two shook her head; the younger of the two turned beet red.

She slipped from the room when Lan received a call.

Esmé pulls a quick breath and lowers her voice, "I think Marin might have snooped into Watch Ledge the night Lan MacTavish said someone broke in and tossed the place. That was the same night he said he was with Danielle Rayburn."

June misses the point and goes off on a little tangent, "We all snoop. You would have snooped, Esmé." She scoffs in Jenny's direction, "You wouldn't snoop, but most everyone else would."

"Not the point, June," Jenny lawyers. "If Marin snooped into Watch Ledge that particular night, she might have seen it being trashed by someone other than Lan MacTavish. If that's the case, she should have told the police back then. They would have had to investigate whether someone else was involved in the events that night. Because she didn't say anything, the prosecution was able to use the house-trashing as a suggestion that MacTavish was enraged after he killed Danielle. That incident was used to prove his state of mind on the night of the murder."

"Pues, si. Marin should have said something," Esmé sighs.

"...**if** Marin saw something," June reminds.

"What are you three whispering about?" Marin asks as she enters the hallway looking as though she'd been in a street brawl, her hair all tangled and her eyes rimmed dark with exhaustion.

The women jump and scream at the intrusion.

The sleep-slogged one shakes her head and moves along to the bathroom. When she returns, the first-floor is empty. She grabs a cup of coffee and makes her way to the widow's walk where she finds her telescope pointing toward Watch Ledge. "What the eff?" She bends and takes a peek at the perfectly aligned scope and immediately pulls away from the eyepiece, "Are you fucking kidding me? There's someone inside Watch Ledge? Who? Lan MacTavish is in jail." She bends forward to take another look, changes her mind, runs inside and downstairs, then heads to the patio. She finds three partially empty mugs, but no women. She moves to the ledge for a peek-see of Stony Beach and immediately turns her head toward The Spot when she hears voices, "Oh. My. God."

The women would know they arrived at The Spot even without the remnants of police tape hanging from bramble bushes. They recoil at the rustle and *snap-snap* of the faded yellowed strips and shiver at the thought of what happened there. Jenny and June reflexively pull on the back of Esmé's shirt when she ventures too close to the edge, "What are you doing? You're afraid of heights and it's dangerous! Step back, Es!"

The woman begins shaking, "Hijo de puta, Cliff Man," she utters on a push of air.

Jenny and June search one another's faces for a dawning, then each shrugs a shoulder. "Who's Cliff Man?"

"I don't know who he is, but I know he was standing at this exact spot when Marin took his picture from down there, on Stony Beach."

"And ...?" June prompts.

"And I wonder why he was standing *here*. Joe fell from this exact spot."

"Do you think Joe saw the pictures Marin took and was drawn here because it's so pretty?" June asks, then answers her own question, "Well that doesn't make sense, Joe came here at night."

"After a rain storm."

"By himself."

"Even though he hated heights."

"Nope," they unison, then Esmé finishes her thought, "Joe came to this spot – that night – for a specific reason."

"And we're going to find out what that reason is," Jenny declares.

"Damn-straight we are," June adds.

Watch Ledge

Dale does an abbreviated search of trinket boxes and 'catch-all' places on the first floor then goes upstairs to Laire's bedroom, "Earring and a piss-stick. Look for those two items and ignore everything else." He opens drawers, moving aside anything that isn't a tiny box or a velvet jewelry bag. "I was part of the WPD search of this stuff before Lan's trial began. Nothing but colorful rocks and Scottish coins and shit in the drawers. Think outside the box—think like a teenage girl. Where would she hide something she didn't want her brother to find?" He stands in the center of the room and casually eyes the walls and furniture. He takes a picture of a poster hanging above her bed,

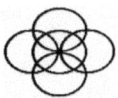

and adds commentary about the rest. "Blue and black tartan throws and Scottish heritage crap all over the place." A memory from something Lan said pushes in...

"In Scotland and other places for sure, the coat of arms is serious business, passed down through ancestral rights and protected by the Lyon Court, a standing court of law which regulates heraldry. A man who fucks with a Scotsman's coat of arms ends up a dead man, or one wishin he were dead, or one who could spend enough time in jail to become dead."

Dale scoffs, "You'll spend enough time in jail to become dead when all is said and done, and it's not gonna be because of some Scottish bullshit." Dale takes another look around and settles on a throw pillow with beautiful, embroidered words, "Non Oblitus." He picks up the pillow then drops it to the floor when the smoke detectors blare. "Fuck. That'll get a response from WFD." He bolts from Watch Ledge.

Sheryll O'Brien

~~*YOU'D BE WISE TO STAY AWAY*~~

Day Three
Sunday, July 2
Waxing Gibbous – Illumination 66%

Tom dropped Priscilla at home after the 9 AM church service and headed to Wind Ledge. He's making his way to the porch when he hears talking from the back, so he heads in that direction. He gives the obligatory throat clearing a try, "Excuse me, ladies."

Esmé hops from her seat with a friendlier than needed greeting, "Oh, Detective, come on back, have a seat. Can I get you something?"

Team JJ raises a brow at their friend. June offers a more normal welcome, "Take a load off, Detective, and try not to read too much into whatever the hell that nervous crap was."

He smiles wide, "Please, call me Tom, and I'm feeling a bit anxious, myself."

Jenny and Esmé share a look. June scoffs, "Well, you did just arrive at the scene of a crime—" her abrupt stop courtesy of Jenny's swift kick.

Tom's attention goes to the woman rubbing her shin.

She addresses the crowd, "I'm sorry, but are we going to pretend that Joe's plunge off the cliff was an accident?" She addresses her cohorts, "Last night, you two were all about finding out why Joe was on that cliff – in the dark – all alone – when the man was straight up terrified of heights. Open your eyes, Jen and Es, there's a detective within spitting distance. This is not the time to go all silent and shit."

The detective drags a chair to the table. "Okay, who wants to go first?"

Esmé is quick to set parameters, "Marin is jogging Stony. We can talk until she gets back— and the second she does you need to leave, no chit-chatting, no pleasantries sent her way."

"Understood. Now, someone start talking?"

Esmé makes brief introductions, "The mouthy one over there is June Fletcher, and this is Jenny Stuart—"

"Attorney Stuart," June brags up her wife.

"A lawyer. Criminal law?"

Jenny shakes her head, "My specialty is intellectual property law, but I've seen the inside of a courtroom or two. Currently, I'm on Whisper to help Esmé find answers."

"To what questions?"

The three women silently check with one another, then confirm their next step with nods. Esmé begins, "I don't know why Joe ended up at the bottom of that cliff." She tears a bit, pushes them back, and swallows them hard. "That's the most important question I have, but the questions that bother me most involve his being there in the first place. For nearly a year, I've been wondering why my husband, a man who feared heights, and who spent his entire time cliff side looking out toward the horizon and never down, left Wind Ledge soon after a thunderstorm, and meandered along a steep and slippery cliff walk in the dead of night?"

"And tell him you think Joe was pushed? Don't forget that part, Es."

Jenny shoots a warning eye June's way.

Tom shoots a question, "That's the second time in a handful of minutes you've suggested Joe's fall might not have been accidental. Anyone want to tell me why?"

The lawyer turns the tables, "Why don't you explain why you think it was accidental."

"What makes you think I do, Attorney Stuart?"

Marin gasps when she sees the detective seated with the women. She remains perched on the last step of the access ladder until he casually extends his goodbyes. She climbs to the landing and scowls at the women, "What the hell was he doing here?"

"He told me he'd stop by once we settled in, just to make sure we were okay. Why do you dislike him?"

"I don't dislike him. I hate this fucking place, and I wish you didn't force me to come here." She storms into the house.

June leans forward, "Can you imagine how pissed she's gonna be when you tell her you want to move here?"

Jenny takes hold of Esmé's hand, "You aren't still considering that, are you?"

The widow looks out at Casco Bay and gets lost in thought…

"Your land and seascapes are breathtaking, Es. If things settle, maybe we should think about moving here permanently. I could teach at the high school, and you could paint, paint, paint. Okay, let's make a promise. Come hell or highwater, we move to Whisper next summer and make this our permanent home."

"Deal."

"I promised Joe we'd move here this summer."

"Yes, but that was before he—"

She raises her hand again, "Don't. You two might not understand, and I know Marin won't understand, but I need to honor my last promise to my husband. I am going to live on Whisper Island." She tears at a memory that keeps her up at night—the one that torments any slumber she finds. "The last words I said to Joe were, 'Love you, Joe,' not 'I love you, Joseph' and the last word I heard from the man I loved more than life itself was ditto." This time, the tears that fill her eyes, silently trail her cheeks. "The seconds it took me to utter those few words are the ones I'd trade all of my tomorrows to do over. My casual ending to a phone call haunts me. The promise I made to Joe was anything but casual. In a very big way, I think my moving here is my way to say a proper I love you to Joseph."

J & J each take hold of the widow's hand and give a little squeeze as tears fill their eyes. "Okay, but you don't have to live at Wind?"

"No, and I don't want to."

"Okay, will you sell it, rent it, or what?"

"I don't give a damn about Wind Ledge, Jenny. It could tumble from the cliff for all I care."

Day Four
Monday, July 3
Waxing Gibbous – Illumination 75%

Tom stepped into Town Hall shortly before 2 PM and bumped into Donna Abbott sending a stack of files free from her hands and scattering them across scuffed-bare, warped, plank floors. "Thought I might run into you, Donna, but not like this."

She smiles wide and chuckles, "No worries, Detective."

"Retired, remember?"

She rolls her eyes and groans, "Yeah," her tone full of meaning.

The two former coworkers busy themselves gathering the ream of papers with minimal commentary. He walks a stack her way, "Getting ready for a bonfire?"

"Nope." She snaps, then casually looks both ways, finds the corridor empty, and grouses a bit, "Since you left, I've somehow become a file clerk and photocopy girl."

He bends near, "Who's doing dispatch?"

"Me. All this crap is above and beyond, Detective." She silences pretty quick when the chief enters the scene.

"Well, this explains the delay."

Tom stands, hands an untidy grouping of papers to Donna, and addresses his former boss, "My fault, Vernon. I took a wide turn and bumped into the file-laden dispatcher."

The chief offers an explanation. "We're all doing double-duty, Tom. I'm spending my days training your replacement."

"Though no one could ever fill my shoes. You forgot that part, Chief."

The men share an uncomfortable laugh then the chief tosses a bone, "It'll be a long while before anyone works a case as well as you." He bends to help Donna, "Tell me, Tom, what brings you to Town Hall?"

"I have a little business with the Court."

The chief straightens, "Find yourself on the opposite side of the law already?"

The men share another uncomfortable laugh, then the detective tosses a bomb, "Finding myself appointed legal representative for Lan MacTavish, so the next time anyone from WPD wants in to his place, make sure you contact me first." He walks away.

The chief does too.

Donna continues cleaning the mess by herself.

Wind Ledge
Esmé tapes a note to Marin's bedroom door reminding her that she and the Js are heading to town.

"Does Marin know you got a call from the real estate agent?"

"No, and please refrain from motor-mouthing about it."

The loquacious one laughs her response, "I've already been put on notice by my lawyering wife. She suggested I keep my mouth shut for the remainder of our time here."

"I don't expect her to follow that dictum, Esmé, but it's worth a try," Jenny scoffs.

"I appreciate the effort. Let's go!" Esmé pulls an excited breath. "I really hope the place is still available. I've seen the property from Main Street, but I've never been inside. After speaking with Mr. Crane, it sounds perfect for me the homeowner and me the artist."

Jenny sort of blocks her friend's forward movement, "After yesterday's conversation, you still want to make a move to Whisper, a permanent move?"

"Only if I move to the sandy side of the island."

"And away from Death Ledge," June blurts, then takes a scowl from Jenny. "What? I'm just saying what you two are thinking."

The gobsmacked ones nod and move on.

Marin's been on Stony Beach since early afternoon. She's had her ass parked on her rock and has taken countless pictures of Stonehenge visitors and their creations. She thinks about going back to Wind, looks at the clock on her camera, and changes her mind, "Mom and the

Js To-The-Second-Power have already left for their meeting in town, and I **really** do not want to be at the cottage alone, so…" She pushes from her stone seat, straps her camera messenger-style across her chest, and starts jogging, westerly. She bypasses Walker Ledge and continues toward the far end where it curves toward the Kingston estate and marina. "Never been this far before," she pants then plops her duff on a respectable size square of sand. "Huh. The island starts to get sandy at the bend." She looks at the shoreline, "Hardly any rocks." She pushes to her feet and goes for a closer look. "I could actually…" She strips off her tee to her sports bra, kicks her feet free of her running shoes, and wades in. She stops when she's waist deep remembering her father's familiar refrain, *Don't ever swim alone.* She heeds his warning with a look skyward.

She wiggles her feet into the sandy bottom and enjoys cool waves that splash chest high, then giggles at the tickle of sand when its pulled back to sea by undertows. She recites a bit of what she knows, "Waves are caused by wind that blows across oceans, lakes, and rivers. Tides are caused by the gravitational pull of the moon and the sun. The ebb and flow of waves and tides are the life force of our world ocean." She laughs at the scholarly recitation, stops laughing when she remembers why the words fall so easily, "I practiced that information a hundred times and used it at the exact right time during my interview for a spot at Woods Hole

Oceanographic Institute. But I'm pretty sure it was my passionate ramble about the moon and the ocean, and how I'd been working on a collection of drawings showcasing the two that got me selected for the coveted spot at the marine science research center."

Her smile of accomplishment fades pretty quickly, "Time is running out. I need to tell my mother about my change of plans." She pulls a deep breath and exhales it as she recites the litany of things her mother doesn't know. "I withdrew my admission to UMass, a deposit to WHOI is due on July 15th, and I'll be staying in Oxford until January 2018." A pit forms in her belly when she remembers the promise she made to send a copy of her sketches to the admission's director. "I said they were at our summer place on Whisper Island. I neglected to say I haven't a clue where they were hidden."

She's knocked a bit off kilter and takes a mouthful of salty water courtesy of a particularly rough wave, coughs a bit, then sets her feet in the sand and sets her course, "I need to find that sketchpad. It's not in my bedroom, or in the first-floor bathroom, and it's not on the stairway leading to the widow's walk, and it's not up there. I doubt Dad hid it in the parental bedroom, or the kitchen, or the master bedroom art studio, all places Mom calls her own. So that leaves the living room, the front porch, the second-floor guest room and bathroom, and Dad's shed."

Her verbal mulling comes to an end when a double-hull, mint-green and white catamaran moves slowly around the bend heading past cliff side bay waters toward the Diamond islands. She raises a hand to block the lowering sun and to get a good look at the beautiful vessel. Her movement catches the boater's eye. The shirtless dude stands a little taller, nods in her direction, directs his attention back to the waterway, then speeds off once he's beyond a rocky jetty. "Well, this certainly is an enjoyable part of Stony." She pushes back to shore, pulls her tee onto her wet self, ties her sneaker laces together, loops them over her shoulder near the strap of her camera, and heads for home. "Time to find my sketchpad and tell Mom I'm going to WHO-ee!"

Echo

Hours later, Edward docks the catamaran under the watchful eye of Ruby. "I heard you were back from the mainland and that you're staying put awhile."

"Actually, I'm just back from Big Diamond, and maybe I'll stay awhile. Where's King?"

"He went to the main house with Vernon."

"An expected visit from the lawman?"

"No, and the chief looked very hot under the collar."

Edward takes hold of Ruby's glass and pulls a generous sip of the icy liquid. He coughs a bit, "Shit, Ruby, have a little 'Ade' with your lemon vodka next time."

She smiles and shrugs a shoulder, "Whatever it takes, Edward. Now that you're back, maybe I'll slow the drinking a bit and indulge in my other addictions."

"Do what you need to do, Ruby. Right now, I need to shower and get ready for a meeting in town."

"It was good seeing you, Heir."

"You too, Ruby."

King's office door doesn't need to be open for Edward to hear the heated words coming from inside.

"Tom Martin has legal authority over Watch Ledge."

"Since when?"

"This afternoon."

"God damn it all, Vern. Kathleen's second earring is in that house."

"Quit shitting bricks, King. Tom won't find it, and even if he does, you'll say you had no idea the earrings were missing and that Lan must have stolen them when you had the Memorial Day party at Echo. In the meantime, you might want to take the portrait of Kathleen down."

"Which painting? And why?"

"The one in the foyer near the stairway, because she's wearing the earrings in the picture. You don't need to advertise that they belonged to a Kingston."

"How big a problem is Tom Martin?"

"I can handle the detective." He leans his hands onto King's boat-size desk and makes his warning clear, "No one is to mess with Tom in any way shape or form, King. If a single hair on his head gets ruffled, I'm coming for you. Do you understand?"

"Yeah, but your loyalties are out of whack, Vern. He'd bust your balls in a heartbeat."

"—because I got pulled to the fucking dark side during the Christie Anderson shit fest. If I hadn't pushed Lan as a fall guy, Tom and I would still be on the same side of things."

"What do you suppose he thinks about all that?"

"He knows I was getting pressure from the mayor and the bigwigs in the vacation industry to solve the Anderson case. He probably thinks I reached for a suspect to appease."

"And our association?"

"He knows I think you're an asshole." The chief delivers his final warning. "Don't do a fucking thing regarding this fucking mess without fucking consulting me."

Edward sprints upstairs to his suite and makes a call. "We have a problem. Tom Martin has legal authority over Watch Ledge. No one can go in without his approval .... Yeah, but this is where things get interesting. The chief knows where the second earring is. He said he hid it, and if Tom finds it the chief will make it look like Lan stole it from Echo. That's all I heard, but they'd been talking for a while before I got in earshot. You need to stay away from Watch Ledge .... Okay, I've got to shower and head into town. I'm getting my girlfriend from the Abenaki."

Ruby was close enough to Edward's room to hear the very end of his conversation. She makes her way back to the end of the hallway and is at the balcony above the foyer when King takes Kathleen's portrait off the wall and carries it away. She sits on the top step and asks herself a few questions. "Why did King remove that picture? Who the hell was Edward talking to? And who the hell is his girlfriend?"

Edward parks his Jag at the Casco Bay Lines parking area and leans against the bumper. A loudspeaker announces the 6 PM arrival of the Abenaki. He smiles when the tall, leggy, henna-haired woman inches her way down a sloped ramp. He smiles wider as every man's head swivels in her direction. He finishes with a smile that cramps his cheeks when she notices him and beams. He pushes from the Jag, makes his way to her, and kisses her, "It's good to see you, Quinn."

"You too. Have to tell you, this first date is already off to an interesting start, Edward."

"Yeah, about that."

The beauty's smile broadens and her cashmere-blue eyes brighten, "Is someone on this island under the impression that we've been dating?"

"Everyone on this island thinks I've been in a relationship with someone from the mainland for the last year."

"And I'm that someone?"

"I hope so."

Quinn brushes Heir's wavy hair from his forehead, "I'm in."

"Good." He takes her bag and her hand and settles her into his two-seater, F-Type, Jag convertible.

"Where to now, darling?" she says as she runs her fingers through his hair again.

"School."

"School?"

He smiles. He winks. He takes hold of her hand and kisses the top, "It's time you learned a thing or two about Edward Kingston IV, aka Heir—but don't ever call me that. I hate it."

"Tell me Edward the fourth, will there be lessons between the sheets in this school of yours?"

"I hope so."

"Me, too." She laughs a laugh full of abandon when he puts the Jag in overdrive and manages the narrow roads up the eastern side of the island, across the length of Cliff Road, and down the western side. He parks on the circular drive, takes hold of Quinn's hand, rushes her to the dock, helps her onto his catamaran, starts the engine, turns on its lights, and eases away from Echo. "We'll head out a bit and talk. That way, no one will hear us."

~~I WILL HEAR YOU EDWARD~~

He smiles at his date, "Did you say something?"

She slips off her shoes, walks behind him, and wraps her arms around his waist. "I don't think I said it out loud, but I was thinking how much I enjoy the rocking of this boat. Can we curl up and sleep out here?"

"This Power Cat isn't good for an overnight, so we'll crash at the house tonight. Tomorrow, I'll grab a big-ass catamaran, and we'll spend the night at sea. There's a pretty decent fireworks display over the ocean. We'll have dinner, share some champagne, and enjoy the show." He eases along the western side of the island toward the sandy side, and within minutes he drops anchor and trou, and eases into his faux-girlfriend.

From Primrose to Watch

Tom has dinner with Priscilla, kisses her cheek, and heads out, "I'll pick up coffee and pastries on my way home. Call me if you need me. And get some rest, Miss Prissy, you look tired."

She waves off his concern, "You be safe on the cliff side, Thomas. No walking the bramble. And be home early."

"I've been waiting a long time to get inside Lan's place. I don't have any intention of leaving Watch Ledge until first light."

He is pulling onto the driveway when Jenny toots and stops. "Welcome to the cliff side, Tom," the mouthy one greets from the passenger seat.

"Thank you June. Just so you know, I'm taking care of Lan's place while he's away, so we'll probably be bumping into one another. If you gals need anything, just let me know." He grabs his wallet from his pocket and hands a few cards to June who hands one to Jenny and one to Esmé.

"We need to get back to the bungalow, Tom, but we also need to continue our conversation," Jenny pushes in, "especially now."

"Care to explain?"

June raises her hand to silence her travel companions, "Unless we talk her out of it, Esmé is buying Sand Art."

"That's a beautiful place. No prettier piece of real estate on the sandy side. And the gallery, will you keep it and run it?"

"She plans on displaying her work," June prides.

"You're an artist?"

June laughs, "Some detective you are, Tom."

He laughs big and raps the roof of the Mercedes. "Have a nice night."

June hollers back, "Head to the window in the comfort room at 11 PM and wave goodnight. We'll be watching through the telescope from the widow's walk."

A smile spreads Tom's face as a memory with Joe bangs...

"Any chance there's a visual into Lan MacTavish's house from up there?"

Joe was quick to answer—too quick to answer, "No."

"You sure about that, Joe?"

Silence.

"Because if someone other than Lan was in his house the night he was visiting Danielle Rayburn, and someone can testify to that fact it'd certainly help keep him out of a courtroom. Right now, Lan's been fingered for tossing his own place, and he can't prove otherwise."

"What reason would Lan have for doing that?"

"Two theories: one, he freaked out and tossed his place after strangling Danielle because the walls are closing in, or two, he tossed it early in the night so he could suggest a mystery someone was in his house while he was in bed with Danielle. Look Joe, the bottom line is this: if your daughter knows anything about anything she needs to come forward. Otherwise, she's going to help convict an innocent man."

"It's not too late to fix this. I just need to convince Marin Baxter to tell me what she knows." Tom spends some time picking up things tossed about during police searches. He's in the kitchen pouring the last of a pot of coffee when he remembers June's directive. He checks the clock. "Almost eleven." He takes his brew to the westerly-facing window in the comfort room and gives a wave, "Nice women." He pulls a sip. "Smart women." He pulls a sip.

"Maybe too smart for their own good." He gives a second wave then drains his cup, "Maybe with their help I can move this case along." He gives one final wave, makes his way back to the kitchen, puts his coffee down, and starts thumbing through a stack of bills and reading a shitload of legal documents and financial papers. "Lan got a sizeable inheritance from his parents and half of the proceeds from selling the family place in Speyside. He stands to inherit the same amount when Laire is declared dead. This gives the prosecution a lock-stock-and-barrel motive. Shit to hell."

Day Five
Tuesday, July 4
Waxing Gibbous – Illumination 83%

It's well after 1 AM when a bitter cold air greets Tom in the upstairs hallway. "Must be an open window somewhere." He peeks into each room and comes up empty. He shakes off a sudden push of heebie-jeebies and enters Laire's room. "Doesn't look like this place got much attention from WPD." He walks to the center of the room, picks up a throw pillow from the floor, and places it on a nearby chair. He reads the embroidery, "Non Oblitus. Pretty sure that means not forgotten." A cold breeze pushes against his back. He checks behind though he knows he's alone, shakes off another creepy feeling, then gets back to business. He eyes an array of Scottish pride on display. "Okay, Miss MacTavish, let's find out who you were and what you were up to before you went missing. He pulls his little book from his pocket, reads his jotted notes, and sets his plan. "Okay, first up— find the missing earring." After a good two-hour search, he doesn't find it. In fact, he doesn't find anything that suggests a teenage girl ever lived in the room, "Maybe the place *was* picked clean by WPD."

He heads to the bathroom for a once over and comes up empty. He's about to step into Lan's room when he notices the throw pillow is back on the floor in Laire's room. He doesn't bother trying to ignore the spine tingle; he just heads inside and picks it up. Before dropping it onto the chair, he feels something hard inside and turns it over, "A zipper." He slides it and reaches inside the stiff linen cover. "BINGO! A packet of birth control pills." He flips open the plastic container, "Full. If Miss MacTavish got these pills, there was a reason—could be any number of reasons," he reminds himself. He reads the prescription fill date and the pharmacy name. "Peduzzi. She got them in town on the 5th of June, but she didn't take any. There's no way of knowing if this is the first package of pills she got, or if she'd been on them for a period of time." He tucks the container back inside the pillow and opens the pocket calendar. He reads notations made in a very pretty script beginning in January. "Mostly school-related stuff and hand drawn hearts here and there with names written inside. Lan. Ma and Da. Caillen. Finnea. Probably birthday and anniversary reminders." The detective finds the months of June and July particularly interesting. "Almost every dated square contains a pretty five-point star with letters, or the word WEFA written underneath. Above the highest point there's a circle or maybe the letter O."

o

W. E. F. A.

The detective jots a couple notes and talks himself through them: "Lan told the chief Laire might have left to meet up with some guy. Looks like his suspicion might be right, but what made him think that? Confirm the names inside the hearts. Ask if—" Tom drops his notebook and bolts from the room at the sound of a blood-curdling scream.

Wind Ledge

J & J bump full-body into Marin as the three scramble to Esmé's room. June turns and heads to the front door when Tom bangs and demands they open up.

"Who screamed?" he asks as he pushes in.

"Esmé, but I don't know why. Come on."

Marin starts to retreat to her room when the detective fills the hallway. He points his finger in her direction, "You, stay put. You are at the center of whatever is going on, and you are going to come clean." He walks past her and finds Esmé in Jenny's arms grabbing at breaths that are full of pain and grief. He listens for a few.

"I know it was a nightmare, Jenny, but it was so real and someone, something touched my cheek and woke me." She raises her hand and skims it along the path of the ice cold sensation. "Right here. I swear someone wiped my tears." They start again.

Tom steps forward, "Esmé, do you think you can tell me about the nightmare?"

"You!" she points a shaky finger. "You were part of it. Joe said you came to see him to ask if we heard anything at Lan's house the night it got tossed."

"That's right."

"He said you were glad that Marin and I went home and that you were worried about him being on cliff side by himself."

"That's right."

"He regretted telling me about your conversation because I would worry about him." She pulls a ragged breath and lets it shake back out, "I reminded him that we don't keep secrets from each other." She sobs her last words, "I was wrong. Everything about our lives at Whisper was shrouded in secrecy."

Marin flashes back to her conversation with her father at Sandy Beach...

"I need you to listen, really listen. Okay?"

"Okay."

"Your mother and I have been married almost eighteen years, and in all that time I haven't lied to her or kept secrets from her. Not once, Marin. And now, every word that comes out of my mouth is a lie. I hate what I'm doing, and I will pay dearly when all of this comes to light. So, while you're stewing about whether to tell me or not to tell me what you know, make sure you consider the collateral damage being caused on this end."

"Okay. That's it," Tom declares. "We all need to sit and talk, why don't you take a minute, then join us in the living room, Esmé."

She takes ten and when she arrives, she addresses Marin in a similar tone to the one Tom used. "Marin, some horrible things happened on Whisper last year. Since then, I have replayed every conversation I had with your father, analyzed every look the two of you shared, questioned whether I missed something, and berated myself for leaving him alone. I am certain that something was going on behind my back. If my husband were here, I'd force him to come clean. He is not, so I am asking you. No, I am demanding that you start talking."

Marin falls apart.

Primrose Priscilla

Miss Prissy is sitting smackdab in the center of her solid mahogany, four-poster bed, surrounded by stacks of burgundy colored journals. On one side there's a small stack she just finished reading, and on the other side there are four stacks of unread stitch-bound scripted accounts of her life with Tom. On the floor across the room are several boxes filled to the brim with more and more books. Priscilla started her read-through hours ago looking for a clue as to who fathered Dale Jacobs, but she got grabbed by the emotional rollercoaster she and Tom were on when they were trying to conceive, so she abandoned her search and went back to the very beginning, to the very first journal she filled—the one Tom gave her on the day of their wedding. She reads the words he wrote on the inside cover.

**I promise to help you fill these pages
with love and joy.**

Priscilla stops to have a good cry for herself over the love and joy she had with the man she adores, and painfully accepts, once again, that she missed having the love and joy of children. When she's cried herself dry, she cracks the spine of another journal and begins reading another chapter in the life of Mr. and Mrs. Martin.

Wind Ledge

Tom takes lead, "While Marin pulls herself together, why don't you tell us more about the nightmare."

Esmé stops to organize her thoughts, finds there's just no way, so she pushes in. "It was a jumble of things, so I might bounce back and forth, and I'm not too sure how much sense I'll make."

"You just talk. We'll pull threads later."

"One of the reasons we bought Wind Ledge is because I'm an artist. During the five or six weeks we were here, I painted several land and seascapes. I decided to shake things up, so I painted a picture of Marin that I call, *Girl on a Rock*. I planned to give it to Joe for Christmas. The piece is really good, and it inspired me to paint other works with figures in them. I borrowed Marin's camera so I could take pictures of people at Stonehenge, but I found some shots on the camera that Marin had taken of a man standing on a cliff—"

Marin gasps from behind.

All eyes turn her way.

She shakes her head.

Esmé continues, "I decided to paint Cliff Man because the structure of the photography is wonderful. His face is obscured, but I still saw a raw edginess to the faceless form and was inspired to paint him. In my nightmare just now, Cliff Man went from being intense and mysterious to menacing and murderous."

Tom knows there's more, he nudges her along, "Continue."

"That's it."

"No, Esmé, it isn't. Find the end of story and tell it."

A shiver runs, and she sort of sinks into herself. "In the pictures Marin took, Cliff Man is standing in the exact spot where Joe was when he—"

"Was pushed."

All eyes turn to June and burn with an array of emotion: anger, shock, fear, disbelief.

Marin turns and storms from the room.

June raises a hand and says her piece, "Everyone in this room is on the same page— Marin knows enough, or she knows everything, about the things that took place here. We are not helping her or protecting her by letting her think we are clueless OR that the people who killed her father are clueless. The person or persons who have blood on their hands know Esmé and Marin are back on Whisper. The only chance we have to keep these women safe is to push that girl into telling us what the hell happened. So, be mad at me if you want, but you all know I'm right about this."

Tom gets up, "Marin is going to need some time to reconcile some things." He checks his watch, "It's a little after 2 AM, let's try to get some sleep and reconvene at 9. I'll bring pastries; you put on the coffee. And do not discuss the case without me. We all need to stay on the same page, as June would say."

The women nod their agreement. Esmé stretches out on one end of the couch, and Jenny does the same on the other end. June grabs a blanket and follows Tom.

"Are you sleeping on the porch?"

"Nope. I'm heading to the patio. Someone needs to make sure Marin doesn't sneak out the window."

"I'm starting to like you, June Fletcher."

"Right backatcha, Tom Martin."

Echo

Edward and Quinn join King and Ruby at the rattans shortly before noon. Brief introductions are made and are quickly followed by Happy Fourth of July expressions. The women are somewhat discreet in their sizing up of one another; the men are very obvious in their women-watching. After several minutes, King gets up and offers his hand to Quinn, "Let's take a stroll."

Ruby waits until they are out of earshot before taking a swing, "You should let Howling Henna know walls are only so thick. King and I were up most of the night listening to the two of you."

"Been there. Done that." He tosses a wide smile. "You could have been making a racket of your own if you popped the old man a little blue pill. Then he could have been UP most of the night with Roaring Ruby. By the way, you and I—well, there isn't a you and I anymore." He laughs at her expense, jogs to the shoreline, and takes a quick dip. She goes off in a huff.

King walks Quinn to a shaded veranda, "Can I get you something?"

"Iced tea or lemonade if you have it. Otherwise club soda is fine."

"I have it all. Would you prefer it straight or spiked?"

She offers a wide smile, "I think I should keep my wits about me."

He laughs big, "You're expecting a grilling are you?"

"Not sure what to expect, Mr. Kingston."

"King."

She smiles. She sips. She waits.

"So, you and Heir."

"God he hates that name," she laughs. "I wouldn't dare call him that."

"A benefit of being his father, I suppose." He takes a pull of scotch whisky, "Tell me how you two met."

"We were introduced by our broker. Edward had just finished a meeting with Brandan Brash and the two were in the lobby saying goodbyes when I arrived a few minutes early for my meeting with Brandan. Honestly, after our brief introduction, I never thought twice about hearing from Edward."

"Why's that?"

"He was somewhat rude during the encounter. My second impression of him was completely different." She takes a sip and smiles, "When I finished with Brandan and was walking back through the lobby, Edward appeared out of nowhere and offered an apology. He said he was distracted during our first meeting and wanted to correct my impression since he felt he fell short."

"It must have worked."

"It helped. It wasn't until he wooed me off my feet and into his bed that I fully forgave him."

The two share a hearty laugh, then an even harder laugh when a dripping Edward shakes ocean water at them.

"How's the water?" she asks.

"Wet," he answers.

King excuses himself, "I'll leave the two of you to this captivating discussion. I need to check with Cook about the clambake this evening. You will be joining us. Right?"

Edward and Quinn silently check with one another, then agree. "We'll be on shore until 9 PM, then we're taking the Big Cat out for a night at sea," the son answers.

"Good for you. The bay is a perfect place to watch the fireworks."

"And to set off a few of our own." Edward takes King's vacated seat and traces his fingers along the top Quinn's hand, then weaves them with hers.

She laughs her wonderful laugh.

From on high, Ruby watches.
She sure as hell isn't laughing.

Day Six
Wednesday, July 5
Waxing Gibbous – Illumination 89%

The Baxters et al and Tom Martin rescheduled their get together to the day after the holiday. He arrives right on time carrying the pastries he promised. Marin greets him at the door and steps onto the porch. "I've decided to tell you what I know." She raises her hand when he starts to say something. "I don't know if Mr. MacTavish has committed any crimes, but I do know he was not the person who trashed Watch Ledge the night Danielle Rayburn was murdered, though I'm not really sure how I know that since the man wore a black ski mask." She reaches for the pastries, "I'll take these and meet you on the patio. My mother and the Js-Times-2 are already out there. How do you take your coffee?"

"Black, one sugar." He joins the others, "What happened to her?" he tilts his head toward the house.

Esmé starts to get up, "Que la? What do you mean *what happened*?"

He smiles, "Marin met me at the door and said she's ready to talk."

All eyes turn her way at the slam of the screen door.

She hands June the box of yummies and Tom his cup of brew then raises her hand. "I have a lot to say, but I'm afraid I might be criminally responsible for some things. I've been reading online," she adds sheepishly.

Tom pushes in, "I'm no longer an officer of the law. I'm here strictly as a civilian. You have legal representation right there, so if you're nearing the line, she won't let you cross it." He silently checks with Jenny. She nods his way, then to Marin.

The soon-to-be eighteen-year-old walks to the cliff, clearly carrying a load that most never burden. She stares a good few minutes then takes the empty seat at the table. "On July 21st last year, I climbed out of my bedroom window, something I'd been doing for weeks, and went to my special spot to sketch the phases of the moon." She pulls a deep breath and exhales it fully. "I saw a man on a boat dump a body into the ocean." She tears and welcomes the touch of her mother's hand. "After many minutes, I crawled on my hands and knees back to Wind Ledge and was sneaking through the window when Lan called out to me." She looks to Tom, "Can you ask me some questions because I feel a ramble coming on?"

He takes out his pocket notebook. Jenny reaches into her briefcase and removes two big-ass legal pads. She gives him one, "I think you'll need this."

"When did you first arrive on Whisper?"

She shrugs.

Esmé answers, "June 21st."

"And you'd been sneaking out to draw the moon for weeks?"

"Yes. I had a sketchpad with a collection of drawings I named *Moonlight Over Midnight Ocean*."

"*Had* a sketchpad?"

She lowers her head, "My father found it and hid it."

"Why?" Esmé asks with another touch of her hand to Marin's.

"Because he knew I was keeping secrets about the night Laire went missing. My secrets made him keep secrets from you. He was afraid you'd find the sketchpad and—"

"Demand answers."

"Yes. Mom, if I had told Daddy what I saw, he would have told you," she looks at her mother, "and you," she looks at the detective. "And Daddy would still be alive today."

She falls apart.
Completely apart.

Cliff Road

Rookie detective, Dale Jacobs, drives past Wind Ledge for the third time in an hour. "Tom's truck's still here. He could be paying the widow Baxter a social call. If so, he should be leaving soon." That thought is replaced with another when he nears Watch Ledge. "Maybe I should do a quick look inside." Another thought, a more reasonable thought, settles pretty quickly, "Nope. Tomorrow is Thursday. The detective has been going off-island every Thursday for months. I can spend all day at the bungalow looking for the earring and the piss-stick tomorrow. Edward said the chief hid the earring in Watch Ledge, and if it was found he'd make it look like Lan stole it from Echo. That means it's most likely hidden in Lan's bedroom. That's where I'll be spending my time."

He's back on the sandy side in time to see Edward escorting Quinn to the Abenaki. He pulls the cruiser over and watches the faux couple do the whole 'can't wait to see you again' ritual. "Heir sure got himself a banging hot babe to pass time with. Good. Now he can go to the condo in Portland and stay for a while. I've got some shit to handle, and it'd be easier if he stayed off island."

Echo

King is in his office checking on a few things. "Brandan Brash, please. Tell him it's Edward Kingston III."

The young broker is on the line within seconds, "Mr. Kingston, it's a pleasure."

"Call me King."

"Will do. Is this an introductory call, or are you looking for a new firm?"

226

King laughs big, "I like your style, Mr. Brash, but I'm looking for information."

"On?"

"Quinn Hughes."

"You do know Quinn's already been claimed by a Kingston."

The King enjoys the comment, "Yes. I know. I actually met the lovely woman at our July Fourth celebration. If my son is bringing her to family affairs, then I suspect he's quite enamored. He said you introduced them last year, so I wanted to thank you."

Brandan's delight at being pulled into a Kingston family affair is on display—of course he'd already been pulled into the charade by Heir earlier that morning. "If I'd given any thought to pairing Edward with anyone, it would have been Quinn, but it was purely a chance meeting in a lobby. Sometimes organic encounters work best."

"Like this one."

"How so?"

"I'm working on a few things in the Casco Bay area, and I might like to have a local financial whiz on board. I'll be in touch in a few weeks."

"Look forward to working with you, King."

Ruby skedaddles barefoot from her listening post outside King's office and heads to her room. She tosses her clickity-clackers onto the floor, grabs her iPad and gets to work. "Quinn Hughes," she keys in the name and starts reading, "Age thirty-one, originally from Alvarado, Texas, graduate of Harvard Law, managing partner of Hughes and Creighton Law, with two locations, one in Portland, ME the other Portsmouth, NH." She gets into a fit of giggles, "A lawyer. Well that explains the uptight, anal-retentive vibe. Based on King's end of the phone call, Quinn and Edward met last year in the lobby of a brokerage firm." She grabs a calendar from her end table and flips back to the first time she and Edward bedded, "July 23rd last year. When exactly did they meet because he's been fucking me for almost a year?"

Wind Ledge

When Marin returns to the patio, Tom starts right in, "You saw a man on a boat dump a body into the ocean."

"Yes."

"Tell me about it in as much detail as you can."

"I went to my special spot to sketch, but I forgot to bring my flashlight, so I just leaned back to gaze a bit. Movement from just outside the tail of light reflecting off the ocean pulled my attention. It was a small craft lifting and slapping on waves."

"What direction did it come from?"

"From the east. At first I wondered if it was adrift, then I saw a man crouched on his knees. I started to get up, but I got an instinct that I shouldn't be seen, so I immediately squatted and went flat onto the ground."

"Do you think the man saw you?"

"Yes. He stood and stared in my direction for many seconds, maybe for a full minute. He waited until the boat bobbed beyond the lighted swath, then took hold of a body and dumped it overboard. Within seconds, the boat's engine started, and it moved slowly toward the westerly end and around the island's bend. My first thought was that whoever was in the boat knows the stony waterway. My second thought was I needed to get home."

"You said you initially thought the boat was adrift."

"Yes."

"So you didn't hear a boat's engine before you saw it move into the illumination?"

She thinks a second, "No, the first time I heard an engine was after he dumped … after he put the body into the bay."

"Can you tell me anything about the man's appearance?"

"He wore a hat. I think it was a ballcap, and I think it was a dark color."

"Tell me about the pictures of Cliff Man."

"At 3 AM that morning, Lan MacTavish came to Wind Ledge and told Daddy that his sister was missing. Later that morning, Daddy went for a walk with Lan, and when he returned he was in a really bad mood. He said he was going to work on screens and that I should head to Stony and spend the day there. When I came home for lunch, Daddy was alone at the cottage. That's when I learned he had spent the morning searching my bedroom. He found my sketchpad of drawings and a pile of dirty and blood-stained clothing I wore on my crawl through the bramble. I lied when he suggested I saw something or knew something about the missing girl. He begged me to confide in him—really pushed me to confess about my secret trips out my bedroom window. He kept pressing me, but I couldn't tell him that Laire might be at the bottom of Casco Bay, so I said nothing. Then he asked about the muddy and bloody clothes and whether they got that way from a trip through the bramble. I lied and said I wore them to Stony and scraped my leg on my rock. That's when we heard Mom come home from a trip to town. Daddy said we weren't to say anything to you until he had all of the facts, and that I'd better keep my butt in my bedroom at night."

Jenny pushes in with a question, "Joe found your sketchpad, then he took it and hid it?"

"Yes."

"Any idea where?" three women and a cop ask in unison.

"I haven't a clue, but I need to find it as soon as possible."

"Why?" her mother asks.

Marin addresses the detective, "I think you should leave. I'm about to set my mother's hair on fire, and I don't want any witnesses."

He stands and tilts his head in the direction of J & J, "What about them?"

"One is a pacificist, so she won't rough and tumble over this or any other news—"

"Not true, I rough and tumble over environmental issues," June clarifies.

Marin nods, "True. As for the other J, she's a wuss outside a courtroom."

He smiles at the spunky one, "Okay, I'll leave, but let's review the ground rules. No discussing the case without me. I usually go to Portland on Thursday to see Lan, but the discussions we're having are more pressing, so I'll be back tomorrow at 9 AM." He's at the driveway when June calls after him.

"Bring some more yummies."

"Will do Miss Motormouth."

"That's Ms. Motormouth, thank you very much."

Marin gets up, "You three meet me in the living room." When she joins them, she has a large yellow envelope in hand, and a story in progress. "I need to find my sketchbook because I promised to send copies of my work to the admission's director at Woods Hole Oceanographic Institute. I landed a coveted spot at the marine science research center beginning January 2018. As much as I hate Whisper, I fell in love with the ocean and island life when I was here. I love the connection between its movement and the moon. And I want to do my part to help conserve the ocean and marine life. Mom, I have accepted admission to WHO-ee. I need to send a deposit by July 15th. I withdrew my spot at UMass. And I'll be staying with you in Oxford until the first of the year."

The women bust a gut laughing.

When Esmé tells Marin she is selling the house in Oxford, has put an offer on a home on the sandy side of Whisper, and is moving there as soon as papers are signed, Marin storms to Cliff Road for a run. She's just about at Watch Ledge when she sees a WPD cruiser do a slow crawl past Lan's bungalow. The car gains speed as it passes her. Shivers run up and down her spine as she runs easterly. Instead of staying on the road, she jogs to the patio in back of Watch and gives a holler, "Hey! Detective! Are you here?"

He yells down from on high, "On the walk. The stairway is through—"

"The master bedroom. Got it."

The good-size man is sitting in one of two lawn chairs, his feet perched on a rail. He smiles when he sees her, "That was fast."

"Yeah, well my bomb wasn't nearly as big as Esmé's. Apparently, the Baxter women are buying real estate on the sandy side and moving to Whisper."

"Yeah? She's going through with the purchase?"

"You knew?"

"Some. I saw the ladies returning after they toured the Crane place, one of the most beautiful places on Whisper, it should be noted.

It's really a perfect property for your mother because of her artwork."

Marin offers a shoulder shrug. "I can't imagine why she wants to live where her husband died."

"Maybe she needs to stay close to your father. They bought Wind Ledge for a reason, probably scrimped and saved to get it. Regardless of whether she lives here or in Oxford, or on the moon you love so much, she's going to have memories, some will be comforting, others not so much. Maybe the sun, sand, and surf will be healing for her."

"Yeah."

"I'm just speculating here, Marin, but your father probably left her some life insurance. Maybe they discussed what they'd do if one of them found themselves alone. I know Miss Prissy and I have had those conversations. They are tough to have. I don't want to think how tough it would be for one of us to be left alone. My advice to you, though you haven't asked for it, is to listen to why she wants to be here." He takes a good long look at the bay then continues, "Why are you moving here? I thought you were heading to UMass in the fall."

"There's been a change of plans."

"Ah, the 'setting her hair on fire' news."

She laughs, "I'm headed to WHO-ee."

"As in the marine institute at Woods Hole?"

"Yeah."

"Well, good for you. Just getting accepted there is a huge accomplishment."

She smiles really wide, "It is, isn't it."

"It is."

It's her turn to take a ponder at the bay, "You know who would have loved hearing this?"

"Your dad."

"Yeah."

"Didn't know him well, Marin, but he was a good man, and he loved you and your mother deeply. And before you start guilting yourself over what happened, you need to remember this. The only person who bears responsibility for your father's death is the person who caused it. And that person is not you." He plunks his feet onto the decking and pushes up, "Come on, I'll see you out. I've got a wife at home waiting my arrival."

"Miss Prissy?"

"The one and only. I'll mention to Priscilla that I'd like you two to meet. She'll do the inviting. She's very proper about things of that nature. I think you two will hit it off very well."

He opens the front door for her and she stops cold.

"What's wrong?"

"Nothing, really, I just got a little spooked earlier. That's why I stopped at your place."

"What spooked you?"

"A police car. Just seeing it made me think about the night Lan got arrested. There were several police cars blocking our path when we were heading to the ferry line. We had to turn around and go down the western side of Cliff Road. That was the night Mom and I left Dad alone. I never saw my father again."

The detective nods, "Come on, I'll give you a lift home." Halfway there he sees Dale Jacobs drive by. The men give a quick toot and wave. "Was that the officer you saw earlier?"

"Not sure. I really didn't see his face then or now."

"Well, if that's him, his name is Officer Jacobs, and he's a good guy."

Week One Comes To An End
Thursday, July 6
Waxing Gibbous – Illumination 94%

Edward is surprised shitless when he arrives at the condo in Portland and finds Dale inside. "What the fuck are you doing here?"

"I went to the dock to make sure Tom got on the Abenaki for one of his Thursday trips to Portland. He didn't set sail. I can't go to Cliff Road to satisfy my curiosity because I was seen on patrol there twice yesterday, once by Marin Baxter when she was out on a run, and once by Marin and Tom when he gave her a ride home from Watch Ledge. Since I can't get into MacTavish's place, I thought I'd visit my brother at his swanky digs."

"You swiped my keys and made copies?"

"Yeah."

"How'd you get past the lobby manager?"

"Jesus, Edward, I waited until he needed a piss. This isn't rocket science."

"There are cameras in the lobby."

"I should hope so."

"You'll be on video."

"For a couple of weeks, then it'll be taped over. Forget the damned lobby surveillance, we need to talk about Marin Baxter."

"What was she doing at Lan's?"

"What do you think?"

"I think we have a problem, Dale."

"Yeah, one that I have to handle. Marin Baxter will be taken care of very soon. You need to stay on the mainland. Spend the next few weeks playing 'fuck the henna' for a while." He walks to the door and calls over his shoulder, "I mean it, Edward, don't come back to Whisper until I tell you to."

As soon as the door slams shut, Edward races to the bedroom, pulls open the bedside drawer, and exhales a sigh of relief. "Baby Bro didn't find the pregnancy stick."

As soon as the elevator door slides shut, Dale slumps back against the wall, bangs his fist hard against it, and groans. "The goddamn fucker kept the pregnancy stick."

Wind Ledge

Tom makes and early morning delivery. It comes in two parts: donuts from the Boardwalk, a Main Street hole-in-the-wall coffee shop, and a directive. "First, eat the yummies," he quotes June. "Second, get ready for a scavenger hunt. We find Marin's sketchpad before we do anything else. She needs it for WHO-ee, and we need it to establish a timeline for her trips to The Spot, so eat up, drink up, and get up."

June is licking sugar and strawberry jelly from her fingertips and muttering, "Who the hell put that guy in charge?"

"I did, so motormouth about it later. Marin, describe the sketchpad."

"It's really a sketchbook. It's 10 x 14, the cover is light brown buffalo hide with a leather strap that wraps around, and it has deckle edge paper inside."

"Where'd you get that?" the surprised mother asks in a surprised mother tone.

"At Pendleton's Art back home. It was expensive, but I used the gift card those two gave me for Christmas."

"It sounds beautiful. Is it embossed or anything?"

"Around the edges and—"

Tom pulls the train back onto the track, "Ladies. Why don't we find the damn thing, and then we'll all take a look at it."

"I'm not looking at it. It's b.u.f.f.a.l.o h.i.d.e. Honestly Marin, I thought I taught you better." She huffs and puffs a bit, "Buffalo hide, leather straps, maybe we should grill up the poor beast for dinner."

"Sorry, June."

"Yeah. Yeah."

Tom yanks the train onto another track, "Marin, I suspect you've already looked for it."

"Since we've been back, I checked my bedroom, the first-floor bathroom, the stairway leading to the widow's walk and the walk itself. My next search was going to be the living room, the front porch, and the second-floor guest room and bathroom."

"What about my room, the kitchen, and my art studio?"

"I doubt Daddy would have hidden it in the places you frequented most, Mom. And besides, I think it's probably in Dad's work shed."

There is a mass exodus. Bodies melding together in a great push through doorways, and down porch stairs, and along the driveway and walkway. The advancing adults pull up short when they find the door locked and turn in unison to backtrack when Marin suggests, "I think you need this." She hands a keyring to the man of the group, "Some leader you are."

He laughs big. "You're a pisser, Miss Baxter." He uses an old-fashioned skeleton key on the bottom lock and another key in a recently added deadbolt lock. He opens the door and befitting the mood of things, it creaks ominously—the movement sending dust particles flying in all directions and stagnant air wafting.

Esmé steps away, "I can't." She makes her way to the patio table, followed close behind by her friends.

"Marin, why don't you and Tom look for the sketchbook," Jenny encourages. An hour later, the lounging lawyer pushes from her chaise and knocks on the shed door. "We're heading into town to meet the realtor. Jasper Crane has accepted Esmé's offer, so we've got some paperwork to do."

"Jasper Crane. Is he the dude who does the handblown glass art?"

"You know him?" Jenny asks dubiously.

"No. But he owns that beautiful place at the end of Main Street, right before you get to Shaky Town."

"Yes. Sand Art. That's the name of his place—of your mother's place."

Marin addresses Tom, "You were right, that property is the perfect place for the artist known as Esmé Clemente Baxter."

Tom nudges, "She must be good if she has three names."

"Yeup, artists and serial killers. Once they make it in their chosen profession, they get to go by three names."

Tom laughs big.

"Still not sure about living here, but at least Sand Art is on the sandy side of Murder Island."

The mother hears her daughter's words and joins her for a hug, "I know you would rather I stay in Oxford or move any place other than Whisper, but I promised Joseph I'd paint, paint, paint. This is where I want to do that. Now that you've begun your own journey as an artist, I'm sure you recognize how important a creative influence is."

"Whisper is your muse?"

She smiles wide, "I suppose it is." She reflects a bit, "It's so much more now." She opens her arms and her daughter folds within. Mom kisses her daughter's temple, "Okay, we're off."

Many hours later, she and the J-Team return to find Tom and Marin in the living room having a coffee table picnic of tuna sandwiches. "From the look of you two, I'm guessing your search was unfruitful."

They grunt.

Darkening afternoon skies set the plan for the rest of the day. "It looks like our search will be inside the bungalow. Rain is expected early evening. There are plenty of places and several rooms that haven't been searched yet, so let's get to work." Esmé moves about the room turning on lights, "Too bad the fireplace isn't working, it'd be nice to have a fire on a stormy night."

A memory bangs Marin hard...

"Hey, Marin, why don't we leave your mother to her work. You can help me with the fireplace downstairs."

Esmé pushed in, "Joseph, you should hire a professional to inspect the fireplaces before you do anything to them."

"I will, but we can do some cleaning before then, and there's a loose piece of mantle I should shore up. Marin can help."

Marin pushes from the couch, sending her drink and sandwich flying. "Mom! Move!" She goes to the mantle and starts tapping.

"What are you doing," Tom asks as he joins her.

"My father said there was a loose piece of mantle. He was going to fix it, but—" A square piece of mahogany slides a bit from the surrounding molding. Tom removes it as Marin peeks inside. Her widening smile screams **Paydirt!** He reaches in and hands it off. Marin clutches it to her chest and starts bawling. She folds into the arms of the man who's becoming an important part of her life.

Esmé joins them, "May I?" She walks away with the sketchpad and opens it on the now cleared off coffee table. J & J join her on the couch, and Tom peeks from behind.

There is complete silence.

It clangs loudly in Marin's head. And with each page that's turned without commentary from the viewers of her artwork, the clang intensifies in volume and reverberation—until finally the group shares their enthusiasm. Esmé exhales her amazement, "These are exquisite, Marin. I had no idea of your talent. Surely your father recognized it when he found this book."

Marin smiles, "He said they were remarkable."

"And they are," the art critics say in unison.

Marin makes her way to her mother's vacant seat and flips through the pages. She whispers each phase of the moon and it's illumination, runs her finger across her scripted *Baxter* at the bottom, and reads the date on the back. When she reaches the end of her collection, she closes the book and remembers, "Wait. There's a missing picture. A drawing I did that I just didn't like. I tore it from the sketchpad, folded it and tucked it under the leather strap in the back. It's gone."

Tom takes his phone, shines the flashlight into the mantle hole and declares, "It's not here."

Marin is quick to wonder, "If it slipped from beneath the leather strap the night of the murder," she stops short and asks Tom, *The Question*, "The body in the bay, it's Laire MacTavish, isn't it?"

"Yes."

"I always knew it was," she points to her heart, "but so long as I never asked, it was just a dead body. Not sure what that says about me—"

"It says you weren't ready to deal. That's all it says, Marin."

"Okay, so now I am ready to deal. Laire was most likely murdered."

"Yes."

"Her death wasn't accidental."

"No."

"And if the man in the boat saw me, and he is Laire's killer, and he's Cliff Man, and he went to The Spot the day after he saw me, and if I dropped the sketch, and if he found it, then—"

"He knows someone named *Baxter* was at The Spot and saw him."

Motormouth speeds right in, "Any chance the killer thought Joe drew the pictures, and that's why—"

"Nope," is the collective answer.

Marin grabs her rain slicker off a peg on the porch, "I need to walk. I'll be on Stony."

"It's going to storm later, Marin," her mother says on approach.

"I'll be back before then. I promise. And I'll stay between Walker and Wind Ledge. Really, Mom, I promise. I just need to clear my head, and I want to do that on Stony."

Esmé silently checks her cohorts, who all nod. "Sas, but please be careful."

"I'll be heading to Watch in a few minutes, Marin, if you need me," Tom offers.

"Good to know." She grabs her cell, puts in her earbuds, pulls her hood up, and walks away.

Dale parked his father's car a couple streets below Cliff Road and hoofed it to Watch Ledge when he saw Tom's truck at the Baxter place. He's been inside for nearly an hour, having made no headway when he sees lights from the driveway travel the walls and ceiling. He double-times down the stairs and sneaks out the back door as Tom enters from the front. Dale is halfway down the access ladder when he sees a young woman he thinks is Marin Baxter jogging westerly. He sets off after her.

The newest admission of WHO-ee is listening to a podcast about Alvin, the institute's Human Occupied Vehicle that takes scientists to depths reaching 4,500 meters below sea level. A series of deep breaths ensues at the thought of doing deep submergence research. "Pretty sure that's not in my future." She waves to an older couple strolling past, picks up her pace and heads toward her little square of sand at the bend of Stony, having forgotten her promises of 'Wind to Walker and no further'. Striding in that direction, she remembers her promise, makes an abrupt turn, and slams full-body into a young man. She yelps in surprise as her feet are uprooted, and grunts an exhale when her ass thuds onto wet, hard sand. The strolling couple stop their forward momentum and come back to offer help." Are you okay?" they call out.

The bumping-man, whose body is most definitely worth bumping a time or two, offers Marin a hand up and repeats the question, "Are you okay?"

She rights herself and begins slapping at clumps of wet sand on her jeans, "Yes. I'm fine. I'm so sorry. It was my fault. I didn't know you were behind me." She grabs the buds from her ears. "I guess I was caught up in the podcast." She smiles meekly at everyone, takes a step and immediately thumps against the dude's chest when her ankle buckles, "Owww." She lifts the injured foot and does a little hop in place.

"You've hurt yourself."

"Yes."

"Can you walk?"

"No."

"Do you live near Stony?"

"At Wind Ledge." She notices a recognition on his face. "You know the place?"

He smiles, "I'm an officer with the WPD."

That's all he needs to say for her to realize *he knows all about Wind*, "Oh."

"Dale Jacobs," he smiles.

"Marin Baxter," she does not smile until another recognition hits, "Oh, you know Detective Tom Martin."

His smile broadens, "Very well, actually. He's a great guy."

She finds her elusive smile, "He said the same about you."

"Good to know."

The couple who offered help to the fallen girl know they are no longer needed and leave when rain begins to fall.

"Oh, shit. Now what?"

"I'll help you back to the access ladder at your place. Maybe by then you'll be able to climb." He turns and squats, "Hop on."

"I. Don't. Think. So."

He stands and turns, "Okay. What's your plan?"

Before she comes up with one, the rain intensifies, the wind picks up, and her cell phone buzzes. She knows it's her mom. She answers it with an "Almost home." The young woman with no options zips the phone into her pocket and relents, "Okay. Piggy-back it is." Marin's thoughts are all over the place as her rescuer schleps her a half-mile with total ease.

Dale's thoughts are laser-focused. *Be the hero. Get invited into the Baxter circle. Work with Tom Martin. Make sure Edward Kingston IV is* crowned Whisper Island Killer—bring down a fucking King—and walk away unscathed.

Week Two – Day One
Friday, July 7
Waxing Gibbous – Illumination 98%

Tom and Dale meet on the driveway of Wind Ledge the next morning. They are both bearing goodies from the Boardwalk, "This is a surprise, Officer Jacobs."

"Yeah. Good to see you, Detective. I'm just checking in on Miss Baxter."

"Why?"

"She had a little injury on Stony late yesterday and I helped her back—"

June interrupts the conversation with a call out, "Continue your chit-chat after you get those donuts inside."

"Yes, Ms. Motormouth," Tom laughs.

The men find Marin on the couch, her swollen ankle ace-bandaged and propped on a pillow. "How's it doin?" Dale smiles.

"Way better, but not fully weight-bearing yet. Thanks again for the lift home."

Dale smiles at Tom, "A piggy-back to the ladder was all she needed. She managed the climb pretty well."

"Liar! It took me twenty minutes in the pelting rain."

"Yeah. Like I said, you managed the climb pretty well."

The women arrive with plates of donuts and muffins and coffee goods. They set it out on the sofa table behind the couch, "You should be able to help yourself from there, Marin." Esmé smiles wide at the men, "Dale, I want to thank you for helping Marin when she was hurt, and Tom, I want to thank you for trying to keep her safe from harm."

Dale's brow silently expresses his confusion.

Tom tilts his head toward the door, "A moment outside, Mr. Jacobs."

They step outside.

Dale goes all preemptive. "You should know there's a push to get Lan MacTavish for Christie Anderson. I've been asked to review your work, and I think I'm seeing things that are different from the files you showed me at Primrose Priscilla."

"Yeah? Like what?"

"Like a witness statement putting Lan with Christie in Diggers the night she went missing."

"Lan wasn't with Christie. And that witness statement is new. What else?"

"A vacationer came forward, supposedly prompted by the bone washing ashore. Her name is Camilla Stephian," Dale pauses.

Tom shrugs.

"She was a teenage girl back then; she's a college student now. Camilla said she was with Christie when they met Lan **on the beach**.

She said there was no way Christie met Lan for the first time inside a bar. Camilla said it was Lan who told Christie to meet him at Diggers, and Christie told him straight up that she was underage. He supposedly told her Diggers lets underage vacationers in and that they should both go."

"Did you talk to this new witness?"

"Nope. The chief is handling new information."

"Okay. Anything else?"

"A couple things, but damned if I can remember them right now."

Tom takes a hip on his truck, "The Christie Anderson case has been hanging unsolved for too long. Whisper bigwigs are undoubtedly leaning on the chief to get it handled, not necessarily solved. Lan will go down for that, especially if I'm not around to push Banks to the facts of the original investigation." He gives his head a good shake, "Not sure I'll have much success given the fact he successfully bottlenecked me out of Danielle Rayburn's investigation. Straight up, Dale, WPD made a mistake on that case, or worse. Lan MacTavish did not kill that young woman."

"I know you think that."

"How about you? Do you think he was a good arrest and prosecution?"

"Arrest. Maybe. He put himself in the shack with her that night, but everything about their relationship seemed real friendly, caring, maybe even loving. I definitely don't think their relationship was on again, off again like the press said." He thinks a minute or so, "I think there was enough of a connection between them that it could have tied up a juror or two and kept him from being convicted. Bottom line, I think Lan's problem was Christie's bone washing ashore right after he was arrested for Danielle's murder. The heat on WPD to make an arrest was intense, and there was just enough rumor-shit for the press to use against Lan. I think that's what moved things in his direction."

"Yeah."

"But."

"But, what?"

"But I hate to think an innocent man is in prison, and the real killer is roaming free."

"Yeah." Tom mulls a bit then asks, "Are you on duty today?"

"Nope. I just started a two-week vacation. Why?"

"I could use some help finding the person who killed Christie, Danielle, and Laire."

"What the fuck!? Laire MacTavish is dead? You know that? How the fuck do you know that?"

"I'll tell you—if you join my investigation." The detective reads the young officer's face, "This is the deal. You give me two weeks to prove Lan isn't guilty of shit. Maybe we hit paydirt and find a suspect, maybe we don't. At the end of two weeks, I'll let you take whatever we find to the chief or the press or anyone else you want."

Dale paces a bit, then extends his hand to Tom. "Deal. For two weeks I'll bust my ass working this case with you. I won't say shit to anyone until my vacation is over. And even then, I'll give you a say in what I tell."

"Fair enough." The detective and the duplicitous rookie detective shake on it. "First order of business, you and I are going to see Lan at the prison next Thursday, so keep that day open."

Echo

As usual, Ruby is snooping at King's office door. "Yes, Vernon, you heard right, Edward is involved with a lawyer from the mainland. Quinn Hughes, she's originally from Texas, but stayed east after graduating Harvard Law. Forget Edward and Quinn, and do your job. Get the Christie Anderson case finished once and for all."

Ruby is in her room when King knocks an hour later, "Hi, King." She notices his overnight bag, "Are you heading out?"

"To Peaks for the night. Guess there won't be a Kingston man to keep you company in that bed of yours," he slings the arrow.

"Then I'll stay up all night studying French for our trip to Paris," she deflects the archer's point. "Oui?"

"Oui. Au revoir jusqu'à demain."

"Au revoir, roi. Oui?"

"Oui. Très bien."

He leaves Echo in search of a new business deal.

She leaves her room in search of a portrait of Kathleen Kingston.

Peaks Island

Edward meets King at the marina for some shop talk and an early dinner. "I'm going to chew and screw, King. I'm meeting Quinn and her law partner for drinks in Portland at 8 PM."

King raises his glass, "She's a beautiful woman, Heir." The father expects pushback at the name, he receives none. "Have you settled into your birth title?"

Edward laughs, "No. I hate it, but I've reconciled that you won't stop calling me that any time soon."

"Well, you're my son. My only Heir."

"Yeah. Lucky me," he laughs big, then pushes in a bit on that comment. "Why didn't you and Mom have other kids?"

"Kathleen had an emergency hysterectomy right after your birth. She never wanted to consider other options—"

"Like surrogacy or adoption?"

King gives a little nod, "Kathleen's greatest joy in life was being your mother, but she didn't want to have children through other means."

The son pushes beyond normal boundaries, "But you would have had other children? By other means?"

"Yes. But that wasn't in the cards."

"You sure about that? Your dalliances are legendary. Maybe there's a sibling out there who can share the kingdom with Heir Kingston."

The King pulls a good long gulp and pays the price with a good long burn. "I assure you, Edward, you are my one and only. And I assure you I'd be more than happy with a bunch of snotty grandchildren tagging along, so find a broad and knock her good." The father notices the change in his son. "I'm sorry, Edward. I didn't mean to push the bruise of Laire."

He offers a quick shrug, "Don't sweat it. That part of my life is dead and buried."

~~DEAD ~ NOT BURIED~~

A sudden gust lifts from the ocean toppling drinkware and sending linen napkins flying across the outdoor eatery. A paper lantern blows free from an awning and sets sail. It lifts and dips, swirls and twirls like a kite across the open space, its jute rope lashing and snapping harshly at seated, ducking patrons. Another gust sends the lantern and its attached rope toward young Edward. It dances whimsically, then twists and twirls angrily around his neck several times, the tail end simultaneously wrapping tightly around the table's umbrella pole. He rises to his feet and tries to pull the tightening bind free. King pushes to his feet, and with the aid of another man, they pull the umbrella pole from the table—the man holding the umbrella, and

King struggling to pull the rope down and off the pole's end. Edward collapses to the floor unable to breathe until the tangle of rope is freed from his neck. He is a gasping heap. When.

~~A RIGHT TASTE OF FAIR PLAY~~

~~YOUR BREATH THROTTLED BY A PROFESSER OF LOVE~~

Watch Ledge

Tom and Dale spend some time over coffee on the widow's walk catching up and opening up. "Lan filed legal papers so I'd have control over his place and his finances."

"I heard."

"I've spent some time here since then, but I've mostly been with the Baxter women."

Dale waits. While he waits, he wonders if the detective is reassessing their plan to work together. It's a good long wait before he prompts, "And."

"And Marin Baxter saw a man in a boat dump a body into Casco Bay the night Lan MacTavish reported his sister missing."

Dale exhales a sucker-punch's worth of air. "How'd *that* happen?"

"She was on the cliff walk drawing pictures of the moon, something she'd been doing for weeks, when the boat came into view."

"Whoever was in that boat knows how to move through that rocky waterway, knows the back side of the island is nearly uninhabited, and thinks it's good for a dumping ground." He pauses and thinks. "So, Marin Baxter is the person Lan MacTavish saw moving in the shadows near cliff walk."

"Yeah. She was pretty sure the guy in the boat saw her, and was too terrified to say anything. The next day, some guy went to The Spot in the bramble where she'd been hiding, and while he was there she was on Stony taking pictures of him."

"And?"

"I haven't seen the photographs, but Esmé Baxter said his face is obscured—he was wearing a ballcap and there was movement when the pictures were taken, but the subject matter is interesting enough for her to paint the image."

"Paint the image?"

"She's an artist, a good one from what I've heard. It's not public knowledge yet, but she's buying Sand Art from Jasper Crane, and she and Marin are moving in as soon as the paperwork clears."

"They're staying on Whisper?"

"Esmé is staying permanently. Marin is heading to WHO-ee in January."

"Holy shit! That's a tough admissions process."

"She's a brilliant young woman and an incredible artist in her own right."

"Damn, detective. You sound like a proud grandpa."

"Sort of feel like one." He pushes from his seat, "Come on, let's do some searching and speculating."

"Yes, sir."

Portland

Edward flags down a deckhand and hands off a line, "Shore her up."

"Yes, sir. Are you alright, Mr. Kingston?"

"Fine. Why?"

"You're green around the gills."

"It was a rough trip."

"From Peaks?"

"Yeah, it's a bitch out there."

The hand looks at the blackening sea, "Can't say what's happening east of here, but our bay sure looks calm."

"Yeah, well it's fucking hell out there, damn near died." He storms off.

The dockhand calls his supervisor, "Any complaints of rough seas here to Peaks?"

"Nope. Why?"

"Edward Kingston just docked, and he's spooked to shit. He said the seas tossed his ass pretty bad, and he looks like he's ready to toss his stomach."

"First I'm hearing of any issues. Make sure you check with whoever docks next, and let me know."

"On it."

Edward steps into Mooring, a dive bar near the marina that's big with dockhands and chicks who like the trolling type. He gets a shot, plows it back, touches his neck where a nasty rope burn announces itself with every turn of his head, motions for another shot, then takes a smack to his shoulder.

"Well, looky here, Edward Kingston IV slumming it in Portland."

Heir recognizes the voice, but before acknowledging it, he plows his second shot. He abandons his stool, stretches a plastic smile on his face, and greets Fred Fuller, former owner of Diggers. "Long time, no see, Fred."

"If memory serves me Heir, the last time I laid eyes on you was the night Christie Anderson went missing."

Edward closes the space between them, "Let's take this outside." As soon as they're beneath the neon Mooring sign, Edward pushes in, "What the fuck, Fred? Mentioning Christie to me ... in a fuckin dive ... where people know who I am."

"Newsflash, Eddie, I'm trying to buy this fuckin dive, and I just decided you're gonna be an investor."

"I already paid you to keep your mouth shut—"

"And you're gonna pay me again."

Week Two – Day Two
Saturday, July 8
Waxing Gibbous – Illumination 99%

Tom and Dale called it quits at midnight. They're back at it at 8 AM, both quietly inspecting this here and that there. Dale reassess and reminds, *I don't need to look for the pregnancy stick because Edward has it. Tom doesn't know Laire was pregnant, so he won't be looking for the pregnancy stick. We're looking for an earring. I know the chief hid the earring, and I'm pretty sure he hid it in Lan's room, but I can't suggest we look there, so I'll continue looking in Laire's room and follow the detective's lead.*

Tom takes a small calendar from his pocket, "I found this zippered inside that throw pillow."

Dale remembers it's the pillow he dropped when the smoke detector went off. *I could have found this.* He pages through the calendar, "June and July are interesting."

"Yeah. It'll be more interesting when we decode the stars and letters."

"Maybe Lan can help. Maybe the symbol is Scottish or something."

"Yeah or maybe it's something teenage girls are familiar with. When Marin's ankle is better, I might have her take a look at the calendar and that symbol over Laire's bed."

Dale already took a cell phone picture of that symbol, but he takes another. "If Marin can't come to the poster, we'll bring the poster to her."

"We're invited to dinner at the Baxter's. You can show her then if you're not busy."

"Not busy."

"Good. Keep looking, I need to call Priscilla."

"Everything alright?"

"She's been a bit off this week. Tired. I just want to ease my mind."

Wind Ledge

Marin is on the widow's walk when Tom and Dale arrive at the bungalow. Her ankle is mostly weight bearing and feels much better, but she has no intention of trekking two sets of stairs just to say hello when she hears them enter through the patio. She stays perched on her mother's painter's stool alternately paging through her sketchpad and watching the rolling ocean. "There's something about being at the shore right before rain moves in—"

"I agree," Dale interrupts from behind, carrying two sodas, "and in the morning after it's rained all night."

She puts her sketchpad aside and eases off the stool. "Yeah, then too."

"How's the ankle?"

"A little unstable, but feeling so much better. Thanks." She takes the soda and places it on the table, then reaches for his, "There are a couple of lawn chairs in that little hallway if you want to grab them."

He does and once they're set at the rail, they take a load off. He hitches his head back a bit, "The book you were skimming when I arrived, it's the one with your sketches of the moon?"

She raises a brow.

He fills her in, "Tom asked me to help Lan by working the investigation with him."

"You don't believe Lan killed Danielle Rayburn?"

"I think there was a rush to judgement. It would set my mind easier if I pulled a few threads, so I went all-in with Tom. He mentioned your trips to the cliff to draw. He bragged at how good your work is."

She smiles and shrugs a shoulder.

"Would you mind if I looked?"

"Nope."

He grabs the leather-bound book and returns to his seat. After several minutes and several passes through he remarks, "Honestly, Marin, these are so lifelike. The detail, and the way the moon shines, or glows, or makes me think it does. I don't know how you did it, but the drawings have an illumination. Is that possible?" He flips through again, "I don't know if you ever tried to touch the moon when you were a kid, but holding this book is like touching the moon. They are remarkable."

Her smile goes ear to ear, and her eyes light and twinkle like stars. "Thank you."

He gets up to return the book and pretends to see the telescope for the first time. "Do you use the scope to help in your drawings?"

"No, that's just for gazing and studying, and," she leaves her sentence hanging.

He laughs, "And snooping."

She laughs, "Not much to snoop on this side of the island."

He looks to the east, then he looks to the west, "Given the bramble cover, I'd say you'd only be able to snoop on Watch Ledge."

She turns a bit red.

"And I'd say you already have."

She hesitates, then confesses, "Since you're working with Tom now, he'll probably tell you that I saw someone inside Lan's place the night Danielle Rayburn was murdered."

He waits it out.

"Whoever it was, he was the one who trashed Watch Ledge."

He sweats it out.

"I didn't tell anyone at the time because I was terrified, but Tom thinks that with some investigating into that and into the man on the boat," she stops herself, unsure if Tom told Dale that part of the story.

"Who dumped the body," he finishes for her.

"Yes. Tom thinks maybe there's enough evidence to make the authorities rethink Lan's conviction."

Dale nods and ponders, "The man in the boat could be anyone, Marin ... it could even have been Lan."

She thinks a bit, "Does he have a boat? I never heard he had a boat?"

"He worked at the marina, so I'm sure he could get his hands on one, hell, anyone at the marina could get their hands on a boat."

She thinks a bit more, "Yeah, but whoever was in that boat that night knew this waterway. I don't think someone who had to borrow a boat would know how to navigate back here. Whoever handled the boat seemed really comfortable on the water, standing and kneeling with ease and stuff."

He laughs, "Those are all very good points." He takes a few minutes to ponder, "So, I guess our killer is someone who has access to a boat, is very familiar with this particular waterway, and is more than an occasional boater." Dale puts his feet onto the rail and quiets while Marin churns that bit of finger-pointing.

Let the Edward Kingston IV framing begin!

When Marin and Dale get downstairs they learn Tom had to leave, "His wife, Priscilla, isn't feeling well, so he went home," Esmé explains, then hands a set of keys to Dale, "he said you should talk to Marin about Laire's room and if the two of you want to check it out, you can."

"Laire's room?" Marin gasps and gapes wide-eyed at Dale. "Tom wants me to see her bedroom?"

"Yeah. You two are contemporaries, so he thought you might understand the things she has lying about, like this." He slides his cell from his pocket and shows her the picture he took, "That's a poster over her bed. Any ideas?"

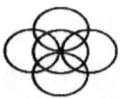

"That's a Celtic Five Fold. It symbolizes earth, air, fire, water, and balance. I have one in my bedroom back home, mine's a little more intricate because it shows the phases of the moon inside the four larger circles, but it's the same, really." She hands his phone back, "Was Laire a lover of the night sky?"

"Not sure, but she's Scottish, so I suppose this being a Celtic symbol might explain her having it. It's one of the things Tom and I plan on asking Lan on Thursday."

"Ask Lan?"

"We're going to see him at the prison."

She blanches and tears, "Can you... Will you... tell him I'm sorry and that I'm trying to help." She turns and hobbles away.

June pushes into the awkwardness, "So, Officer Jacobs, tell us about yourself, and don't bother giving us bits and pieces cause the lawyer over there will pick your bones bare."

All eyes turn June's way, "What?"

"Bones? Really, June?"

"Oh for fucks sake. A bone washes ashore on Stony Beach and everyone needs to censor themselves. Sorry if I offended anyone. Dale, go ahead, save me from this faux pas and spill your guts." She rolls her eyes and pulls a big sigh, "I suppose the guts comment deserves an admonishment from them, so please, just talk before they go all-in!"

"I grew up in South Portland with my mother after my parents' divorce, but came to Whisper during summer vacations to visit my father, so I sort of feel that I'm from here. I was a jock in high school, a smart enough jock to take college courses junior and senior year. I used those credits toward my undergraduate degree from University of New England, a private college with campuses in Biddeford and Portland."

"Were you a criminal justice major?" the lawyer joins in.

He laughs, "No. Far from it. I studied environmental science and sports and recreational management. I originally planned to open a small sport center on Whisper and do hiking and camping tours. I applied to the police academy on a whim, and that was that."

"How old are you?"

"Almost twenty-five. WPD is my first job in law enforcement." He smiles wide, "My father,

Matt Jacobs, is a good friend of Chief Banks. I'm pretty sure he pulled some strings a couple years back."

Marin pipes from behind, "You're almost twenty-five. Are you a Scorpio … you know, your zodiac sign?"

"Yeah."

"So you were born sometime between October 23 and November 22?"

"November 20th. What does that tell you about me?"

"Lots of things, but the most significant is that you're a water sign, and of the three animals associated with your sign, the scorpion, the snake, and the phoenix, I'd say you are most like the last."

"Continue, if you can."

The women scoff, "She can and she will."

"In classical mythology, the phoenix was a unique bird that lived for five or six centuries in the Arabian desert. It eventually burned itself on a funeral pyre and rose from the ashes with renewed youth and purpose." She checks with her audience to see if she should continue. She continues. "From the limited time I've spent with you, I think I can make an argument that you possess the qualities of the phoenix, nothing dramatic like setting yourself on fire, but things like going to school for a somewhat passive field of study and becoming something on the opposite end of the spectrum; and then there's the returning to the place where you were born to renew that part of your story." She assesses.

She still has an engaged audience. She continues. "Then there's the Phoenix constellation, it's part of a star formation known as the Southern Birds: Ankaa the phoenix, Pavo the peacock, Tucana the toucan, and Grus the crane. Ankaa is the brightest star in the constellation. You already identified yourself as a 'smart jock' so this is keeping with the brightness of the phoenix—with a little creative stretching, of course." She smiles and shrugs.

"Can you see the Phoenix constellation from your telescope?"

"If my telescope was set on a widow's walk somewhere south of the Equator," she laughs. A wonderful laugh.

He joins in. "Is your zodiac sign Scorpio? Is that why you know so much about it?"

"Nope. My birthday is September 1st, so that makes me a Virgo. It's one of three Earth signs and is ruled by Mercury, the messenger planet. People born under the sign of Virgo are charming, direct, and their attention to detail is legendary—"

"And they're modest, too," June quips.

"And this particular Virgo is patient, pragmatic, and artistic," the proud mother says as she joins from the kitchen. "Dinner is ready and on the patio, so let's move this zodiac lesson outside."

Dale nudges Marin, "I'd like to know what sign rules the motormouth over there."

June chucks the officer a finger, "How's this for a sign?"

Whisper General Hospital

Tom quietly paces the private hospital room of Priscilla Martin, the love of his life, the woman he found passed out on the floor of their home when he arrived there several hours ago. She stirs when the door opens and a slender, Indian doctor dressed in an unembellished khaki-colored Sari and white lab coat moves lithely into the room.

"Mrs. Martin, my name is Doctor Shenoy." She takes a hip on the patient's bed, "I'll be looking after you while you're here. How are you feeling?"

"A bit tired."

"I'll only keep you a minute, then you can rest. I have a couple questions though."

Priscilla nods.

"You mentioned that you've been fatigued and experiencing some weakness."

"Yes."

"Any dizziness, shortness of breath, headaches, or double vision?"

"Yes."

"To which of those?"

"All of those. From time to time."

"Night sweats, numbness, itchy skin or bruising?"

"Yes."

The doctor gives a gentle rub to Priscilla's leg, "Your bloodwork shows an increase in cells, particularly red blood cells. It's something that needs further examination. My plan is to keep you here for a few days." She gives another rub of Priscilla's leg. "You need your rest, so I'm afraid your handsome husband will need to leave." She addresses Tom, "In a few minutes, no real rush."

He nods his understanding then takes a hip on his wife's bed as the doctor silently leaves.

"Priscilla. The symptoms. Why didn't you tell me?"

"They really come and go and haven't caused much concern. And now, I thought I was fatigued because I've been up the past few nights reading old journals trying to find a thread for you to pull."

He laughs and takes his wife's hand, "A thread? On what matter, Miss Prissy?"

She leans close and whispers, "On who fathered Dale Jacobs."

"I appreciate your efforts, dear, but why don't we work on that mystery when you get home. And when you get there, expect a bit of hovering from your handsome husband."

She giggles. She yawns. She leans back against her pillow.

He smiles. He concerns. He gives her a kiss to the forehead, "I love you." His words are lost to his wife's slumber.

Week Two – Day Three
Sunday, July 9
Full Moon – Illumination 100%

Dale hops onto the porch at Wind Ledge shortly before noon and gives a rap. He is ushered inside by Esmé, "Any news on Priscilla?"

"Only that they're running tests. Tom is staying close and said he probably won't be by for a couple days."

"No. Of course not."

"He suggested I spend some time with you all and get caught up. He apologizes for making you repeat things and said you can ignore the rules about jumping ahead without him. We'll catch him up, later."

"No problem," she swats the air, "the telling and retelling is actually staring to feel therapeutic, at least for me. I'm sorry I can't spend time with you now, but June, Jenny, and I are heading to town to meet with the inspector."

"Because you're buying Sand Art?"

"Yes, but I'm putting Wind Ledge on the market too, so this is a kill two birds with one stone trip."

Dale takes a casual look around, "This is a beautiful piece of property."

She laughs, "You want to buy it?"

He looks again, "Maybe."

"Are you serious?"

"Maybe. When you set a price, let's talk."

"Okay."

"Is Marin around? And is it okay if I talk to her without you being here?"

"Of course. She'll be of legal age in less than a month. She's down on Stony doing her thing."

J & J are on the patio and say their hellos and their goodbyes in the same breath. Dale swings his leg over the cliff and descends the ladder onto a beach that's packed with Stonehenge devotees erecting who knows what. He scans the crowd and comes up empty. "Probably walking or jogging, but in which direction?" He plays a hunch and heads westerly. He eventually finds her waist deep in the ocean, snapping pictures of this and that.

"Hey, Marin," he waves.

She smiles and waves in return, then slogs to shore, waves and undertows, pushing and pulling. "Hi, Dale. Is this a coincidence?"

"Nope. Your mom said you were on Stony. She and the Js-Times-2 just headed to town."

Marin laughs big at the reference, "That's what I call them. Well, that and J-Squared, and J-To-The-Second-Power, and JJ—the list is never ending. It's funny you called them that." Her attention is pulled to the water by the sound of a motorboat. She raises her hand to block the sun and announces, "That guy is on the water a lot."

Dale stares at his brother's boat—the brother who isn't supposed to be anywhere near Whisper. "Do you know him?" *Fucking Edward*, he silently seethes.

"Nope, but I've seen that pretty mint-green and white double-hull a few times. It's really beautiful."

"You can rent a boat like that at the marina if you're interested in getting off shore. Although you might want to cruise the waters on the sandy side, way less treacherous."

"Why do you think he's boating over here?"

"Probably coming in from one of the Diamond islands, or fishing near them is my guess. So, do you want to go out … on the water … for a while? We could talk about the case. Tom suggested we do that, and your mother said it's okay. It's a nice day, so there's no reason why we can't enjoy ourselves while we talk about—"

"Murders and dumping dead bodies over the side of a boat?"

He facepalms, "Shit. What was I thinking?"

"I don't know, but I'm thinking it sounds like fun, the boating, not the talking about dead people. Let's go!"

Kingston Marina

Edward IV is still on the docks when Dale and Marin arrive at the rental booth. He really wants to get in earshot, but the look on his brother's face warns him to steer clear. When their father happens by, Heir turns his attention to King. "You just in from Peaks?"

He nods, "You just in from Portland?"

He shakes his head, "Big Diamond."

King surveys the goings on at his marina.

His Heir apparent watches for a sign of stress given the fact that all three Kingston men are at the same place at the same time. *Huh. Nothing. King sure is a cool muthafucka. If I didn't know any better, I'd say those two have never met, let alone blackmailed each other.*

King steps close to his son, "How's your neck?" He surveys it, "Looks like shit. What a fuckin thing that was!"

"Yeah, some fuckin thing. It hurts like hell."

"Get it checked. Nurse Betty is at the marina today checking on one of the dockhands who cut his finger on a blade. Why don't you head over to the infirmary, then stop by Echo."

"I'll check in with Betty, maybe get a soothing salve or something, but I can't stop at Echo. I'm only here to do some banking in town, and then I'm heading back to Portland."

"Okay. I'll call you later about the Peaks meeting."

"Late afternoon, okay?"

"Sure."

The son watches the father walk within inches of his other son. *Nothing. Absolutely no outward recognition. It's almost as if—* That thought is cut short by the ring of his cell. "Not a good time, Fred. I'm on Whisper."

"Getting my money, I hope."

"Yeah." Edward hangs up, then watches Dale help Marin Baxter onto a catamaran. *Is he gonna kill that girl at sea? What the fuck?*

Sandy Side

As a surprise to Marin, Dale docks at Sand Art. "Is that my mother?"

"Yeah and the J-Twins."

She laughs. "Did you know they'd be here? You had to have known."

The women stroll the beautiful grassy section, then shuffle through the sand until they're at the dock. "Well, this is a surprise! I'm sure there's a story, and since we're done with the inspector and since I own this place, why don't we grab some lunch from town and picnic. We can christen The Promise, our new home with a new name." Mother opens her arms wide, and daughter nestles close.

"You renamed the place. I'm sure there's a story," Marin sniffles.

"Let's grab some blankets from the SUV, and I'll tell you how I decided on the name."

June and Dale get lunch orders, hop into the SUV, and head to the Beach Bum. "If I move to Whisper, I'm looking for a place in Shaky."

"A shack in Shaky. The houses here are called shacks, and only shacks, no matter the cost."

"There are some pretty nice shacks."

"Yeah. And a few are for sale."

"You've been looking at them?"

"Yeah."

"Esmé said you might be interested in buying Wind Ledge."

"Yeah."

"Where do you live now?"

"At my father's place, Jacobs Jolly. It's a sweet little cape inland on the west side. Dad was diagnosed with early onset dementia a few years ago, and he still lives at home courtesy of a health aide, but he needs more care now. I just put his place on the market, and as soon as it sells, I'll set up a trust for his care and get a place of my own. I work in town, so I'm thinking I might like the quiet of the outer easterly bend or the cliff side."

"Well, I know the owner of Wind Ledge, and I might be able to get you a good deal," she singsongs.

"Nice," he smiles wide. "Speaking of nice, this vehicle is pretty sweet." He rubs his hand along the beautiful leather interior, "I'm guessing this is the lawyer's ride."

"You're guessing right, my friend. I drive a shit-box F-150, thank you very much. Although I've been eyeing your Harley, and I could see myself on a bike tooling the island roads."

"Well, I say we see you on a bike as soon we get back to the ledge. You up for a trip around Whisper?"

"So up!"

Dale takes a call on his burner phone when he enters the Beach Bum, though he does not want to, "Why. Are. You. Calling. Me?"

"I saw you two together."

"Are you still at the marina?"

"No. I'm heading back to Portland."

"Good. Things are getting intense here. I want you to dump the burner phone into the ocean as soon as we hang up. That's where my phone is going, so don't bother trying to get in touch. Make. Sure. You. Dump. It. And don't call me on any other phone. I'm putting things in place on this end. I'll be in touch when I need your help." He hangs up and heads back to the Mercedes with takeout containers for five. "If you enjoy this eatery, June, then you're a good fit for Shaky. How about Jenny? Would she move to a bohemian village on a tiny island in Casco Bay?"

"Since her best friend and daughter are moving here, and if her wife wants to, then she'd move in a heartbeat. Jenny could set up shop and lawyer people here, maybe not in her field, but in the other stuff."

"What's her field?"

"Intellectual property law."

"And you, what do you do?"

"I write shit."

"What kind of shit?"

"Whatever people want me to write. I've got a pretty big customer base in the environmental industry, so I mostly write white papers, you know, stuff like: This white paper highlights the importance of verifiable data as the infrastructure of sustainability ... Blah. Blah. Blah."

"Shit. I'm having a flashback to my environmental studies in college."

"I bet."

"That's pretty cool though."

"Yeah, and the good news is, it could be pretty cool anywhere since I work from home."

"Looks like the town of Oxford might be four-short soon."

"And Whisper might be up-four soon after."

They are laughing and nudging when they join the others on a couple of picnic blankets.

"You two are hitting it off," Jenny smiles.

"We are. And as soon as this sandy side excursion is over, Mr. Jacobs is taking me tooling on his Harley."

"Oh. Good. Lord. She's gonna want one before the day is over."

"I think she already does," Dale laughs.

Wind Ledge

Long after the Harley rides are done, Dale finds Marin on the widow's walk, her face pressed close to the telescope. "It's beautiful," he announces from behind.

277

"It's perfectly full, 100% illumination." She steps back from the eyepiece, "Do you want to look?"

"Absolutely."

Marin smiles at the little gasp he makes when he sees it up close. "I bet the little kid in you wants to touch it."

"Yeah, but the man in me wants to walk it, explore it, and conquer it." He grunts.

She laughs.

"It's really amazing." He gets lost in its beauty for a few minutes. "You know," he stops and steps away.

"What?"

"Okay. You're about to see a whole different side to me, like the dorky, nerdy side, so be kind."

"I live on the dorky, nerdy side of life, Dale," she laughs, "so go for it."

"When I was in South Portland, I'd look at the moon and I'd feel closer to my dad because I knew he'd be seeing it, too."

"Pretty sweet thing, Mr. Jacobs." She quiets for a minute, "I think I might adopt that sentimentality ... Hey Dad, if you're watching from on high, you don't need to worry about Mom and me. We have new friends on Whisper who will help keep us safe."

FLASHES OF HEAT LIGHTNING
BLAZE THE SKY

Week Two – Day Four
Monday, July 10
Waning Gibbous – Illumination 97%

Marin descends the ladder at Wind, jogs to Watch, and ascends the ladder there, all within minutes of her wakeup call from Tom. She waves from the landing platform and gives a holler to the men standing on the widow's walk. "Permission to come acliff?"

"Permission granted," Tom hollers back.

She gets steady footing, then bounds through the bungalow. "How is Mrs. Martin?" she asks as she takes to the widow's walk.

"Miss Prissy is feeling right as rain." He lies.

"Oh that's great!" She throws her arms around the big guy's neck and buzzes his cheek. The action keeps her from seeing the sad eyes that travel from man to man. "Since we're all here, why don't you show me Laire's bedroom? Did Dale tell you that the poster over Laire's bed is a Celtic Five Fold that symbolizes earth, air, fire, water, and balance? And that I have one in my bedroom back home? And that mine shows lunar phases?"

"Nope, this is the first I'm hearing about it. What else have you been up to?"

"We took a Cat from the marina and went to the sandy side. We met up with JJ and Esmé at Sand Art, which is now known as The Promise. We had a picnic lunch, then some of us took rides on Dale's Harley while others paced the bungalow floors."

"My guess is you and June were the riders, and Esmé and Jenny were the pacers."

Marin nudges the man, "Wow, those detective skills of yours are still pretty sharp."

He swings his arm over her shoulder, "I missed you, kid."

"I'm sure you'll get your fill pretty quick, Mr. Martin, since I'll be joining Mrs. Baxter on the sandy side of Whisper until I head to WHO-ee in January. And did you hear this dude might buy Wind Ledge."

"That so?"

"Yeah, well, I need to sell my father's place to pay for a secure living spot at Pleasantvale, first."

Tom shakes his head, "Not sure I follow, Dale."

"Dad has early onset dementia. It's gotten bad over the past year or so, and he needs more help than I can give."

"Gee, Dale. I had no idea. I was just mentioning your father to Miss Prissy. A nicer guy would be hard to find."

"Thanks for saying so. Not many people know Dad is suffering since he's always been a private man, but news will spread now that I put the house on the market. As for Wind Ledge, I made a quick comment to Esmé about the place, and before I knew it, June decided I'd buy Wind and she and Jenny would buy a place in Shaky Town."

Marin. Busts. A. Gut. "Are you kidding me? Jenny Bean and June Berry are going to invade the boho part of town. I love it!"

Tom interrupts the frivolity. "Here." He hands Marin the calendar he found in Laire's throw pillow. She silently flips through. During her second and third flip, she concentrates on the dates in June and July. "This symbol," she points with her finger,

W. E. F. A.

"it's obviously a star, and the alphabetical letters are undoubtedly for wind, earth, fire, and air,—"

"Is that what those letters stand for?"

"That's my educated guess. I haven't seen this particular symbol before, so I'm just guessing that the zero, or the degree symbol above the star might be for balance, in keeping with Celtic Five Fold meanings. I'm thinking Laire was very into the elements or she was dating someone who was. Maybe she was dating a pirate," she jokes as she hands back the pocket calendar.

"Or someone from the marina," Dale casually suggests, "or someone associated with the ferry system. This is an island, and most everyone has a boat or knows someone who does."

"Yeah, but let's pull that thread," the detective pushes in. "The boater came from the easterly side of Whisper, then after dumping the body, he headed west."

"Toward the marina," Dale reminds.

"Or past the marina and back to the sandy side or easterly bend out past Shaky," Tom suggests.

"So the directional route tells us nothing," Dale concedes. "Unless someone rented the boat from the marina."

Tom gives a shake of his head. "Unless things have changed, a marina rental would have to be returned by 11 PM. Marin said everything took place after that."

"Okay, so the guy might not have rented a boat, so maybe he has dock space at the marina."

"If the guy owns the boat that was used, then he most likely does have space at the marina. The King of Whisper, and owner of Kingston Marina has done a bang up job pulling strings with the town council to change ordinances over the years. There once was a time when boat owners docked at their own places. The ordinances now say boats have to be docked at the marina midnight to 6 AM. Very few islanders have overnight docking privileges anymore."

"The Promise has a dock, and Mr. Crane has a boat," Marin counters.

He nods, "Jasper docks his Cat, Shattered Glass, at his place because his rights are grandfathered in. I'll be surprised if his permit transfers to your mother, so don't plan on keeping a boat docked there overnight."

"Well that sucks."

The men laugh, "Welcome to Whisper, where everything is ruled by The King," Tom carps.

"Well, if The King set up a boating kingdom, and most every boat on Whisper is docked at the marina overnight, then you two know where to head for information," the young woman explains.

"**If** we were investigating this case, we would. We're not working this, remember?"

"Then what's your next step, Detective?"

"We get a description of the boat the killer used."

"From who?" She pauses. "From me?" She speculates. "I don't know anything about boats."

Dale pushes in, "You identified a double-hull, yesterday."

"Because I can count to the number two, not because I know boats. Watch and learn. One hull. Two hull. See, easy-peasy. Counting hulls is different than knowing about boats."

283

"You don't need to. All you need to do is tell us what you saw," the detective reminds.

"I saw a B.O.A.T. Something that's crafted for water use. Beyond that, I haven't a clue."

"Did it have a mast for sails?"

"No, but it had some type of awning."

"At the middle of the boat?"

"No, closer to the front."

"And when the man lifted the body and dumped it, was it all in one motion?"

"What?"

"Did he lift it from the deck and send it immediately over the side, or did he lift it, rest it on a side bench, and then roll it overboard?"

Marin closes her eyes. "He lifted it … huh. I thought he immediately dumped it over, but he paused."

"Did he rest it on the side?"

She opens her eyes. "No. I think he might have cradled it, or hugged it. Like for only a second, but there was a pause and not a resting of the body onto something pause. Does that make sense?"

"Maybe. We're starting to think Laire was involved with someone. If the killer had feelings for her, he might have cradled her before—"

Marin shakes from a heebie-jeebie. "Before dumping her murdered body overboard!" Marin's body has a full-out shake attack. She runs from the room.

"Shit. She's so intelligent and poised I sometimes forget she's a teen herself," Tom admonishes.

"She headed to the widow's walk. I'll check on her."

"Okay. I'm gonna head to the hospital and check on Miss Prissy. If Marin settles enough to answer some questions, see if she remembers anything about the guy who trashed Watch the night Danielle was murdered."

"On it." *Or not.*

Echo

Ruby slides Kathleen's portrait back behind a big-ass wall unit in a big-ass first-floor den when she hears King's car pull onto the circular drive. She turns on the T.V. and stretches out on the couch from where she answers his holler, "In here, King."

"Well this is something new—Sunbathe Ruby is inside on a day like today and perched on a couch watching … what the hell are you watching?"

"The weather channel."

"Why?"

"I was bored."

"Maybe because you're watching the weather channel."

She laughs. She moans.

"What's wrong?"

"I pulled a muscle doing laps." She pauses, "I pulled a muscle doing an underwater flip before pushing off the wall with my feet."

"*You* were doing laps?"

"Yes, and not very well. I hope you don't mind my camping here, it's more comfortable than my room."

He pours himself a drink, "Don't mind. I'm heading to the office. If you need anything, ask someone else."

She laughs. She fake moans. She gets captured by the drone of the T.V. and bangs the conversation she's been having with herself for the past few days. "Edward sprinted upstairs to his suite and made a call after listening in on a conversation between King and the chief. I arrived outside Edward's suite as he was ending that call. I didn't hear much, but it felt like he might have been telling someone about King's conversation. I left the upstairs hallway and immediately saw King removing Kathleen's portrait from the foyer. Why? And who the hell was Edward talking to? It wasn't his lawyer/girlfriend because he told the person on the phone that he was heading to the Abenaki to meet her. So. Who. The. Hell. Was. He. Talking. To?"

Whisper General Hospital

The Martins are listening intently to Doctor Shenoy. "Polycythemia vera is a rare blood disorder caused by a genetic change that develops over time. It produces an increase in blood cells, particularly red blood cells. The increase makes blood thicker, which can lead to strokes or tissue and organ damage," the doctor says directly, but compassionately.

Tom parks a hip next to Miss Prissy. Their hands find their homes.

"There is no cure for polycythemia vera, but proper treatment can help reduce or delay problems. I have you scheduled for a procedure tomorrow morning. It's done in the Blood Bank and is very similar to the process for blood donation. I'll keep you in until at least Wednesday then send you home. You'll come in once a week as an outpatient for a repeat procedure until we get your body's iron stores reduced."

"And after that?"

"And after that, you'll be prescribed medicines to help stop your bone marrow from making too many blood cells. That will help keep your blood flow as close to normal as possible. Until we get this under control, Mrs. Martin, you'll need someone with you round the clock." She gives another leg rub and a reassuring smile before leaving.

Tom gives his wife's hand a gentle squeeze, "Well, Miss Prissy, some changes are in store."

"Oh, Thomas, you've already taken to worrying about me."

"My dear, I took to worrying about you the day we met. As of this very minute, I'm taking the front lines with you." He is spared further discussion when he's asked to leave by a no-nonsense nurse who's come to discuss medical matters. The detective is in the lobby when he places a call, "Dale, I need you and the Baxter forces at Primrose Priscilla within the hour."

The Baxter forces spend hours rearranging Tom and Priscilla's home. They move den furniture out, leaving a big-ass recliner behind, bring the four-poster bed from the master bedroom downstairs and set it and a Highboy dresser in the room located just off the kitchen. Before they leave, Dale heads out for pizzas, which they hungrily consume outside. On their short jaunt cliffside, J & J are chatting, Marin is researching, and the mother is wondering, "What are you reading so intently, Marin?"

"Miss Prissy has a rare blood disease called polycythemia vera. It's really serious."

"How on earth do you know her diagnosis?"

"Tom told me."

"Why?"

"Because I asked."

"Marin. You didn't. You shouldn't—"

"What? I shouldn't have asked because that makes me seem nosey?"

"Yes."

"I am nosey, but I'm also interested in the health and wellbeing of Tom's wife."

June cracks up laughing, then says proudly, "She gets that from me, you know."

Jenny and Esmé unison, "We know!"

Portland

Edward meets Fred Fuller in an alley near the Mooring. He slaps an envelope onto the blackmailer's chest. "This is it, Fred. Don't ask for another penny."

"Or what?"

"Or you can deal with King."

Week Two – Day Five
Tuesday, July 11
Waning Gibbous – Illumination 93%

Chief Banks leaves Peduzzi's pharmacy, gets into his WPD Land Rover, and heads to Echo. He doesn't knock on the front door or ring the bell; he just storms in and hunts his enemy. He finds him on a rattan having a smoke and a belt. "King, you'd better stay on your ass because otherwise you're gonna be knocked back onto it."

"What's got you so heated?"

The chief lowers his voice, but not his intensity. "Laire MacTavish was pregnant when your son killed her."

"So."

"So THIS, you fucking asshole. When Laire's bones make it to shore and they end up on an ME's table, they might show she was pregnant. I don't know how that shit works, but I do know THIS. If DNA shows who the mommy and the daddy are, instead of the five years Edward would have gotten for having sex with an underage girl, it will be twenty-five years for killing her and a life-sentence for killing an unborn child." He storms back and forth then threatens before storming away, "I'm putting you on notice. You've pissed off the wrong fucking guy."

Ruby moves away from the open balcony seconds before the chief rounds the corner. He looks up when he sees gossamer silk sheers flapping in the breeze. He waits several seconds—just enough time for him to see Ruby step onto the balcony. She nods in his direction. "For fucks sake, she heard." He gives another 'for fucks sake' when he takes the long way back to WPD and sees Dale Jacobs' Harley parked at Watch Ledge.

Dale peeks from Laire's bedroom window when he hears a car pull onto the gravel driveway. "Fuck! Fuck! Fuck!" He quickly slides the invitation to the Memorial Day outing under the corner of Laire's rug, the whole purpose of this visit, then two-steps it downstairs. At the knock on the front door, he exits the back and heads around the house, "Hey Chief. I don't think the detective is here."

"What are you doing here?"

"I heard about Mrs. Martin and thought I'd express my concern if Tom was around. I've seen his truck parked here lately."

"What's wrong with Priscilla?"

"Not sure exactly. But the day nurse who takes care of my father mentioned Mrs. Martin is in the hospital." He lies with ease.

"Doesn't explain why you're here Officer Jacobs when Tom's not here. Help me piece that together."

"I stop at Watch from time to time. I spend a few minutes on the patio processing the case."

"Which case?"

"Laire's case. We already got Lan for Danielle's murder, and he'll probably be charged for Christie's murder, but ...."

"But what?"

"I can see the sex angle for those two women's deaths, but I can't find a motive for a brother to kill a sister—assuming that's what we learn."

"Maybe the sister found out the brother killed those two women. That'd be motivation enough for one sibling to kill another."

"Damn straight it would."

"Good. Now that that's settled, get on your Harley and leave."

"Yes, Chief."

Portland

Edward is hung-the-fuck-over when his cell rings. He tries to read caller ID but can't get his eyes open beyond a slit. "What!?"

"I heard you tied one on at the docks."

"King?"

"Yeah, King! It's worse than I thought. Keep your ass off the pier, Edward, and dry the fuck up. We've got some problems building on Whisper, and you'd better keep your shit together so you can help deal with the fallout— the one you caused!" The father hangs up on the son.

Edward stumbles to the bathroom then back again. "What problems?" He pulls a mouthful of water from a bottle, sloshes it good, then spits it out over the rail of his penthouse balcony. A good gust of wind rises and flaps the slider curtains in his direction causing him to flashback to the lantern rope tied tight around his neck. He leans away from the flimsy cloth toward the open rail, feels a gentle push against the front of his shoulder and tries to get a handhold onto the railing that turns slick beneath his touch. He leans backward just enough to nearly topple over, grabs at the twirling cloth in a last-ditch attempt to right himself, then collapses onto the floor in a heap. "What the fuck?" He peeks through the railing slats and notices a group of people at the pool on their feet and freaked out by the show. He crawls away, rolls himself inside, slides the glass door closed, and flops prone to the floor where he emotionally loses it. "Fuck this shit," he says with a push from the floor, "I need to sober up, and as soon I can, I need to get back to Echo."

~~YOU WILL NEVER SEE ECHO AGAIN~~

He freezes in place. "Laire?" He drops back to the floor as ornamental vases, picture frames, and lamps lift and crash around him. He barely moves out of the way when the drawer from the bedside table flies across the room and lands inches away. He reaches for the pregnancy test, and when his hand is swatted away he moans. "Laire. I'm so sorry."

~~NOT SORRY ENOUGH ~ BUT SURE THAT YOU WILL BE~~

Primrose Priscilla

Dale meets Tom at 9 PM at the house Miss Prissy made into a home. "How is Mrs. Martin?"

"She tolerated the procedure well and is resting comfortably at the hospital. She said to say hello and to have you make sure I'm eating and sleeping. Now that I've delivered her message, you can keep your nose out of my eating and sleeping habits."

"Yes, sir."

"Anything happen today?"

"Ahhhh, well, yeah, about that."

"Aw shit. What?"

"I was waiting at Watch for Marin when the chief parked his Rover behind my Harley. Luckily, I'd just arrived and was still outside. He asked why I was there."

"Aw shit."

"I told him the health care worker taking care of my father mentioned Mrs. Martin's hospitalization, and so I swung by Watch to see if you were around, so I could express my concern."

"Aw shit."

"When he asked why I was there if you weren't—"

"Aw shit."

"I told him I sometimes stop and sit on the patio and work the case. He asked which case, so I said Laire's case since we got Lan for Danielle's murder, and that he'll probably be charged for Christie's murder. I told him I understood the sex angle for those crimes, but I was having trouble finding a reason for Lan to be involved in Laire's disappearance."

"And?"

"The chief offered a motive. He suggested Laire found out her brother is a killer. He said that'd be motivation enough for one sibling to kill another."

Tom mulls the conversation a bit. "Okay, you need to keep your Harley off cliff side. I doubt the chief knows we're working together or that you've become friendly with the Baxters et al, but he might have seen your explanation as a pile of BS—although it is believable BS. If the chief finds out I'm still working the cases, he'll put my ass in the clinker for interfering with an investigation. And if he finds out you're working with me, he'll fire your ass. Since you're on vacation, Dale, why don't you spend tomorrow at sandy beach. Be seen in town. As for our trip to see Lan on Thursday, you're gonna have to go it alone." Tom hands Dale a legal pad that has a series of questions and talking points. "Get familiar with those and add what you want. You get an hour with the prisoner, so make your time count. And under **no** circumstances are you to let him know Laire is dead."

Week Two – Day Six
Wednesday, July 12
Waning Gibbous – Illumination 87%

Quinn joins Edward for breakfast and a relax poolside. She remarks on the rash burn around his neck and the bruising across his back and hip area as soon as he removes his shirt, "Were you in an accident?"

"No, but some freaky shit happened, and I swear, Quinn, had luck not intervened, I might be dead."

"Are your injuries the reason you cancelled plans with my partner and me the other night?"

"Yes."

"What happened?"

"I was having lunch with King on an outdoor patio at Mulligans on Peaks Island when the wind suddenly picked up and sent a paper lantern flying. The rope attached to it swung and wrapped around my neck a few times then wrapped around a table umbrella. Had King and some other dude not been there to help, I would have been choked to death. The bruising on my back is from a slip on the penthouse balcony and a smash against the railing. I managed to grab hold of the slider curtains and pull hard enough to keep from going over."

"Jesus, Edward." Her sentence is abbreviated by the approach of a man.

"Mr. Kingston, I heard about the mishap, yesterday. Thanks be that you are alright. Would you like management to check the balcony fixtures to make sure they are secure?"

"No, Henri, it was nothing more than a slip that could have ended in a fall, but I'm perfectly fine."

Henri points to the bruising, "Not perfectly fine, but thanks be you're well enough for a day of relaxing poolside. If you need anything, Mr. Kingston, please let me know. Ms. Hughes, enjoy your visit."

Edward waits until the man leaves then shares a thought with Quinn, "The pool area was full of spectators. That's how Henri heard about the near fall. I guess it's just a matter of time before King hears."

"So?"

An answer to Quinn's question will reveal Heir's heavy drinking of late, so he takes hold of her hand, "Did I mention how hot you are in that black suit?"

"You did not."

"Well, you are smokin hot, Quinn."

She eyes his bulge, "And you are smokin hard, Edward."

An ice cold touch to his cheek sends a shiver. It deflates his hardon. "Maybe we should cool off in the pool."

"Sure. Let's play a bit down here, then you can push in for a while up there," she points to the penthouse.

"So long as we stay away from the balcony, I'm all-in."

"Well that's not quite true, but it will be."

~~IT WILL NOT BE~~

Quinn inches her mouth away from Edward's non-performing penis, and momentarily thinks about her next move. She pushes from bed, gathers her clothes and heads for the en suite.

"Quinn. Don't." He gets up, shoves his legs into his jeans, and paces a bit, all the while talking to the woman behind closed door, "Quinn. I've had a couple rough days. I guess I'm more freaked out by it than I thought."

She opens the door, runs her hand down his cheek as she passes by, "I get it Edward. Don't sweat it, really. This is just a pretend relationship, and I can pretend it's great sexually too."

"Quinn, come on, the sex between us is great. I know you thought so over Fourth of July."

"Yes, it was great, and it may be great again, but it sure the hell isn't today. When you get your head together and your penis back in working form, give me a call. And if impotence is more than an occasional thing with you, and that's the reason why you need a fake girlfriend, do me a solid and tell me so my expectations are realistic."

He steps in front of her, "Quinn. It. Is. Not. Like. That."

She kisses his cheek, "Good, then things will be different next time. I'll call you." Quinn is at the elevator when she hears crashing sounds coming from the penthouse suite. "A temper tantrum? Okay, it seems Edward Kingston IV has some serious issues. I need to cut my losses before our relationship becomes public knowledge."

Edward would have answered Quinn's breakup call ten minutes later if he weren't dealing with a really pissed off spirit.

Sandy Side

Dale called Marin when he got back from Tom's place the night before. He updated her on Priscilla's condition, said he had to stay away from the cliff side for a few days, that he was heading to the public beach the next day, and was going to Portland to see Lan on Thursday. She told him to head to The Promise if he saw Jenny's SUV there.

He roars down Main Street, then parks his bike at the farthest end of the public beach as close as possible to the Baxter's new place. He picks a plot of sand within eyesight of the docks, unrolls a beach towel, drops his gear onto it, runs to the shore, and throws himself into the surf. He swims from the public beach waters to those in front of The Promise several times before seeing Marin sitting on the dock. He breaststrokes in her direction, "What are you doing here, alone?"

"I remembered something, then thought about something, and the women said I should tell you. I knew I wouldn't be seeing you until Friday at the earliest, so I took a trolly off the cliff. Mom and J-Squared are coming to get me later."

"Should I come out, or is it something quick?"

"Out. Nothing about me is ever quick, Dale."

"Right." He puts his hands onto the dock and pushes himself up bringing a good amount of ocean water with. She gets a good splashing and a **good** eye of his physique. If he notices her reddening cheeks, he doesn't let on. He sits next to her on the edge and nudges, "Okay, spill."

"I was thinking about the Celtic Five Fold and the star symbol. Both have prominence with the number five, the circles in the Five Fold and the points on a star. When Laire labeled the star, she referenced four alphabet letters which stand for the elements: earth, water, air, and fire. She omitted mentioning balance which is part of the Five Fold."

"Go on."

"If I were labeling something and there was a part that didn't matter enough to include, I'd omit it. So I'm thinking balance was an irrelevant component to Laire's thinking. That leaves us with four elements." She swerves the conversation a bit. "You were an environmental studies major, so I'm sure you know a lot about the elements, but bear with me."

"Okay."

"Ancient Greeks believed everything was made up of earth, water, air, and fire—except Aristotle who believed there was a fifth element, ether, because it seemed strange to him that stars would be made out of earthly elements. He was wrong of course."

Dale laughs big, "Aristotle was wrong? How?"

"Stars are made up of many elements found on earth, and they burn with the heat of fire, all the time, so that is their element," she realizes she has veered off track, so she pulls herself back on. "Bottom line, every visible thing in the universe is made up of some combination of earth, water, air, and fire. Hippocrates went on to theorize that the four elements describe the four basic temperaments of human beings, you know, if someone is grounded they are like the earth, if someone goes with the flow they are like water, if someone is untethered or flighty they are like air, and if someone is intense and quick to burn with emotion they are like fire. He believed that a bit of all temperaments are needed for a person to be in balance; to be mentally and physically well."

"So?"

"So maybe Laire thought the guy she was dating possessed all four elements, but since she omitted balance from her star drawing, maybe she thought her guy was a bit off-balance, or—"

"Or maybe it's simpler than that. Maybe the number four is important, not the elements." *Take that Edward.*

"Ooooo, I never thought of that, but yeah. Maybe Laire met him on the fourth, or he was born in the fourth month, or it's his favorite number. God, the possibilities are endless."

For now, but we'll get to IV. "What were you going to say before I mentioned the number four?"

"I was going to suggest the four elements are prevalent in Shaky Town, and he might be from there, or they might have met there. There's all kinds of zodiac, mystical, new-agey stuff in Shaky."

"New agey?" he laughs.

"I tend to make up words. New agey sounds like it should be on the pages of Webster's Dictionary. It's out in the universe now, so it exists."

"Yeah, between us."

"Gotta start small, Dale."

They turn at the sound of a horn from behind. "That's my cue to leave. Thanks for the information, Marin. I think you're definitely onto something. Keep at it." He gives a wave over his shoulder to the women, stands on the dock, and dives in.

Marin watches until he's back at the public beach. He waves when he gets to his spot.

As the women make their way to the dock, June says what everyone else is thinking, "Marin has a crush on Dale. How do we feel about that?"

"So long as the crush is only one way, I'm fine with it," the mother decides.

Jenny pushes in, "I'm actually getting a protective older brother vibe from him."

June guffaws. "That's because you're a lesbian."

"Ditto."

"I admit I'm not completely versed in boy/girl stuff, but as soon as she's eighteen, I expect there'll be movement between those two."

"He's too old for her," Esmé counters.

"Practically the same age difference as for you and Joe."

"Yesss, but I was almost nineteen when I met Joseph."

"And you were married and a mom within a year."

"Things were different back then."

"Boy/girl things never change, Esmé. A crush is a crush no matter what century it's in." She laughs at her dig.

"Okay, but even if Marin has a crush, it doesn't mean Dale is interested, and besides, she'll be leaving for WHO-ee in January."

"Good thing," June scoffs.

Dale heads back to the shoreline, grabs a handful of small rocks then sits on his towel.

"Let's make sure Edward Kingston IV pays for the crimes he's committed, and few others." The brother who is eager to throw his half-flesh-and-blood under a bus or over the side of a boat checks for eavesdroppers then places a stone onto the sand. "Heir thinks King knows I'm his son. The stupid fuck thinks I blackmailed King to get a job at WPD. Seriously? The trust-fund fucker thinks I'd blackmail the richest man in the state of Maine for a lowly police job at a rinky-dink force on an island in the middle of Casco Bay. And he thinks King got me the job so I'd keep my mouth shut about my paternity. The fact that Heir believes that shit shows how ignorant he is."

He places another stone on the sand and continues. "Heir thinks I just happened by the dunes at Cliff Cove the night he killed Christie Anderson. Granted, he was all freaked out having just choked the life out of that beautiful blonde babe, and clearly wasn't thinking straight when he begged me to help him, but Jesus, he's had two years to pull a thread or two on that shit. I was following Heir that night to fuckin kill him. Helping him dump Christie turned my short game into a long game—the one I'm playing right now."

He places another stone on the sand and continues. "Heir thinks I'm going to cut the final thread to the night he killed Laire by killing Marin, the witness to his dumping a pregnant teen at sea. The stupid fuck isn't even thinking I might be working against him. He isn't even trying to figure this shit out." Dale has a good laugh at his brother's expense. "Edward Kingston IV doesn't know he's at the center of a deadly game, and he won't until seconds before it's over." Dale takes a good long look out at the water then gets back to work—serious work. "Time to review the moves I've already put into play:

- I told Tom there's a push to get Lan MacTavish for Christie Anderson's murder and implied the WPD might be messing with parts of his investigation. That aligned me with Tom in the pursuit of justice. The detective mentioned way back when that he thought the chief was pushing Lan as a suspect because the mayor and town council wanted an immediate arrest. But now that there's still a push to get Lan on trial and convicted, I wonder if Tom is considering whether the chief might have other reasons for dirtying up the original investigation. I wonder if Tom Martin thinks Vernon Banks is a dirty lawman?
- I told Tom I'm not convinced Lan killed Danielle Rayburn and there might have been a rush to judgement, opening the door for Tom to ask me to work with him which will keep me in the loop on any clues Tom stumbles upon.
- I reminded Tom and Marin that the guy in the boat headed toward the marina after he dumped Laire. That unraveled the

discussion about islanders and docking permits and suggested the killer most likely has an association with the marina. That's sort of a given, but I wanted everyone looking at the marina, the one owned by the Kingston family.

- I put the invitation to the Memorial Day event at Echo under Laire's rug. If that thread gets pulled, it will put Laire and Edward at the same event, and with a little more pulling it will be revealed that's where they met.

- I suggested the four elements might have something to do with the number four. A little pulling on this thread, and it will lead to Edward Kingston 'the fourth'.

- I haven't told Tom that Laire was pregnant, but I know where the pregnancy test stick is located, and when the time comes we'll find it and get it analyzed for DNA. That will tie up that loose end. Since I'm not supposed to know about the condo in Portland, I'm gonna have to say I saw Heir on the mainland and followed him to The Claremont.

- I haven't told anyone that Edward found the sketch Marin dropped from her backpack on the cliff walk. I'm pretty sure Edward said it's hidden in his suite at Echo, so there's no way I can get it now. But once he's found dead, WPD will search the entire estate and find it.

- I haven't told Tom that the earrings Chief Banks found in Laire's room belonged to Kathleen Kingston or that the chief hid one in Lan's room in a preemptive move to accuse him of stealing them from Echo. A little pulling on this thread will tie the earring to Heir and to his teenage girlfriend.
- The most significant thing I haven't told Tom is that the chief is working with King—full-out. I suspected Banks was on the wrong side of the law since my first day on the force, but Heir confirmed it when he said he overheard the men plotting about the earrings, amongst other things."

Dale gathers the stones, walks to the shore, and skips them one by one across rolling waves. *When the time comes to investigate Heir's sudden death, there will be plenty of other threads to pull—all of them leading to the indisputable conclusion that Edward Kingston IV killed Christie Anderson, Danielle Rayburn, Laire MacTavish, and Joseph Baxter. Seems only fitting that the killer of Christie and Laire will carry those sins to his grave and that he shoulders my sins for killing Danielle and Joe on his behalf. When the Heir to the Kingston throne commits suicide off the cliff near Wind Ledge, there will be no lingering questions about his guilt.*

Sheryll O'Brien

And since no one knows I'm his brother,
I'll be free and clear.

Week Two Comes To An End
Thursday, July 13
Waning Gibbous – Illumination 80%

The prison meeting is set for 11 AM. Dale Jacobs is battling some nerves when he shows at the dock for the Abenaki's 7 AM run. The young detective isn't concerned about the trip across the bay—it's the sit down with Lachlan MacTavish that's causing some internal havoc. Tom Martin's words fuel the constant bang in Dale's head, "You get an hour with Lan, so make your time count." Those words precede Dale's simpler, more straightforward warning to himself, "Don't fuck this up. Don't fuck this up. Don't fuck this up." With every go around his anxiety ratchets, and within twenty minutes after setting sail, the ferry docks in Portland. The young man bounds down the plank and gets a pretty decent distraction—Fred Fuller is heading toward Mooring. Dale sprints Fred's way and gives a shout-out, "Yo, Fred."

The brand new owner of the not-so-fine-establishment turns and gives a shout-back, "Second damned Whisper flashback this week."

"Yeah? Who else is in town?"

"Heir."

"No shit? You've seen him here on the docks?"

"More often than not, my friend."

"He's bending the elbow some?"

"Bending both I'd say. So tell me, Officer Jacobs, what brings you to the mainland?"

"Vacation day. I'm meeting some friends from South Portland. How about you?"

"Just bought Mooring." He points to the neon.

"No shit."

"Shit you not, my friend. I figure I'll give bar ownership another go."

"Little advice, Fred, keep the young ones out of your place. The law on this side of the bay isn't nearly as accommodating as on Whisper."

"Advice heard. Advice taken. The shit with Christie has never set right with me, and …"

"And?"

"And nothing, Dale. Look I've gotta get inside for a meeting."

"Yeah. See ya around, Fred."

Dale walks away and starts banging that conversation for all it's worth.

Wind Ledge

Esmé Clemente Baxter is in her second-floor art studio at Wind Ledge sitting with her pieces—in other words, she's cross-legged on the floor in the center of the room in deep analysis of her work. Her land and seascapes are perfectly spaced from one another and leaning against the walls courtesy of June's decision to set the room as a gallery. In an almost rhythmic way she inches and turns her butt across the floor, stares at the picture directly in front of her then inches and turns her butt a bit to the left, starting the process anew. She's been doing this for more than an hour. June and Jenny have been watching the process for nearly all that time.

"Hey Es, do you want to clue us in?" June breaks the spell.

"Trying to decide what the feature piece of work will be at Clemente, my new gallery."

"You named it. It's perfect, Es."

"She pushes from the floor. I'll want the piece to be prominently displayed, and I'll probably use the image on my website, social media, and print materials, so the image has to be really special."

Marin pushes into the room and into the conversation, "The image should be this," she holds out *Girl on a Rock*. "You painted this for Daddy, and you're staying on Whisper because of the promise you made to him, so this is really the only painting worthy of being your signature piece." Marin hands it to her mother who turns it toward J & J. They gasp at the wonder.

"Oh, Esmé. It is exquisite," Jenny exhales.

"It really is," June agrees, "even if it's of the pipsqueak over there."

Marin walks to her mother and holds out the envelope she found inside the painter's portfolio. The widow's hand trembles as she takes it, and her eyes tear as reads the front,

"Joseph, I Love You." She slumps to the floor; her friends and daughter join her in an embrace.

Jenny knows where her friend's thoughts are, "Joe didn't see the painting, or that letter, or read the words on the envelope, Esmé, but he knew how you felt about him during every minute of every day that you two spent together. When you falter in believing that, please remember this. You are uprooting your life and moving to a place that is the source of your loss and pain all because of a promise you made to the man you loved more than life itself."

Esmé accepts her friends' embrace until she's too spent to hold herself upright. She lies on the floor and curls into a fetal position. June tucks a pillow under her head, and Marin covers her with an antique quilt, then the J and M squad head to the widow's walk fully aware Round Two of pain and guilt is about to begin.

"It's my fault," Marin reminds as she marches east and west across the platform. "If I'd just told Dad about the man in the boat, or the man on the cliff walk, or the man tossing Lan's house, or any of the other crap I kept secret, he would have told the police, and they would have kept us safe. They would have kept Daddy safe after my mother and I abandoned him."

"You're rewriting parts of history, Marin," Jenny counters. "You did not abandon your father, he sent you away to keep you safe. Your reasons for keeping secrets may seem difficult to understand now, but you had very good reasons for staying silent."

"Yeah like a homicidal dude knowing you saw him dunk a dead body."

"June," Jenny sighs heavily, "go a bit easier."

"No, Jenny, I will not. Marin was a sixteen-year-old kid when this shit happened. She was naïve, a bit sheltered, and only interested in the moon and the solar system—and some questionable music choices, but that's a topic for another day." She steps in front of Marin to stop her back and forth. "You did what most teenagers would have done, and your father did what most men would have done. You need to stop blaming yourself for his death. The only person who bears responsibility for the things that happened is the killer. Your only responsibility is to accept the painful loss and let go of the guilt."

Marin slumps to the floor; her friends join her in an embrace.

Portland Prison

"Where's Tom?"

"He's with Priscilla. She has a medical issue that needs tending."

"A serious one for him to miss two back-to-back meetings."

"He missed last week because we were busy working your cases."

"We?"

"Yeah. Why else would I be here?"

"To tell me WPD is ready to frame me for another murder."

"They are, but I'm inclined to reconsider you for Danielle, and I never thought you were good for Christie."

Lan leans back and thinks a bit, "Tom sent ya?"

Dale reaches into his pocket and pulls the page he ripped from Tom's legal pad. "He wrote some questions and talking points."

"Then go ahead and ask 'em."

"You've said all along that you thought Laire might have skipped out to meet a guy. Why'd you think that?"

"You askin for reasons other than the bonnie one is a teen caught by hormones?"

"Yeah."

Lan is quiet for a bit. "I'm sure Laire was carryin a love bite on her neck the week before she up and left."

"A hickey? She had a hickey?"

"Yeah."

"And you think she up and left willingly?"

"I need to think it, Officer Jacobs, else I'll go mad in this shithole."

Dale nods. "Tom found a pocket-calendar inside a throw pillow Laire had in her room."

Lan leans-in.

"It has a few names written inside hand drawn hearts. Your name in January, Ma and Da in February, and Caillen and Finnea in April."

"My birthday. My parent's anniversary. Probably the Aitken twins' birthday. They were

Laire's friends comin up in Speyside. Was there anything else in the calendar?"

"Beginning in June and through July, this symbol is under most dates." He points to the symbol on the page he brought in.

o

W. E. F. A.

"I get the star, Laire was keen on dark skies and horoscopes, things of that, but the letters? Don't expect my help."

"They stand for wind, earth, fire, and air."

"The elements. And you might be thinkin what?"

"Marin Baxter thinks—"

"Hold up, Dale, and explain some."

"Marin and Esmé Baxter are helping us."

"How?"

"Marin finally broke and confessed to seeing a man toss Watch Ledge while you were with Danielle."

Lan's eyes fill seconds before he gets hot under the collar, "Why the fuck didn't she say somethin before now?"

"She was scared."

"Yeah, well her pussy-footin probably cost Joe his life."

"She knows. There are parts of that girl that are broken. The other parts are trying to help you, so shut the fuck up."

315

"She's your friend now, is she?"

"She's part of the team trying to free your ass. She thinks the star symbol and letters might be a reference to whoever Laire was seeing."

"Let me see the star again." He shrugs, "If the Baxter girl sees somethin, she might be the only one who does."

"Changing gears here. Did you ever rent a boat from the marina?"

"No need to rent one. If I needed one for business, I signed one out."

"On a log or something?"

"Yeah. And when the boat was brought in, it needed to be logged and cleaned. There was a deadline for return, but not sure exactly of that. Danielle used to handle that shit, ya know."

"Didn't know. What about taking a boat out for pleasure?"

"Don't find pleasure in that, Dale, so no."

"Any experience with Laire taking things that didn't belong?"

"Don't know of any. The bonnie one isn't greedy. She doesn't pine for what others have. Laire is ruled by her heart, and it probably got her in trouble deep."

The words plunk a chord with Dale.

Lan thinks a bit, "Are you askin if she thieved cause of the earrings?"

"Yeah."

"If she did take 'em, it might'a been from Echo the day we visited for a remembering day party. But I rightly don't know how she'd manage a thievery. I kept a tight rein on the lass that day."

Dale takes a look at his notes.

Lan has a thought. "About the earrings. Don't think you were in earshot when I mentioned the chief goin into my bedroom the night he came to Watch."

Dale shakes his head. Dale smiles inside.

"The chief searched Laire's room as he told he would, but he did a fair move about my room. Seein he came down with one earring, I'm wonderin if he left the other in my space for a bit of framin."

"Strong accusation, Lan."

"Sittin my ass in prison for a crime I didn't do, Dale."

Moonlight Over Whisper Island

King storms across Echo's perfectly manicured grounds raging into his cell. "Call me! You need to explain why I got a call from Quinn Hughes ending your relationship. Apparently, she thinks you need an intervention or some assistance from your father. Your father is going to assist your ass real good, Heir. Fucking call me!"

Tom paces across his crabgrass backyard having just checked on his slumbering wife. He offers a Heavenly plea, "My nightly talks with you, dear Lord, are to thank you for the most important blessing I have ever had—Miss Prissy. She's in need of some loving care, and I hope you and I can work to see her through this challenge. Amen."

Dale leans against a blue painted rail at the bow of the Abenaki banging the events of the day. "There's a lot of shit that plays heavily in my favor. Running into Fred Fuller was huge. He places Edward in a dive bar on the docks of Portland, and when the time comes that WPD needs Fred to testify, I know where to find him. More important, it's entirely plausible that I stumbled across Edward's condo after Fred tipped me off to Edward's frequent trips to the dock. I'll have an easy go of explaining how I know where the Whisper Island Killer lived before he offed himself. And then there's Lan, he gave me the piece I needed—a way to get Tom looking inside Lan's room for Kathleen Kingston's earring. Once the detective sees how expensive the gems are, he'll know Heir gave the earrings to Laire. It'll be an easy jump to figuring he's the one who fucked and killed the underage girls."

Marin gazes at the moon from the widow's walk at The Promise. She finally does the thing she's wanted to do for nearly a year, she talks to her father. "I miss you, Daddy, every minute of every day, and I will miss you for all eternity." She moves to the railing and watches one shooting star after another after another. Her heart lifts a bit at the sight, "I accept that you are gone, Daddy, but I believe your energy is constant. That's how I know you are part of our lives, watching and knowing all that we do and feel. It must make you happy to know Mom is fulfilling the promise she made to you—and I promise you, here and now, that I'll accept that Mom and I are staying on Whisper—on the sandy side." She laughs. "No more terrifying treks and drives to the cliff side for Esmé Clemente Baxter. And J & J are with us, and we had a celebration tonight in our new home—in Mom's new gallery, Clemente. She hung a painting she did of me for you. It's really wonderful. You should check it out, Daddy."

FLASHES OF HEAT LIGHTNING
BLAZE THE SKY

That bit of illumination means different things to the people of Whisper.

Marin pulls a comforting breath, "I know you hear me."

Dale uses it as his driving force, "Just a matter of time now."

Tom finds spiritual confirmation, "I believe you will bless us."

King knows, "There's an end coming."

Week Three – Day One
Friday, July 14
Waning Gibbous – Illumination 71%

Dale stops in to say hello to Priscilla, who's resting in her new first-floor room, before heading to the backyard. He parks his ass on a chaise and is out cold when Tom smacks his foot many minutes later, "Tough day at the prison?"

The young man shakes the cobwebs and pushes up, "Not really. It was very productive, but the shit banged through my head all night, so I'm fried."

"There's coffee inside."

"I'm good, thanks. Why don't I just do an information dump and get out of your hair."

"Dump away."

"I got to Portland around 7:30 AM and immediately ran into Fred Fuller."

"No shit."

"Shit you not. Fred's the brand new owner of Mooring."

"I've seen the place."

"Apparently, Edward Kingston IV has been a regular patron lately. Fred said Heir's been doing his fair share of double-elbow-bending."

"The Heir of Whisper has been on the docks?"

"Yeah. But there's more. After my meeting with Lan, I spent the afternoon and early evening doing a little sightseeing along the waterfront, hoping I might get lucky and see Edward. I was heading back to the docks for the last Abenaki run when I saw him heading out of The Claremont, a swanky condo complex on the waterfront. I followed him to the docks, he stepped into a bar, not the Mooring."

"I wonder what's sending Heir Kingston in search of low grade booze when he could be drinking the good stuff?"

"Not sure, but it looks like he might be living in Portland. And I'm wondering why he made the move."

Tom nods, "You've got a good head for this, Dale."

"Yeah?"

"Yeah. Now tell me about Lan."

"He thought I was at the prison to tell him WPD was ready to frame him for another murder."

"Did you tell him about Priscilla?"

"Just that she had a medical issue that required your attention, and you decided to send me since we're working his cases. Naturally, he was skeptical. I had to show him your written list of things before he budged. I asked him why he thought Laire might have skipped out to meet a guy. He first mentioned teenage hormones, then said he saw a hickey on her neck the week before, so he made the very simple leap. He said he's hoping she left willingly and is still alive." He shakes his head and quiets.

"Feeling like shit keeping the truth from him?"

"Yeah, but he said if he knew otherwise, he'd go mad."

"He would. Go on."

"I told him you found a pocket-calendar belonging to Laire. He confirmed the red hearts with written names were for birthdays and anniversaries of her family and friends. Then, I showed him the star and letters. He said Laire was keen on horoscopes, so the star made sense, but he didn't have a clue about the letters. When I told him Marin Baxter thought they were letters associated with the elements, he pushed in, all-in."

"I imagine."

"I told him Marin confessed to seeing a man toss Watch Ledge the night he was with Danielle. He got emotional. Then he got pissed. He said her pussy-footing cost him his freedom and Joe his life. I pushed back hard and said she's broken over everything, and trying to make amends by being part of our team. After some back and forth about Marin, I asked him if he ever rented a boat from the marina. He said there was no need since he isn't into boating for fun, and if he needed one for work, he'd log one out with Danielle."

"So, that was her job?"

"I guess."

The detective thinks a bit, "Danielle might have known who was on the bay the nights Christie and Laire were dumped, but since she didn't know they were dead or at the bottom of Casco Bay, it didn't matter to her who was cruising the waters on those nights. But—"

"But, if a bone suddenly washed ashore, and it belonged to Christie or Laire, then…" Dale does a bit of thinking. "Do you think that's why Danielle was killed, because it was only a matter of time before bones came ashore?"

"Could be." Tom notices something cross Dale's face and plays a hunch, "There's more."

"Yeah."

"Something good."

"Yeah. Lan said he was thinking about the missing earring. He said he thinks the chief planted it in his room. I guess the chief went into his bedroom the night he searched Laire's bedroom."

"He did. Lan said he heard a floorboard creak overhead and that it was from his room. He said the chief moved about then came downstairs with a baggie of Laire's things. One of those things was an earring. Lan's suggestion that the chief planted evidence in his room is a strong accusation."

"That's exactly what I said."

"And?"

"He said he was sitting his ass in prison for a crime he didn't do."

"He's right about that."

"Yeah."

"I'll be sticking close to home, Dale, so we'll have to talk by phone. I really don't want your Harley seen at my place. As far as the Baxters et al—"

Dale cuts him off. "I made plans with June to pick me up this afternoon and take me to Wind. I'll do a little cliff walking between the cottages so I'm not seen on Cliff Road, and I'll spend the day inside at Watch. I want to get a jump on looking for the earring."

"Good. Maybe Marin can help. She's got an intuition on things."

"Sure. I'll ask."

"Okay, keep me in the loop."

"Tell Mrs. Martin goodbye for me, and if you need anything…"

"I'll call."

Along The Ledge

Marin and Dale push through the bramble between Wind and Watch. He offers her his hand when they near a particularly narrow section of cliff walk. "Don't look down."

She looks down, grabs tighter to his hand, and shivers, "I am soooo not afraid of heights, but that drop is terrifying."

He laughs, "Any drop off this cliff is terrifying because it's deadly." He immediately wishes he could pull back the words, "Oh, Marin. I'm sorry." He stops and blocks her path.

She lowers her eyes so he can't see the tears.

"Shit. Don't cry. I'm sorry. I totally forgot."

She tries to move past. He grabs hold of her forearm. "Marin. Don't. You need to calm down and take it slow."

She nods and wipes away tears that have started southward. "I can't wait to get to the sandy side, and when I do I'm never coming to this fucking side of Murder Island again."

Dale laughs big.

"What?"

"I never heard you swear. It's like hearing a bunny fart or something."

She growls and pushes past. "Jerk."

He's still laughing when they head inside Watch.

She's still pissed. "So why are we here?" There's a bit of foot stomping.

"Tom wants us to look for something in Lan's bedroom."

"What?"

"An earring. A very expensive earring."

"That's it? That's the description?"

"It has a post."

"Well that's a start I guess."

"I figure since it's an earring, and since we're looking in a man's bedroom, we don't really need to know what it looks like. It should be the only earring we find."

"Okay." She peeks into Laire's room on the way past and sees something white sticking out from under the corner of a throw rug. "What's that?"

"What?"

"That. It looks like a piece of paper or something."

"That paper or something might have been overlooked during the original searches. Same thing for the earring, provided we find it. I'll be right back." He returns with a baggie on his hand, bends and pulls the Memorial Day invitation from under the rug.

"What is it?"

"An invitation to a party at Echo, the Kingston estate. They have a Memorial Day bash every year. Lan works for the marina, or he worked there, so it's probably his invitation."

"Doesn't explain why it's in Laire's room."

"No. It doesn't," he slides the invitation into a separate baggie and shows Marin.

"It's pretty. White, navy, and mint-green. Do you think those are the company colors for the marina?"

"I don't know, why?"

"The man in the mint-green and white catamaran. Maybe he's from the marina."

"Maybe." *Definitely.*

"So what makes you think there's an earring in Lan's room?"

"Not sure, but Tom wants us to look. He said to trust your intuition."

"My what?"

"He said you're intuitive about things?"

"I am not. I'm pragmatic, thoughtful, determinative, very much an earth mother. I am not some flighty, airy, intuitive being."

"Maybe you're operating under Hippocrates' four element thing. You feel all earthy, but Tom sees an airy intuitiveness, and you damn near singed me with your fired up swearing, so all we're missing is a water theme, then we've got you all balanced out."

"A water theme?"

"Yeah."

"Like a career in marine biology? Would that count as a water theme?"

"Yeah, I guess it would."

The two snoops head back to Wind around seven after an unsuccessful earring search at Watch. This time, they walk Cliff Road. "Did I tell you we're going home Sunday to pack some things? I guess there's a buyer for the house in Oxford."

"That's a good thing, right?"

"If seeing your childhood home for the last time is a good thing, then yeah."

"I didn't grow up on Whisper, but I was born here, and I spent all of my vacations here with my dad. He's failing with dementia, and I recently put his house on the market. As soon as it sells I have to admit him to a long-term care facility. So, my childhood home will be gone soon, too."

"I'm sorry, Dale."

"Yeah."

"That's why you're interested in Wind Ledge."

"Yeah."

"I heard the women talking. Mom's going to give you a good deal if you're serious about buying it."

"Yeah?"

"They're gonna say something tonight."

"Good to know."

"Yeah, Dale, good to fucking know."

He touches her arm, "What just happened?"

"Nothing," she pulls her arm away, and storms into the bungalow, "Well, it looks like the stars are aligning or we're playing a weird game of, 'Hey! Do You Know Where I Live, Cause If You Do, I'll Sell You My House?' Esmé Baxter buys Sand Art, so she needs to sell Wind Ledge. Dale Jacobs needs to sell Jacobs Jolly and wants to buy Wind Ledge. There's an offer to buy the Massachusetts abode of Joseph and Esmé, which of course means Jenny Stuart and June Fletcher will uproot their lives in central Massachusetts and move to Murder Island." She slaps her hands together, "And just like that, we all get to wipe away everything we've ever known, everything that has ever mattered." Four pair of eyes fix steadily on her. She responds with a flash of anger, "What? Am I wrong? Isn't that what's happening here? Life has dealt a whole lot of 'Shit Happens, So Move The Fuck On', so we're all moving the fuck on."

She storms to her room and slams the door with absolutely no idea why. She paces a circuitous route, grabs her backpack, makes sure her sketchpad and flashlight are inside, moves her curtains, climbs out the window, and heads to her spot—The Spot. She settles in, looks at the moon, and mellows. Just. Like. That. "Hello, Waning Gibbous at 71 percent illumination. Let's get you on paper." Clouds immediately block the lunar light and heat lightening cuts across the sky. "Looks like it's an unsettled night all around."

~~GO HOME~~

A BOLT OF LIGHTNING
CUTS THE SKY

Four people at Wind Ledge take turns knocking on Marin's door. Dale is last up. "Hey Marin, I'm heading out." No answer.

"She'll come out when she's hungry," Mama Bear suggests.

"Unless she snuck out the window," June smirks, then gets caught in the mad push out the door. The troupe realize she did exactly that when they see her curtains flapping in a gusting wind. Just then deep rolls of thunder and vivid streaks of lightning precede the pelting rain by mere seconds. "Stay here," Dale orders. Aided by only the beam of his cell phone flashlight, he takes to the cliff walk.

"Be careful!" The women yell from their huddle.

Dale knows every twisted root, every pricker vine, rock, tree, and rut from his walkabouts before he sent Joe hurtling toward death. Several yards shy of The Spot, he comes across a knocked out cold Marin. He drops to his knees and feels for a pulse, "Good. Good. Marin, can you hear me?" He gently slaps her cheeks, "Marin." He grabs her backpack and swings it over his shoulder, lifts her, cradles her against his chest, and moves out. As he nears the lilac bushes that border the Baxter property, he calls out, "She's unconscious! Open the doors to the house!" He hurries her inside and to her room. She comes to within seconds of her head finding her pillow.

"Marin. Look at me."

"Get the flashlight out of my eyes, and I will."

"Oh, thank God," June smirks. "The bitch is back."

Dale gives a chuckle and continues his exam. "You've got a good lump on your head."

"Bet I got it when I fell," she rolls her eyes.

"Marin," her mother admonishes.

The patient slaps Dale's hands away, "I'm fine."

"You were unconscious. You need to be checked at the hospital."

"I do not."

"You do," the insisting party unisons.

Dale steps away, "She needs to get into dry clothes. You guys get her ready. Don't let her sleep, and don't give her any pain meds. Let me know when she's changed, and I'll get her to the

SUV. And let's hope part of what changes in this room is the bitchy part."

Jenny preempts her wife's comment, "He's not bossy, June, he's a man of action."

"I was gonna say he's a hoot."

Marin snarls. "Officer Jacobs is not a hoot. He is bossy, and he's a pain in the ass."

"Pot. Kettle. Miss Baxter," he calls from the hall.

Week Three – Day Two
Saturday, July 15
Waning Gibbous – Illumination 61%

Marin was kept overnight and is sitting in a wheelchair grousing because she's sitting in a wheelchair. "I am perfectly capable of walking."

"You're perfectly capable of yakking, that's for sure," Dale pushes back. "Just quiet down and enjoy the ride."

"Hardly."

When he moves her into the elevator and they are behind closed doors, he pushes down on the handles, causing the front of the chair to lift. She squeals and laughs, "Okay, then, this isn't so bad."

June and Esmé are parked at the curb, and as soon as everyone is settled, Mom begins, "First, remind me to do a bit of yelling about your sneaking out of the cottage and going on one of your dangerous strolls."

"I was pissed and needed to get away from—all of you."

"I'm aware. People who are pissed and need some time away generally use a door and then slam it behind them. That is your new practice. Understood?"

"Understood."

"Your discharge orders are going to keep you on Whisper for the foreseeable future."

"But we're all leaving for home. Tomorrow."

"Jenny and I are leaving for home. Tomorrow. She and I will pack up our things, handle the sale of the house, and travel back as soon as we can. Since June works from wherever she is, she will be staying with you."

"At Wind Ledge?"

"Absolutely not! Since The Promise isn't set yet, you'll be staying at the little cottage by the water. That's where Mr. Crane's daughter stayed when she visited. He left the place furnished, so you and June will be perfectly comfortable, and Dale has agreed to stay with you two."

"As what? A babysitter?"

"No, Marin. As a favor to a concerned mother. You need to have someone with medical know how check for concussion-related problems, and the fact that he's a cop doesn't hurt, either. So please thank the nice officer in advance of his services and apologize in advance for your surliness."

"Yeah. Thanks, Dale."

"Yeah. You're welcome, Marin."

June cracks up. "Well this ought to be fun." She swings by Jacobs Jolly to drop Dale off then heads to Wind. The women pack clothes, and toiletries, and basic provisions, and Marin's backpack, and June's computer, then Jenny and

Esmé schlepp them to the sandy side. "Dale said he'll get here sometime after nine. Jenny and I will stop by to see you before we board the ferry in the morning. In the meantime, Marin, make a list of what you want me to bring from home. Most everything else will be put into storage until I decide what I want for The Promise, so you'll have plenty of time to pick through those things."

"Okay. I want everything in my room."

"You can have it, just not when we return, so choose wisely."

"Back up a bit. Did you say when **we** return? Jenny's coming back? She's not just meeting June in Portland?" She eyes the conspiratorial trio, "Oh. My. God. J & J *are* moving to Whisper? For real? To Shaky Town?"

"Not quite, but let's save that bomb for later," June smiles wide. "I'm going on record right here, right now—this island will never be the same with all of us in residence."

Marin scoffs. "Good 'cause the island pretty much sucks the way it is right now."

Portland

King steps onto the mainland dock shortly before 2 PM and huffs his way to The Claremont. It's been four days since he's heard from his son, and three days since Quinn called to say Edward needed an intervention. That point is proven when he enters the penthouse condo and finds the place in total shambles. He storms to the manager's office, "Henri! What happened in the penthouse?"

"Is your inquiry about the fall Edward almost took from the balcony?"

"What fall!?"

"I called and left a message for you to contact me."

"Yes. Yes. I was tied up in negotiations. Tell me now."

"Come, Mr. Kingston, you may view the video."

King watches the captured images of a flailing, flapping Edward a half-dozen times, ending each viewing thinking the same thing, *He looks bat-shit crazy.* "When was the last time you saw my son?"

"Wednesday. He stormed from The Claremont early evening."

"Are you aware that the penthouse is in total ruin?"

"No. Edward cancelled maid service. Said no one was allowed in. I can send a cleaning crew up, of course."

"Please." He hands a business card to Henri, "Call me the second you see my son. I don't care what time it is."

"By all means." Henri heads to the penthouse the second King leaves. He is overtaken by a creepy sensation when he enters, "A veil of evilness dwells. What could have happened here?" He steps around toppled furniture and smashed décor, shards of glass crunching beneath his feet. He stops when his shoe kicks something across the floor. He bends to retrieve it, "A pregnancy test. Ah, perhaps Ms. Hughes is pregnant and the news was not welcome." He scans the destruction, "Very unwelcome, I'd say." He tucks the pregnancy test strip into his pocket for safe keeping. "Perhaps the news will settle, and they will welcome their child. They will want the remembrance of the test. One can hope, anyway."

Echo

Chief Vernon Banks is waiting in King's office a little before 8 PM. As soon as King enters, he starts interrogating, "When was the last time you saw Heir?"

"Sunday at the marina."

"Six days."

King nods. "He'd just arrived from Big Diamond, and I'd just arrived from Peaks."

"What was he doing on Big Diamond?"

"He didn't say."

"Maybe business?"

King shakes his head, "It's possible, but there wasn't anything pending, certainly nothing that required a Sunday visit. I told him to stop by Echo so I could tell him about a meeting I had on a Peaks project we're working. He said he couldn't and that he was only on Whisper to do some banking—"

"On a Sunday? Don't they have ATMs on the mainland?"

King gives it a quick thought. "That never occurred to me."

"Why not?"

He shrugs, "I was distracted by a bad rope burn on his neck from a freak accident the day before."

The chief takes a hip on the corner of King's desk and crosses his arms over his chest, "Accident?"

"We were at Mulligans having lunch on the outdoor patio when a huge gust of wind sent everything flying, including a paper lantern decoration that'd come untied from an awning. The lantern rope twisted around Edward's neck several times, and then around the damn table umbrella. The fuckin thing tightened and almost choked him to death. Some guy and I managed to get him free, but it was close. Anyway, when I saw him on Sunday, I told him he needed to get the burn checked by Nurse Betty."

"Did he?"

"I don't know for sure."

"Go on."

"Since he couldn't come to Echo, we went our separate ways. I told him I wanted to discuss the meeting, and he said to call him later that afternoon. I got tied up on a matter and never made the call. Monday came and went without our speaking which is unusual in general terms, but more so because we really needed to touch base on that matter. I was up to my eyeballs in negotiations all day and just didn't get a chance, so first thing Tuesday I called, and he was either really hungover or still drunk. I told him to dry the fuck up because there were problems developing on Whisper, and he needed to be clearheaded to help with them. Vern, I just found out that immediately after that call, Edward almost fell from the penthouse balcony. The manager of The Claremont showed me video of the event after I found the penthouse destroyed."

"We'll come back to today's events, but finish the timeline first."

"So Tuesday I called, and he was drunk. I didn't hear back from him for the rest of that day or all day Wednesday. On Thursday, I received a call from Edward's girlfriend, Quinn Hughes, saying she was ending her relationship with Edward and that she thought he needed an intervention or at the very least assistance from his father."

"Because of his drinking? Or what?"

"She never really said. She was classy and shit, but guarded. The conversation was awkward, sort of a 'you know your son, so read between the lines' exchange. I immediately called his cell and left a rage message demanding he call me. He didn't call Thursday or Friday, so I dragged my ass to Portland today and found the penthouse trashed—no, I found the place destroyed. I went to the manager's office and asked him when he last saw my son. He said Edward stormed out of The Claremont on Wednesday. That was sometime after Quinn Hughes left. I asked Henri what happened in the penthouse. His response was along the lines of, 'Is your inquiry about the fall Edward almost took from the balcony?' I had no idea what he was talking about so he showed me a video of the event. I watched the damned thing over and over, not believing what I was seeing." King pushes from his desk and goes to his office bar to pour a belt.

"Don't, King. Finish the story, first."

"Edward looked crazed, maybe spooked or possessed, I don't know. There was all this movement, flapping of arms, pulling at curtains, and at least twice, he almost went backward over the rail. I asked the manager if anyone had been to the penthouse since Wednesday, and he said Edward cancelled maid service and no one was allowed in. I left it with the manager that he send a cleaning crew up."

The chief picks up King's phone, "Call him. Tell him to leave the penthouse the way it is. Then give me Quinn Hughes' number."

The Promise

Dale parks his Harley in back of the main house, away from prying eyes, and heads to the little waterfront cottage currently known as Sand Castle. He finds Marin asleep on a chaise on the wrap-around deck. She stirs when he moves past to put his gear in the corner. She groans when she sees him.

"I'm starting to get a complex," he chuckles.

"Starting? I expected more from you Officer Jacobs."

"Huh. We're back to formalities, I see."

"A rose by any other name, or when in Rome. I don't know, you pick."

"Mixing your metaphors, I see."

"I've recently been concussed, so I might be a bit sloppy in my verbal delivery."

"How are you feeling?"

"Tired, achy, mostly in the head and neck area. Grumpy."

"Yeah. I got that part."

June joins them outside, "It's nearly midnight. You should hit the hay, Marin."

"Okay." She sways a bit on standing, but is quickly righted against the rock-solid chest of Officer Jacobs. "What are the sleeping arrangements?" she yawns.

"You and I will share the bedroom. Dale can camp out on the sofa."

"It's an awesome night, so I'll probably crash outside on the chaise."

"Good, then I'm taking the sofa," Marin says as she moves past.

"Is it because I'm a lesbian? You don't want to sleep with a lesbian?" June calls after her.

"Don't mind sleeping with a lesbian. I mind your never-ending chatting and your snoring."

"I do not snore!"

"Yes. You. Do."

Dale grabs his gear, rolls a beach towel into a pillow, and parks his ass on the chaise,

"Do you think the Grump-Ass will kill me in my sleep if I start snoring?"

"I'm not a gambler, Dale, but I'd go all-in on that bet."

Week Three – Day Three
Sunday, July 16
Last Quarter – Illumination 50%

It's a little past midnight when the chief heads back to King's office. "Quinn Hughes is not and never has been Edward's girlfriend. They've known one another for over a year, and have been in one another's circle a handful of times during that year, but the first time they spent any measurable time together was over the Fourth of July break."

"Why'd he lie?"

"I think we know why he lied about having a woman, an appropriately aged woman, in his life."

"Okay. Why'd she lie?"

"He sprung the ruse on her when she arrived on the Abenaki. She readily agreed, thinking it would be fun and because she enjoyed his company. After spending time with him on Wednesday, she decided he wasn't all that much fun, and she no longer enjoyed his company, especially between the sheets. She said he had an impotency problem. She was willing to concede that 'his issue' might have been caused by his two recent near-death experiences. She said he was really freaked out by them. She also said rumors of his drinking are becoming legendary in certain Portland circles. That's why she reached out to you. For what it's worth, Quinn seems genuinely concerned about Edward and really does like him, but she said he's too much of a risk personally and professionally."

King starts pacing. It's many minutes before he asks, "Now what?"

"Now we consider the possibility that Edward is suicidal."

"Are you fuckin kidding me right now?"

"I am not."

"Explain how you made that leap."

"Right off the top, Edward doesn't have the mind of a criminal, or the constitution of a murderer, and yet he is both. Granted, he killed Christie Anderson in a fit of rage, but he killed Laire MacTavish during a premeditated act. Granted, he did it because you forced him to."

"I—"

"Save it King. Edward killed two women and an unborn child. Any chance that young man might have had a normal life is fucked. Spending time with someone like Quinn Hughes probably brought it all home."

"Brought what home, Vern?"

"What he is and what he could have been," he scoffs, "if he'd been raised by—"

"Who? You?"

"By Kathleen."

"Fuck you."

"We're both about to get fucked. Edward is an emotional mess, he's drinking heavily, is away from home because The King banished him. That's a perfect storm for suicidal thoughts. The freak accident at Mulligans might have put something in motion. You said he almost died. Maybe he started thinking about how easy his almost-death was. Maybe the event on the balcony wasn't an accident. Maybe it was a failed suicide attempt."

King can barely pull the breath he needs to say a single word, "Heir."

Vern scoffs at the emoting man and storms out.

Ruby reverses her descent down the center stairs and sneaks around a hallway corner when she hears someone marching toward the foyer. She's surprised to hear Vernon Bank's voice.

"You and I are heading to Portland on the 11 AM Abenaki. Meet me at the ferry. Pack for a couple of days. Get some rest, and stop drinking."

Ruby takes a step toward her room, stops when she hears Edward Kingston III sobbing and his plaintiff call to his son.

"Heir, where are you?"

The Promise

Esmé and Jenny shout from the deck of the main house, "Coffee and donuts are here!"

There's a mass push from the Sand Castle. June and Dale traverse the sand and lawn quickly, and Marin brings up the rear. "You'd better save me a honey-glazed," she hollers.

"First come, first served," the guy hollers back then hands her an ooey-gooey honey-glazed when she arrives. "Here."

"Thanks."

Esmé hands Marin a coffee, "How are you feeling?"

"Fine," the word lifting at the end with faux enthusiasm.

"Uh. Huh. Let's try that again. How are you feeling?"

"About the same. Do you think that's a bad thing?"

"No. The doctor said you'd feel crappy for a week or two, with incremental improvement during that time period. I want you to promise that you'll rest while I'm away. If you feel like going for a walk or a swim in a few days that's fine, but, Do. Not. Go. Alone."

Dale offers, "I'm off from the PD until next Sunday, so I can stay until you two get back. Any plans on that end yet?"

"We should be back by the weekend."

"We'll make sure we're back by then," Jenny concludes.

Dale addresses the lawyer, "How is all this happening? Did you quit your job?"

"I gave notice that I'm leaving at the end of the year. Until then, I'll work remotely as often as I can and go to my office in Boston when I need to meet with clients. In the meantime, June will be looking for the perfect place here."

He laughs, "Damn, you Baxters and Baxterettes sure do move fast."

"Baxterettes! I love it!" Jenny enthuses.

"You would," June groans.

The Abenaki

Jenny and Esmé stay inside a rental SUV until Chief Banks and another man exit a WPD Rover and leave the hull for the deck above. "I wonder why the chief of Whisper is heading mainland." And just like that, the first round of speculation begins.

"I wonder who the other guy is. He's very handsome for an older man," the artist remarks.

"Whoever he is, he's obviously very well off."

"The richest man on Whisper is Edward Kingston III. Maybe that's him. He goes by King."

"How completely unpretentious of him," Jenny laughs big.

"And if that's him, how completely odd that the owner of several marinas and a gazillion boats is on a passenger ferry."

"They must need a car on the mainland, otherwise why ferry it? And maybe they didn't want a rental for some reason."

"And maybe they *wanted* to be seen in a police vehicle. Remind me to tell Dale we saw his boss today. It might take some pressure off about his being seen with the Baxters."

"And the Baxterettes," Jenny nudges.

Esmé laughs and rolls her eyes.

"You look just like Marin when she does that."

She repeats the gesture. "Let's get to the promenading deck and do a little—"

"Promenading?"

"Yesss."

Their leisurely stroll is immediately shortened when the chief approaches. "Mrs. Baxter," he looks around presumably for Marin, "Are you and your daughter leaving Whisper?"

"No. In fact, I recently purchased Sand Art, so we're staying put."

"Jasper's place?"

"Yes."

"It's a beautiful piece of property."

"It is."

"And Wind Ledge, what are your plans for that place?"

Esmé heeds her friend's gentle squeeze of her arm, "I really haven't decided."

"Might be a difficult sell—what with its history and all."

Esmé ignores her friend's gentle squeeze this time, "Yesss. On the matter of my husband's death—"

"Accidental death."

"Yesss, well. Perhaps there was a rush to judgement on that finding. When I return from the mainland, I'll be requesting a sit down and will most likely ask for a reopening of his case. Have a pleasant trip, Chief Banks." The women stroll off, arm in arm.

"Jesus, Es, you put him on notice. You definitely need to call Dale. Like right now."

The Promise

Dale and Marin are poppin-a-squat in low lawn chairs at the shoreline when Esmé's call comes in. "I've got you on speaker, Esmé. Marin and I are in earshot. Did you forget something, or do you miss us?" he jokes.

"Neither."

"Wow, harsh. What's up?"

"Your boss and some man who I think might be The King of Whisper are on the Abenaki. They parked a WPD Rover in the hull."

Dale cracks up laughing, "No shit. Last I heard, King owned a fleet of ships that could carry his ass mainland or to Thailand. Wonder what's up?"

"We think they might have brought their own car so they wouldn't have to rent one on the mainland."

"Okay, that makes sense."

"We weren't up on deck a minute when the chief approached. He looked around for Marin, then asked if my daughter and I were leaving Whisper. I sort of blurted that I bought Sand Art, and we were staying put. He immediately asked about Wind Ledge and suggested it might be difficult to sell considering its history. I threw caution to the wind and told him that I thought there was a rush to judgement on Joseph's death, that I wanted a sit down with him when I return, and that I would be asking him to reopen the investigation."

"Holy shit!"

"That was Jenny's general reaction."

"Okay, listen. You two need to ignore those two men, and no matter what, Do. Not. Follow. Them. when you get to Portland. As far as you two are concerned, they do not exist. Got it?"

"Got it."

"Good. I'm gonna give Tom a call and fill him in. Head on a swivel. Head on a swivel."

"What?"

"Stay alert and be aware of your surroundings."

Dale makes the call. He tells Tom that Esmé and Jenny are heading home for a few days, and about the happenings on the Abenaki, and about the invitation Marin found in Laire's bedroom, and about Marin's escape out a window, and about her subsequent fall, and about her concussion, and about her overnight stay at the hospital, and that he, June, and Marin are staying at Sand Castle. Then Dale asks about Mrs. Martin.

"Miss Prissy is up and at 'em more and more. She tires easily and is getting a bit stir-crazy."

"Do you think she's up for company? I could bring Marin and June by for a visit, and you and I could tackle Lan's room for a bit."

"I think that's a perfect idea. Priscilla is napping right now. I'll check with her and get back to you, but plan on it being tomorrow. Preacher Paulson is stopping by later this afternoon to sit with his congregant."

"I believe there are two congregants living at Primrose Priscilla."

"This congregant will be mowing his crabgrass during tea time."

The Claremont

Chief Banks and Edward Kingston III sit with the condo manager for several minutes watching the captured video of an almost-tragic-fall.

"I'll want a copy of that tape," the chief says.

"Of course."

"And videos of the lobby for the past week."

"I'm sorry Chief Banks, but I can't provide that, privacy issues, you understand."

King starts to say something. The chief stops him with a shake of his head, "We'll be heading to the penthouse."

"Yes. Of course. A cleaning crew began some work but stopped when I received Mr. Kington's request for a cessation of service. I had all of the bagged trash and broken articles that'd already been collected left in the living area for your inspection."

"Does your cleaning crew wear gloves."

"Yes, although you will find my prints. I went to inspect the area after my meeting with this Mr. Kingston, to make sure I ordered the correct cleaning service. I'm afraid I did not wear gloves."

"Okay." The chief walks away, but halts at the manager's next question.

"Should I be notifying the Portland police department?"

"No. I'll handle that."

Chief Banks walks the penthouse without comment, pulls open drawers, looks in cabinets, checks medication labels, reads paperwork, rifles through closets, and peeks under beds. He spends a good chunk of time on the balcony before taking another walkthrough of the rooms. "Come on." When they arrive back downstairs, he asks the manager to get a list of names of the people who were at the pool and witnessed Edward that morning. "I'll be back by 7 PM. Will that be enough time for you to prepare the list?"

"By all means."

"We'll be leaving a WPD Rover in one of Edward's spots overnight."

"Oui. I'm glad you mentioned that. When Edward left on Wednesday, he exited through the lobby to the street, not to the garage. That means he did not take his car at that particular time. I noticed his blue Jaguar was in his assigned parking spot Wednesday night when I left from work around 11 PM. The Jag was gone Thursday when I returned. There are no cameras aimed near his parking space, so we cannot be sure who took the car, but there are video cameras in the lobby and at the door leading to the garage. All tenants are required to go through the lobby to get to the garage. None of the videos show Edward returning to The Claremont on Wednesday night or Thursday morning to take the Jag or to do anything else."

"Okay. Thank you, Henri."

The men step onto the street, immediately stilled by their own thoughts.

"King, you're more familiar with Portland than I am. What hotel is good?"

"The Coastline. It's five blocks from here."

"Check us in. I'll meet you there in an hour or so. While you're waiting, see what you can find out about Edward's banking on Whisper, and ask Nurse Betty if he stopped to see her about the rope burn, and what her assessment was of his demeanor." He takes off his WPD navy blue wind breaker, cuffs his long-sleeves back to his elbows, and puts his shield on the hip of his jeans. He hands his jacket to King. "Give me your slicker." He pulls on the blue, white, and mint-green jacket, zipping it halfway to hide his shield, "I'll be back."

Vernon Banks enters Mooring and bellies up to the bar. Fred Fuller audibly groans when he recognizes him. "What are you doing this side of the bay?"

"Where'd you get the money to buy this place?"

"My Great-Auntie None-Of-Your-Fucking-Business died and left me a boatload of Benjamins." He walks away to pour a few brews for a table of customers. He heads back toward the chief several minutes later, "You ordering or loitering, Vernon?"

"I'm looking for Heir. You seen him, lately?"

"Might have. Word is he lives in Portland now."

"Word was he was on Whisper doing some emergency banking—on a Sunday. I'm pulling that thread, Fred, and when I learn his finances have something to do with the purchase of this place, I'm coming back to find out what you had on him. So you'd better start concocting your bullshit now."

Fred leans across the bar, "You and I both know what I had on Edward Kingston IV. Now get the fuck out of my place, and don't come back. If you do, Chief Banks, you can accompany me to the Portland PD and give a listen while I tell a tale or two about the kingdom of Whisper—about its King—about its Heir—and about the jester in Town Hall who flashes his shiny gold badge right before he plays the fool for the royal lot. Consider yourself banished from **my** kingdom. Get out, Vernon."

Week Three – Day Four
Monday, July 17
Waning Crescent – Illumination 39%

June and Marin join Priscilla in the screened-in patio late morning. Tom makes introductions, settles everyone with glasses of iced tea and a plate of square, fig cookies lined in a row like tiny, sticky soldiers. The wife gushes over his efforts and sends him on his way. Dale greets him on the driveway, gets a grunt in return, and follows the guy on a mission inside Watch. "Something wrong?" Dale treads softly.

"An innocent man is in jail, and I'm starting to get a whiff of shit coming from Town Hall and the western part of the island."

"Care to explain?"

"Not sure I should, Dale. You work for WPD. You're only on loan here for another handful of days. If you know too much, you might slip up. You need to think about your future."

Dale nods and quiets a bit, "How about I tell you what I think, and if I go too thick in the weeds, you pull me back."

Tom nods.

"Pick a subject, Tom."

"Let's head to Lan's room and search while we talk … Okay, first subject, the new push by WPD to get Lan for Christie Anderson."

"I think the push could still have something to do with the chief getting pressure from the town bigwigs. It can't be good that there are two unsolved missing girl cases, but the messing with the original investigation and the sudden appearance of new witnesses doesn't make the chief look too good. If that's what happening."

"New subject, Danielle Rayburn's murder."

"I thought Lan was good for that. He was with her that night and there wasn't any good explanation for his trashed bungalow."

"But?"

"But now I know Marin saw some dude inside Watch at the time Lan said he was with Danielle. Add to that the fact that Danielle handled marina rentals and might have known something about boaters being on the bay on the nights of Christie's and Laire's disappearances. That makes me think there's another angle that needs looking at."

"New subject, the invitation to the Memorial Day event at Echo."

"Lan was an employee of Kingston Marina and would have been on the invitation list. His sister could have found the invitation and saved it for whatever reason, maybe she met some dude there and wanted to have a keepsake, although Lan said he kept a tight rein on her that day. Still, the party was at the end of May, and her calendar started showing the star drawings at the beginning of June, so the timing might be right. And Lan said Laire had a hickey before she went missing, so that suggests she was seeing someone. It doesn't have to be a guy though."

"It was a guy. Laire had a package of birth control pills," Tom casually drops the bomb.

"Well, shit then. When did you find out about the pills."

"A while back. I was about to tell you, but we got interrupted, then everything happened with Priscilla."

"Tell me what you know about them."

"The prescription was filled at Peduzzi's on the 5th of June, but none were taken before she went missing a couple weeks later. I don't know enough about contraception to venture a guess about what that means."

Dale laughs at the old guy, "Well don't look at me. All I know is they prevent pregnancies if they're taken correctly. We should ask someone on our team about them. Probably Esmé. I'm guessing she's the only one who might have actual experience with birth control." Dale steps out of the closet he's been searching to look at the man who's suddenly gone v.e.r.y. q.u.i.e.t. "Hey, Tom, where'd you go?"

"Pregnancy. You don't suppose Laire could have been pregnant?"

"Shit, I don't know, but I guess anything is possible." *Paydirt!*

"New subject, why is Edward Kingston IV living in Portland? Why did Fred Fuller tell you he saw Edward on the docks? And why did he say Edward's been hanging in a dive bar? And if you've got answers to those questions, why don't you tackle the big question?"

"Which is?"

"Why are Chief Banks and The King of Whisper in Portland?"

"Maybe Edward doesn't live there, maybe he's on a long-term stay for business. Or maybe he really does have a girlfriend in Portland, like it's been rumored, and his being mainland is about proximity to her. As for Fred Fuller, maybe he mentioned Edward because I was the second person he saw from Whisper in a matter of days. Maybe Edward was on the docks because he just arrived on the mainland. And maybe he was in a dive bar because he wanted a belt before going home."

"That's a lot of maybes, Dale."

"Yeah, but there could be a million other maybes to explain that shit."

"Here's a few maybes for you. Maybe Edward met Laire MacTavish at Echo. Maybe they started seeing each other. Maybe he gave his new plaything a pair of really expensive earrings and a hickey or two. Maybe he tired of her, or maybe she got herself knocked up. Maybe he killed her. Maybe he took a boat from the marina or from his very own dock and brought her body to the quiet side of Whisper. Maybe he dumped her overboard in a waterway that few know well enough to make their way through. Maybe he saw Marin on the cliff walk.

Maybe he killed Joe Baxter so the Baxter women wouldn't come back to Whisper. Maybe he's living in Portland so he doesn't run into the Baxter women. Maybe he killed Danielle Rayburn because she knew he was on the water when both teenage girls went missing. Maybe he was the guy people saw Christie Anderson with at Diggers. Maybe Fred Fuller knows that and used the information to his advantage. And maybe Chief Banks has been working with Edward Kingston III to keep Edward Kingston IV out of jail."

Bingo! "Well fuck, Tom. Maybe that's enough shit to blow this whole island to smithereens."

Tom goes to the window to stare at the bay while he processes his ramble. He pushes aside a pair of curtains—a small thud comes from the hem of one as it hits the sill. Tom takes hold of the tartan material and pinches along the hem, moving something along inside. He tilts the curtain sideways and waits for the beautiful diamond and sapphire earring to fall from its hiding place. "Well I'll be damned."

"The perfect hiding place," Dale suggests.

"Almost perfect," Tom corrects.

Portland

Chief Banks spent the morning interviewing residents of The Claremont who were poolside during Edward's freak event. Slightly more than half think it's very possible he was on that balcony to commit suicide. One woman is so sure he'll come back to do it, she's refused to return to the pool area. After the interviews are concluded, he heads to the manager's office. "Henri, any luck accessing the video footage for the camera at the parking garage exit?"

"No, but I think I found something useful." Henri presses a few console buttons and runs the lobby video on slow loop, "I am showing you this because no resident of The Claremont is on the video." He stops the tape, "There. That woman is not a resident, and I have never seen her before. I know most visitor's faces, and I make sure to remember new guests, such as Ms. Hughes. This woman is new as of that night. I checked other videos to make certain."

"Run it again and stop when she first appears ... okay, the time stamp is 4:12a. Now run the wide angle video from inside the garage ... okay, it doesn't capture Edward's parking space, but it shows most of the other cars. Bring the tape to 4:10 AM then go slowly through .... Okay, there she is walking into and out of frame."

"And she is heading in the direction of Edward's parking space."

"Yes. Would you please print several freeze frame pictures of that woman?"

"Oui. One last thing, Chief Banks."

"Yes."

"Please shut the door. The walls have ears, they say."

"What is it?"

Henri reaches into his pocket, "I found this in the penthouse and removed it for safekeeping. You should have it. Perhaps it will explain why Edward was upset."

The chief takes the pregnancy test strip. He nods, gets up, and starts to leave. "How long do you typically keep video before taping over it."

"One month. I can keep it longer if you think it will help."

"It would be very helpful."

South Portland

Edward Kingston IV pulls his blue Jag onto the lot of Bob's Boat Trader just before closing. He asks for Bob and is pointed to a small building where he finds a man in his fifties, feet on his desk, and a porn magazine open on his lap. Heir laughs, "Please tell me I'm not interrupting anything."

Bob tosses the magazine onto a nearby shelf, plops the feet of his chair onto the floor and snarls, "Nothing that can't wait a while."

"Good to know. I'm looking to make a trade."

"What for what?"

"My F-Type convertible Jag for a Cat I saw on your lot."

"What's the catch?"

"No catch, but a couple of stipulations."

"I'm listening."

"You need to take the boat to the marina, tonight, get it in the water under your name, and you can't drive the Jag until August."

"That's it?"

"That's it."

"You own the Jag?"

"Outright."

"Come on, I'll show you what I've got."

"I'll take the 2012 Cat75, unless you object."

"Nope."

Edward hands a scribbled Bill of Sale and the Jag's registration to a very happy dude named Bob, follows him to the marina, and heads to open waters.

Week Three – Day Five
Tuesday, July 18
Waning Crescent – Illumination 28%

The rulers of Whisper return to Echo, each with a plan. King heads to Ruby's suite. He enters without knocking. "King!" she startles, then reads his face, "What's wrong?"

"You need to leave."

"What? Why? Did I do something?"

"No. You just need to leave." He hands her an envelope. "There's ten grand inside. I bought you a place in Shaky, not too far from where you used to live. Go there and do whatever until I handle some shit."

"King."

"Pack your shit and meet me downstairs. Ten minutes, Ruby."

Her bodacious booty drops to the mattress. Her shaking hands clutch her stomach, "Does he know about Edward and me?"

In a suite down the hall, Chief Banks is searching for something that might explain were Heir is. He's also leaving behind something that will tie Edward Kingston IV to the dead pregnant teen currently residing on the floor of Casco Bay. "The only man going down for the crimes committed on my island is a fucking Kingston."

The Promise

June, Marin, and Dale head to Beach Bum for some takeout. On the way back Dale notices a Kingston Marina SUV parked at the boarded shack that belonged to Danielle Rayburn. He tells June to pull to the side of the road. Dale turns in his seat. June eyes Marin who shrugs a shoulder. "Hey Dale, what are we doing?"

"Shhhh."

The women in front get in on whatever it is that they're doing. They twist in their seats and watch—nothing—until they watch—something. Something very explosive.

King bolts from the shack. Ruby is tight on his heels screaming, "You bought me a murdered woman's shack? Danni Rayburn's shack! And you want me to live here? I swear on Danni's murdered soul, if you leave me here, I'll make you and your son sorry!"

King drags his ass back out of the SUV and charges toward her. He grabs hold of her arms and begins shaking, "Don't you EVER threaten me or Heir!" He has his hand raised when Dale grabs it from behind, twists it and locks it against the back of the breathless man. Dale orders Ruby. "Get in the shack or on the beach behind the shack. Now!"

King starts yelling at Dale, who slides his phone from his pocket. He calls Marin, "Go home." Then he calls dispatch. "Donna, it's Dale. I'm at the Rayburn shack. There's a dustup between a woman and Mr. Kingston III. You need to get the chief here, now!"

Dale is sent from the scene by the chief. He hoofs it back to The Promise, heads to the waterfront cottage, and tells June and Marin he needs to leave. "I'm taking my Harley to the public beach parking lot so when the chief calls to ask me why I was at the scene of the altercation. I can say I was at the beach and went for a walk. I'm pretty sure King and Ruby were too busy fighting to have noticed me getting out of the Mercedes. I'll be back as soon as possible."

Week Three – Day Six
Wednesday, July 19
Waning Crescent – Illumination 18%

Dale returns to the tiny waterfront cottage shortly before sunrise. He finds the women asleep on side by side chaise loungers. Marin barely opens her eyes before asking, "Do I smell honey-glazed donuts?"

He laughs then hands off a dozen-mixed.

"Are you just getting back?" June asks as she reaches for the box of yumminess. "Ooooo, jelly-filled. Calling dibs on both of them."

"While you two slackers were camped at the water's edge, I spent my night at WPD in the chief's office explaining why I parked my Harley at the public beach, and instead of walking the sand, I was walking tar on the main drag in Shaky near Danielle's shack. I fed him some bullshit, which he read as bullshit, but he was mainly interested in hearing an explanation for my intervening in a minor altercation between—"

Marin pushes all the way in on that, "Minor altercation? That man was raging mad, and he would have hit that woman if you hadn't stop him."

"We know that, but since you two Aren't. Going. To. Involve. Yourselves. it comes down to a he-said-he-said, my word against Edward Kingston III's word."

"What about the woman?"

"Ruby?" he laughs big. "She's working out a settlement with King."

June laughs at the turn of events, "She gets money, he gets her silence, you get your ass reamed by the chief. Just another day on Whisper."

Dale laughs his next question, "Are you sure you want to live here?"

"I don't," Marin is quick to answer. She tilts her head in June's direction, "But the hours-long phone call that one over there had with Jenny suggests their move to Murder Island is imminent."

"Yeah, I'm going to look at a place tomorrow."

"In Shaky?"

"Nope on Main Street."

"Not gonna find living quarters on Main Street. It's commercially zoned."

"Good, cause I'm looking for office space for Jenny, and I'm thinking I might set up shop there, too."

"Sweet."

"Yeah, sweet," the honey-dipping young woman grunts.

He ignores her. "So you'll look for a shack in Shaky?"

"Nope."

367

"I know you won't look for a place on cliff side, so are you moving inland?"

"Nope."

"Not much on the western end, so are you two pitching tents somewhere?"

Marin grunts in, "Wow, those rookie detective skills need some serious work. Read the room—or the twelve rooms in the main house—and you'll figure it out."

Dale hands Marin a second donut, "Figured it out, now eat this. It'll help with the bitchiness."

"Stop talking about my early-morning-low-blood-sugar moods and finish telling us what happened last night. What was the fight about?"

"The Kingston shit is hitting the fan. Apparently, Edward Kingston IV has gone missing, and his father is off-the-charts concerned." He leans in, "I heard the word *suicide* mentioned." He sits back up and warns, "You did not hear that from me. I guess the concern is high that Heir is emotionally off, and that's why Chief Banks and The King went to Portland. They did a search, came back empty-handed, and in King's case, came back a bit unhinged."

"Where do you think Edward is?" Marin asks with a note of concern.

"I haven't a clue. I don't know him. I know of him because he's a bigshot on the island, but we don't exactly swim in the same bay, if you know what I mean." He eyes Marin, "Do you know Edward Kingston?"

"I met him, twice actually, on the day he busted my telescope, and the night he delivered a new one to Wind Ledge. He's very nice."

Dale bites a chocolate frosted and raises a shoulder.

"Did you ever find out what the fight was about?"

"The woman, Ruby Norman, has been living with King for a couple of years. He plucked her from obscurity out of a bevy of beauties who live and work in Shaky and brought her all the way up in the world. Rumor has it she has a suite of rooms at the estate and free-reign over the place. Or that was the case until last night. The way I'm piecing together the shit I heard at the station, King came home in a fit and told Ruby she had to leave. He bought her a place in Shaky, and gave her ten-grand to tide her over. She freaked out when she learned he bought her Danielle's shack."

"A murdered woman's shack. Honestly, men are so damned stupid," June grumbles.

"Present company excluded, right?"

"Jury's still out, Dale."

"Ouch."

Marin shoves the last bite of her second donut into her mouth, licks a finger so she can push a button on her cell, and utters a stuffed-mouthed, "Hello. You're on speaker."

"Honey-glazed donut?" her mother laughs.

"Yeup. Too bad you're not here, there's a cinnamon."

"Save it. We'll be back tomorrow night. Jenny and I have tickets on the 7 PM ferry out of Portland for the two of us and two-packed-full-to-the-brim vehicles."

"Wow. Everything's done? The house … everything?"

"Our belongings go into storage later today, the house is in escrow pending an inspection that everyone expects will go through without a hitch. So yesss, everything is done."

There's some silence, then a semi-happy, "That's great, Mom, and we'll have the Baxter Mobile here, so that will be great, too."

"So tell me how you're feeling."

"I'm good."

"That's good. Anything interesting happen since we've been gone?"

June and Dale give hearty shakes of their heads, Marin ignores them, "Yeah, The King of Whisper got into a brawl with some bleach-blonde-bimbo in Shaky Town, a suicide watch and warning has been placed on the Heir to the throne, and Dale almost got arrested. News at eleven."

Esmé cracks up laughing. "Sorry to have missed that. So, Dale?"

"Yeah."

"Any thoughts on buying Wind?"

"I'm all-in Esmé."

"Great. I want to make you another offer."

"Go for it."

"Take Marin to the bungalow, have her pick and choose what she wants to bring to The

Promise, help her get it there, and in return you can keep all of the furnishings at Wind."

"Sweet deal."

"The only things I want are my paintings and Joe's tools. I'll pack up my artwork and studio pieces when I get back. But if you could transport all the rest before then, the place is yours. You can move in before the sale goes through. If you want."

"Sounds great, Esmé. Thank you."

"Do you think Marin's up for the grunt work?"

"I think you should ask Marin that question, Mom."

"Okay. Are you up for the grunt work?"

"I'll have to ask my babysitter and get back to you."

June drops Dale and Marin at Wind, "I'll be back to get you and your first load by four. Work on getting the small stuff to the driveway. Anything big, the five of us can schlepp tomorrow."

Marin nudges Dale, "Do you think this crap will ever end?"

"The packing and moving crap?"

"The getting dropped off so no one knows you hang with us crap."

"Yeah, it'll end, pretty soon I think, but I have to tell you, riding in a Mercedes is pretty sweet."

"Riding a Harley is a lot sweeter."

"Yeah, that bike is tits."

She laughs.

He apologizes, "Sorry for the slip. I've been working overtime on keeping my language PG."

"Ha! So there is a bad boy under the squeaky-clean Boy Cop routine."

He. Laughs. Big. "You have no idea how bad."

Primrose Priscilla

Tom answers Dale's call and heads outside, "Heard there was a dustup in Shaky last night."

"You've got yourself a pretty deep mole if you know already."

"I'm still plugged in. I heard you had your ass on the hot seat most of the night."

"Yeah. The chief made it very clear I overreacted to a situation. Last I heard, Ruby and King were in financial negotiations over something that never happened, but it's what **might** happen that is the huge story."

"Should I park my ass on a chaise for this shocker?"

"Yeah. Let me know when you're comfy."

"All set, Officer Jacobs."

"Edward Kingston IV is missing, the chief and The King went looking for him in Portland, and there are whispers of a potential Heir suicide. King is coming apart at the seams and took a shitload of frustration out on Ruby."

"Huh. Wonder what's caused the emotional downfall of the Heir apparent?" His question is laced with sarcasm.

"Maybe it's all those maybes you listed the other day. Maybe the younger Edward is good for all of the shit that's happened, and there's been a coverup at the highest levels."

"Yeah. So this is how things are gonna go from now on. After this phone call, you and I aren't going to talk and you aren't going to be seen anywhere near Watch Ledge. You are going to keep your eyes on Marin Baxter every minute until Edward Kingston IV comes up for air or we find out he's drawn his last breath. I'm gonna work on getting information into the right hands, so keep an eye on WCWI for breaking news."

"Got ya."

"But really, Dale, I want you with Marin 24-7. If it's an issue with Esmé, have her call me."

"I don't think it'll be a problem, and my being seen with the Baxters isn't an issue anymore because I'm buying Wind Ledge."

"Yeah? That's a done deal?"

"The handshake is a done deal. Paperwork and shit will happen soon. I'm actually at Wind helping Marin pack some stuff. June will be back to schlepp us to The Promise, then Esmé will be by tomorrow to pack up her artwork. She's leaving the place furnished, so I can move in tomorrow."

"Well good for you. Maybe we can get the owner of Watch Ledge back on cliff side so you'll have a playmate."

Dale laughs big, "I'm sure Lan will be happier than shit at that news."

"And broken to shit by the news his sister's dead."

Week Three Comes To An End
Thursday, July 20
Waning Crescent – Illumination 10%

Roxanne Carmichael reads caller ID, steps away from her coworkers, and presses the bright green button, "This is a surprise."

"The first of many, Miss Carmichael. I'm on the deck of the Abenaki heading to Portland. You are on the next ferry heading in the same direction. You are telling no one anything. Not one word, Miss Carmichael. When you get to Portland, make your way to the prison. Don't ask questions. Do not talk to anyone. I'll be waiting for you at the prison gate. Be there before 11 AM or don't come."

Echo

Vernon Banks doesn't knock before entering the home of Edward Kingston III. He knows he wouldn't get an answer, so he just moves through the foyer to King's office. He finds a set of French doors open and sees the man of the estate on the rattans, a drink in one hand, cigarette in the other. The lawman heads in that direction. "It's time to take some drastic steps. I know a guy on the Portland PD. He owes me.

Maybe we let him know Edward is missing and might be suicidal."

"Not happening."

"Why's that?"

"Edward is on a bender—"

"His drinking is out of control."

"He had a fight with his girlfriend—"

"His fake girlfriend."

"He's taking a few days away—"

"He's been missing for more than a week."

"He's licking a few emotional wounds—"

"He's coming to terms with his homicides."

"What! The! Fuck! Vernon!"

"Get your head out of your ass, King. We either find Edward and squirrel him away someplace, maybe with some very nice people in white coats, or we're gonna find his dead body somewhere."

"Dammit, Vern, Heir is not going to kill himself. Period."

"He will when his ass ends up in prison, and that's what's going to happen. The walls are closing in on him, and he knows it. That's why he's spiraling out of control."

King pushes from his seat, "Then what are we supposed to do?"

"Find him. Fast. Send him away and cover our asses."

King charges the chief, "You son of a bitch, you're trying to—"

The chief steps to the side and laughs when The King of Whisper lands on his ass. The lawman pulls his weapon and trains it on the man he hates most in this world. "Tragically, Kathleen's son is fucked. I should have stepped in when she asked me to on her deathbed. Maybe I could have saved him from the likes of you then, but it's way too late to save him now."

"You son of a bitch!"

"This is where we are, you arrogant asshole. Edward's crimes are coming to light. If he's arrested, he will spend the rest of his days behind bars. If he thinks offing himself is the better choice, his crimes are his and his alone. No one else knows we helped him. If you want to go down with him, I've got all I need to put your ass in jail for the rest of your miserable life—and before you throw any threats my way, I've made damned sure none of your shit will blowback onto me."

The King laughs maniacally. "And if he were your son?" he laughs louder, "which choice would you make for Edward? A cell or a grave?"

Vernon raises his gun and points it at the chest of Edward Kingston III, "I already made the wrong fucking choice when it came to that boy."

"Fuck you."

"Right backatcha, you degenerate fuck." He holsters his weapon and walks away.

King rolls onto his back, lies perfectly still on his perfectly kept lawn, at his gorgeous waterfront estate, on an island he considers his own. He bangs Vernon's words, *"I've got all I need to put your ass in jail for the rest of your miserable life—and before you throw any threats my way, I've made damned sure none of your shit will blowback onto me."* And then he bangs a lesson he drilled into Edward a million times, ***Trust no one and keep everything.*** "Let's hope Edward listened." The King of Whisper Island pushes to his feet, walks to the dock, hops into a Cat and heads to the marina, the one that bears his name. "You may have searched the estate suite and home office of Edward Kingston IV, Vernon Banks, but you haven't searched the place where he would keep his treasure trove. It's time I find his shit and take a long look at what **my** son has been up to."

Portland Prison

Lan stops cold when he sees Roxanne Carmichael sitting next to Tom Martin.

"Miss Carmichael."

"Mr. MacTavish."

"Are you here for another whack?"

The relaxed young woman with long brown hair and crystal-blue eyes leans back and crosses her arms, "To be perfectly honest, Mr. MacTavish, I haven't the slightest idea why I'm here."

The two turn their attention to the guy who knows why.

"Miss Carmichael, everything said in this meeting room, by any one of us is off the record. Is that understood?"

"It is."

"An unnamed individual and I have been conducting an investigation into the disappearances of Christie Anderson and Laire MacTavish, and the murders of Miss Anderson, Danielle Rayburn, and Joseph Baxter."

Lan leans in.

Roxanne leans in.

"I'm going to share the results of our investigation, then I want you to do your own snooping, Miss Carmichael. If you pull the correct threads you will end at the same place my partner and I ended. You need to work on this quietly and tread very carefully. You cannot go public with anything without my approval. Is that understood?"

"It is."

"No one should ever wonder if I tipped you off to anything."

"Got it, Detective."

"Okay. Miss Carmichael—"

"Roxanne."

"Okay. Roxanne, I have been investigating Danielle Rayburn's murder because I do not, and never have, believed that Lan was her killer."

"Agreed."

Lan scoffs.

She smiles at her adversary. "I can only report what I'm told to report, Mr. MacTavish. What I do on my own time is my business, and the bits and pieces I've threaded together put you in Danielle's bed. They do not put your hands around her throat."

Tom nods. He turns his attention to Lan, "My partner and I found a couple things at Watch. Though I know the answers to a few of my questions, I'd like you to confirm them for Roxanne. First, there was an invitation in Laire's room to a Memorial Day party at Echo."

He nods.

"Did you take your sister to that party?"

"Yes."

"The party took place at the end of May. Beginning in June, Laire's calendar had odd notations in certain date squares. We think the notations indicate days when she was with someone. We found a container of birth control pills. The prescription was filled at a local pharmacy on July 5th." Tom notices Lan's squirm. He counsels him, "I have a ton of shit to get through, Lan, and none of it is going to settle well. You need to hear it all, so calm down." He gets a nod. "After an exhaustive search, we found the missing earring."

Lan leans-in.

Tom addresses Roxanne. "I'm not going to fill you in on everything right now, but I'll tell you some stuff when we leave. Just try to follow along."

She nods.

"My partner and I have gone as far as we can with our investigation, but as soon as a few threads are pulled by Roxanne and she goes public with some information, the case will crack open, and we'll drive it forward. This is what we think happened, and with a little more thread pulling, we think we can prove the following: 1) Laire met Edward Kingston IV at Echo and began a secret relationship with him. 2) Heir gave his new girlfriend a very expensive pair of diamond and sapphire earrings. 3) Edward tired of his new plaything .... and killed her."

Lan begins shaking and heaving.

Tom puts his hand onto the young man's forearm. "I really need you to hold it together."

Lan drops his head and lets silent tears flow.

"4) Marin Baxter saw a man in a boat, on the back side of Whisper, on the night Laire went missing. The man dumped a body overboard."

Lan breaks.

Roxanne places her hand on his, and he takes hold.

"5) Marin Baxter saw a man tossing Watch Ledge the night Lan was with Danielle. 6) The person who murdered Danielle might have killed her to keep her from connecting a couple dots. Part of her job at the marina was to log boat rentals and dock schedules—so, if anyone knew who was on the bay the nights Christie Anderson and Laire MacTavish disappeared, it would have been Danielle. Pay attention to the timing here. A bone belonging to Christie supposedly washed ashore at Echo **after** Danielle was murdered. We think it was found **before** she died. If Danielle were still alive when news of the bone coming ashore broke, she would have gone to the log books to see who was out on the bay that night. She might have been able to piece together a significant timeline. If that's the case, the killer needed Danielle out of the picture before news broke about Christie's bone. Some of this is conjecture on my part, but I'd be pushing in on this point if I were still working the case. 7) Fred Fuller sold Diggers shortly after an underage patron named Christie Anderson was seen riding the lap of some guy inside Mr. Fuller's joint. We think Fuller knows the identity of the man with Christie that night and might have been paid to leave Whisper. 8) Fred Fuller recently met Heir Kingston on the docks of Portland. Within days of that meeting, Fred Fuller bought the Mooring, a dive bar located on those same docks. 9) Edward Kingston IV aka Heir is missing. The Chief and The King of Whisper made a trip to Portland and spent a few days looking for Heir. When they returned, King evicted Ruby Norman from his estate, bought her Danielle Rayburn's shack and tried to settle her there. Off-duty officer, Dale Jacobs happened upon the scene of a near fisticuff between King and Ruby. He brought King to the station, had his ass reamed by the chief for misreading the situation, was in earshot when King and Ruby entered into financial negotiations about the non-situation, and overheard a discussion about the suicidal tendencies of Heir Kingston."

Lan thumps back against his seat.

Roxanne thumps back against her seat.

Tom wraps things up. "Lan MacTavish, you need to listen to every word I say. You are not to mention Laire's death to anyone. You are not to outwardly grieve her passing. You need to toe the line. No temper flareups. Nothing, Lan. If the pieces fall into place the way I think they will, you'll be out of here by the end of the year provided you don't fuckup. Lan, I **need** to get you out, so you **need** to do your part."

Lan offers his hand.

The men shake.

"As for you, Roxanne, get a burner phone before you leave the mainland and use it if you need to contact me. Tread lightly on this. The people you are going after are very powerful, and every damned one is up to their asses in dirty dealings and outright criminal acts. As for the earrings, steer clear of those altogether. The only people on record who know they are part of this story are Laire, Lan, Chief Banks, King, and the person who gave them to Laire. You've got plenty of other stuff to weed through, so do your work, keep it close to the vest, and when you get a whiff that shit is hitting the fan, try to stay clear of it." Tom Martin gives a good long look at Lan MacTavish. "Hang in there, son."

"Three hundred sixty-four. Laire will be gone a year tomorrow," her brother moans.

"I know."

"How long have you known her bones have been lyin in ocean silt?"

"Weeks."

"Since Marin Baxter returned to Whisper."

"Yes."

"You best be watchin Joe's girl, Thomas MacMartin, otherwise she might end up sharin the depths with the bonnie one."

Wind Ledge

Marin is on the widow's walk staring at the tiny sliver of moon. She startles at the voice coming from behind. "What did you say?"

"The sky and ocean are so dark. I can't even tell where one ends and the other begins."

"Because the moon is at 10% illumination. I know most people love the Full and Waxing Gibbous phases, but I'm all about the Crescent phase. The thinner the better."

"How come?"

She thinks a bit, "Because even though I can't see the moon, its full shape, and its shine, I know it's there. I **see** it even though I can't see it. It's sort of like trying to explain intense feelings, like love and hate. Even though you can't see them, you know they're there because you feel them. I feel the moon." She sighs, "I bet I lost you on that one."

"Nope, I get it."

She steps away from the scope, "Do you want to look?"

"Yeah."

She moves to a lawn chair. He joins her there a few minutes later. "I need to talk to you about something, Marin."

She notices the gun and gun belt for the first time. "What's wrong?"

"Nothing, and you and I are going to work together to make sure things stay that way."

"Okay."

They share quiet space for a while, then Marin takes to the scope again. "Holy crap."

"What?"

"The waves are picking up in intensity. Come look."

"Holy crap."

"That's what I said."

"That's where I heard it," he nudges. "That's crazy." They take turns at the eyepiece. He is at it when a figure rises from a massive wave. He grabs Marin around the waist and positions her at the scope, "Look."

Air pushes out on a word, "Laire."

"What?"

"That's Laire."

He steps away and looks to the ocean. Feels the cold grip of death inch slowly up his spine and grab tight to the nape of his neck.

~~VENGEANCE~~

Marin straightens from the scope, "Did you hear that?"

"What?"

"The word vengeance."

"I didn't hear anything, Marin."

~~SOON~~

Week Four – Day One
Friday, July 21
Waning Crescent – Illumination 4%

The Baxters and the Baxterettes wake to a cold, raw day after staying up most of the night packing boxes and leaving little surprises for the new owner of Wind Ledge to find over time—which was no easy feat since the new owner was under foot most of the time. Still, the women prevailed. Esmé hid tiny tea bags inside cracker and cereal boxes, under a potted plant, hanging from a light string on the basement stairs, inside a paper towel roll, and between the pages of carpentry magazines Joe left about. June and Jenny hid Boardwalk coupons under seashell-shaped magnets on the side of the refrigerator, the stove, the microwave, the steel reinforced door leading to the basement, and any other magnetized surface they could find. Marin went old school and hid an entire package of black plastic spiders in shoes, on cabinet shelves, tucked between sheets and towels, between couch cushions, on top of doorjambs, inside potted plants, drawers, and closets.

After a bit of slow movement, abbreviated chit-chat, and copious amounts of caffeine, everyone is dressed in long-sleeve sweatshirts and pants, sitting on the patio draining the last of their mugs of coffee and easing into conversation. Esmé starts one. "Since Tom wants Dale and Marin side by side until the Kingston issue is settled, Jenny, June, and I will take my artwork to Clemente, then set the main house with some things we brought from Oxford. Marin, you need to weigh in on which room you want. The wives are taking the master suite, and I'm taking the bedroom suite right off of the studio, so that leaves two upstairs bedrooms facing the bay. One has a balcony off a set of French doors, and the other has access to the widow's walk and a fireplace."

"I want Sand Castle."

"Huh. I never thought about the cottage." Adult eyes start finding one another. There are a few nods, a shrug or two of shoulders, a smile or two, or three, then a silent consensus, "Sas, but only through the end of October. After that you need to move into warmer digs. So choose your winter residence."

"The room with the balcony. My telescope will fit, and I'll be able to hop out of bed to look at the moon without using my preferred mode of exit."

"Done!" Mom enthuses. "I'll probably convert the other bedroom, the one with access to the widow's walk into a secondary art studio. It's perfect, really. Okay, now that that's settled, we'll head out and come get the two of you for dinner at the new place." Esmé notices the slight shake of her daughter's head. "Do you have an alternate plan, Marin?"

"Today is the anniversary of Laire's death. I think we should stay here tonight. I know it sounds weird, but there's no one to acknowledge her passing. I think we should do something, or at the very least stay near her."

Esmé takes her daughter's hand, "I agree. I think it's very important we do that. We should probably ask the new home owner if he will permit another sleepover."

"I'm stuck with Marin here or there, so you guys choose."

"Good. That's settled. Change of plans, we take the paintings to town, set Clemente and the main house, get Beach Bum takeout, and eat here. Text me your orders by 5 PM."

The cop and his charge descend the access ladder late afternoon so she can spend part of her last day on Stony Beach. She takes countless pictures of Stonehenge formations and the people who built them, spends a little time sharing her favorite rock with Dale and talking about waves and tides, gets into a race or two with him from Wind to Watch and back, then moves along the water's edge giving and receiving playful hip-chucks and shoulder nudges. When they get to the westerly bend they plop onto her favorite sand patch where they stretch out and drift into a beach slumber.

Marin begins to stir at the first raindrops hitting her face, then shoots to her feet at the sound of a gunshot. She looks for Dale, panics when she finds he's gone. She reaches into her pocket for her cell, slaps at each one, then remembers she left it at the bungalow. She looks up and down the abandoned beach for him, for anyone, then turns filling eyes to the ocean, fearing he went for a swim and maybe … Panic pushes hard and she wonders if she really heard a gun being fired. She starts for Wind, then stops hard when she remembers Dale is her protection. "He wouldn't have left me."

She turns around and moves toward the bend then sees him lying on the wet packed sand far from where she stands. **"Dale!"** She runs to him, screaming when she sees blood seeping from his back. **"Shot!"** She pulls her sweatshirt over her head, rolls it, and presses it to his wounded area. Marin looks around, suddenly afraid the shooter might be hiding behind a rock. *Help! I need to get help.* She runs back to her spot, takes one last look up the beach, hoping she'll find someone. The rain and wind hamper her effort. She takes a step or two toward Wind, then quickly changes her mind, "Use the public access ladder, then run on Cliff Road."

She veers toward the cliff, stumbles around rocks and rock formations, taking hard hits to her legs. Exhausted and breathing hard, she makes it to the cliff, stands below the ladder, and reaches up. Her hand takes hold of a rung, then the next, and the next—her grip slipping free and causing her to fall onto the rocks below. She lands hard, her breath pushed harshly away. She pulls tiny choppy inhales and immediately wishes she hadn't. Pain shoots from her back around to the front.

~~MARIN~~
~~SAVE YOURSELF~~

She hears her name. She tries to call out, but can't get enough air. She rolls onto her side, pushes herself to a stand, then drops to her knees. She tears when she hears her name again,

~~MARIN~~

"Dale, is that you? Over here. Dale. Help." She crawls through the rock field, banging clumsily against mammoth boulders, taking cuts to her legs and hands from the sharp edges. Rain beats her back, her sopping hair covers her eyes that sting with the salt of tears and scratch from ocean grit. She crawls for an eternity and when she feels the packed, wet sand at the water's edge, she collapses — waking only when waves of high tide find her, push her.

She feels the wrap of his protective arms, his weight heavy upon her, "Dale, thank God." She relaxes into his embrace, their bodies held victim to the push and pull of waves. "Dale. Help.

Please." An awareness returns. She remembers his gunshot, "I should be helping you." She swipes hair from her face, opens nearly-blinded eyes, and tries to move out from under him. Their bodies separate on the next wave, and she looks at the man holding her.

She releases a bloodcurdling scream
and passes out.

Week Four – Day Two
Saturday, July 22
Waning Crescent – Illumination 1%

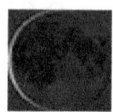

Tom Martin races toward Cliff Road shortly before 1 AM. He's listening to the last of eight hysterical voicemail messages from Esmé Baxter...

"Tom, it's Esmé, again ... it's a little after midnight ... Marin and Dale still haven't returned to the bungalow from a walk on Stony ... they haven't answered any calls or texts for hours ... June and Jenny stumbled along the shoreline ... but it's high tide now ... so they're back at Wind. We've checked The Spot ... and Watch ... and The Promise ... and even Jacobs Jolly ... and nothing. Please call. Tom, please call."

Tom bounds onto the porch and pushes into the house. "I'm sorry I missed your calls, Priscilla—never mind, tell me about your last communication with them."

"They texted late afternoon saying they were headed to Stony to spend some of Marin's last day on the beach. They were going to text us their food order, and we were going to eat at Wind. We never heard from them."

"June and Jenny, did you make it to the far side of Stony?"

"No. It was too dark."

Tom gets back into his truck and races to the public access ladder. He follows a flashlight beam to the cliff's edge, the crash of waves drowning his calls, "Marin! Dale!" He tries to discern shapes on the hauntingly black beach—follows the moving water as it crashes to the cliff below then recedes. He strains to find something in the dark of night. A sliver of moon offers no help, shines no light on what happened on Stony Beach or elsewhere on Whisper. He looks skyward, begs for her help, "Please, Miss Prissy, shine bright. I need to find Marin."

FLASHES OF LIGHTNING
BLAZE THE SKY

AGAIN AND AGAIN AND AGAIN
SHINING UPON HER, AND HIM, AND HIM

Tom places an emergency call. "Donna. It's Tom. I need every available emergency responder sent to Stony Beach at the public access ladder. There may be three casualties." He follows with a call to Esmé, "You need to come to the public access ladder." Within minutes the entire Whisper police, fire, and EMT force is on the beach, battling rough seas and rendering aid to a battered, broken, and nearly drowned young woman and to a critically wounded police officer.

Standing alone on a cliff overlooking Stony Beach is the chief of police. He offers a tearful apology to the hellish night, "I'm sorry, Kathleen. I didn't do right by you or Edward." He moves past his pain when Tom Martin steps near.

"You need to call his next of kin."

The chief nods. Tom walks away.

Vernon Banks takes some pleasure in making this call. "Mr. Kingston, your son is dead on Stony Beach."

King hangs up the phone before asking, "Which son?"

Week Four – Day Three
Sunday, July 23
New Moon – Illumination 0%

Marin Baxter wakes from time to time—she thinks. She hears someone's words, or maybe hallucinates them. *You are safe. Listen to the beep of machines. Push the memories away.* She can't. The claustrophobic crush of a dead man keeps her held prisoner, and drags her to the pits of Hell during her state of oblivion. Esmé, June, and Jenny crescent her hospital bed, stepping away only when Tom steps near. Within the beat of a heart of each of his handholds, she opens her eyes—she thinks. She stares vacantly—she thinks. Then she shuts them tight, the process releasing a well of tears that stain her battered and bruised cheeks until he pats them dry.

Dale Jacobs lies still in a hospital bed not far from the young woman he promised to protect—the one who tried to save him. He's undergone two surgeries to repair damage from a gunshot wound to his back, has been upgraded to stable condition, is expected to live and recover fully, though he has yet to regain consciousness. His mother, Connie, is back on Whisper and is at his bedside counting her blessings. The only person allowed in his room is Tom Martin, who burdens a heavy load of sorrow and regrets.

As for Edward Kingston IV—someone or something caused his death at sea. The body of the Heir apparent to the kingdom of Whisper could have sunk to the depths and spent eternity on the ocean's floor near the spirit of the young woman he abandoned there.

Laire MacTavish would have none of it, and rightly cast him Ashore on Stony Beach.

The End

Please enjoy the teaser for the next Twisted Threads story,

Adrift on Stony Beach

Adrift on Stony Beach

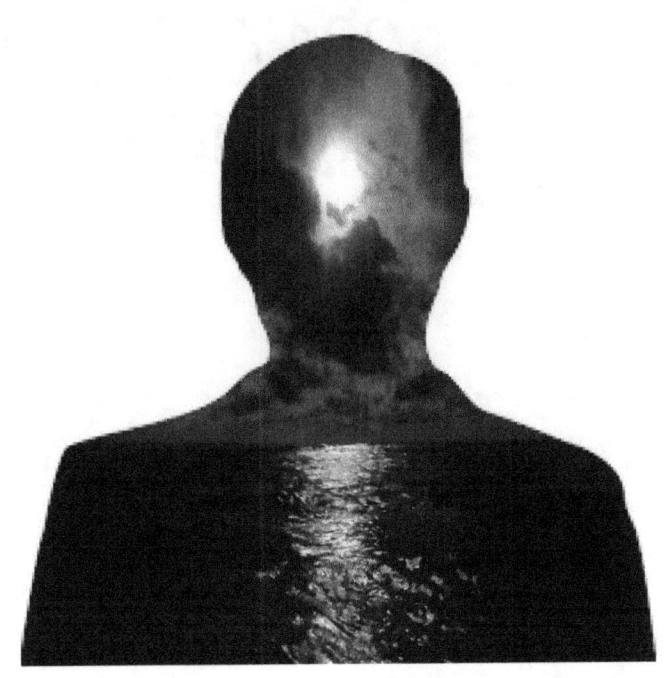

~~~ TWISTED THREADS ~~~
A Novel
SHERYLL O'BRIEN

2017
Sandy Side

Welcome to Murder Island

Esmé Baxter is behind the wheel of a Honda CRV inching along the main street of Whisper Island, a tiny strip of land located in Casco Bay, Maine. The backseat passenger, Esmé's daughter Marin, refers to the isle as, Murder Island. There are very legitimate reasons for the renaming. During the earliest days of the Baxter's arrival on Whisper, a teenage girl went missing, the second in as many years – a young woman was strangled in her beachfront shack – the bone of one of the missing teens washed ashore – the husband of Esmé and father of Marin died at the base of a cliff on the backside of the island – and Marin and a guy named, Dale, almost lost their lives on Stony Beach when their unconscious selves banged relentlessly against massive rocks at high tide. Marin knows the broad strokes of what happened that night because she's heard bits and pieces while in rehab, and because she's been getting her memory back in dribs and drabs, but the circumstantial crux of those events, and how they almost caused her own death, is still lost somewhere in her battered and bruised brain. When she finally recovers those memories, Marin Baxter may very well wish she could forget what happened on a beach named Stony on an island named Whisper.

ABOUT THE AUTHOR

She is not dead.

Sheryll O'Brien crafts characters without constraints. She tells them who they are, then let's them show her better versions of themselves. She gives them life and they live it beyond her wildest dreams.

Sheryll is a lifelong resident of Worcester, Massachusetts, where she is wife to the most supportive husband ever, and mother of two adult daughters, one who refuses to leave her home and the other who refuses to tell her where she lives. Of most significance, she is MammyGrams to the sweetest six-year-old, Hadley.

Sheryll worked several years in the fundraising community of Worcester County, writing grants for non-profit organizations. She began writing for her own pleasure after surviving brain surgery and breast cancer. Happily, for her fanbase of family and friends——she is not dead.

If you have enjoyed reading my book, I would very much appreciate you taking a few minutes to write a review and post that review on amazon.com and goodreads.com.

The opinion of readers can help prospective readers make a purchasing decision.

To learn more, please visit my website, www.pullingthreadsnovella.com subscribe to my blog for updates on future projects.

I would absolutely love to hear from my readers, you can email me at,

pullingthreadsnovella@gmail.com